Prayers, Paws & Providence

**Center Point
Large Print**

**This Large Print Book carries the
Seal of Approval of N.A.V.H.**

Tales from Grace Chapel Inn

Prayers, Paws & Providence

Diann Hunt

CENTER POINT PUBLISHING
THORNDIKE, MAINE

This Center Point Large Print edition
is published in the year 2009 by arrangement with
GuidepostsBooks.

All Scripture quotations are taken from *The Holy Bible,
New International Version.* Copyright © 1973, 1978,
1984 International Bible Society. Used by permission of
Zondervan Bible Publishers.

The text of this Large Print edition is unabridged.
In other aspects, this book may vary
from the original edition.
Printed in the United States of America.
Set in 16-point Times New Roman type.

ISBN: 978-1-60285-412-3

Library of Congress Cataloging-in-Publication Data

Hunt, Diann.
  Prayers, paws & providence / Diann Hunt.
     p. cm. -- (Tales from Grace Chapel Inn)
  ISBN 978-1-60285-412-3 (lib. bdg. : alk. paper)
 1. Bed and breakfast accommodations--Fiction. 2. Dogs--Fiction.
   3. Pennsylvania--Fiction. 4. Large type books. I. Title.
  II. Title: Prayers, paws, and providence. III. Series.

PS3608.U573P73 2009
813'.6--dc22

2008047230

Acknowledgments

With deep gratitude to those who have helped me through this project:

To my agent Karen Solem for stretching me beyond my comfort zone when I wanted to cocoon, and for not allowing me to be satisfied with the status quo.

To my wonderful editors Regina Hersey, Leo Grant and Priscilla Drobes for your editing expertise. I feel blessed to know you and work with you.

To the following Web sites that offered helpful information on assistance dogs:

Assistance Dogs International, Inc.
www.adionline.org

The Epilepsy Foundation
www.epilepsyfoundation.org/epilepsyusa/
seizuredogs.cfm

Midwest Assistance Dogs
www.midwestassistancedogs.org

Heartfelt thanks to my husband Jim Hunt, who always believes in me and keeps a steady supply of chocolate (and mochas) on hand for the difficult days. I love you, honey!

Thank you to my writing friends whom I could never do without: Colleen Coble, Kristin Billerbeck and Denise Hunter. Your constant support, friendship and mutual love for coffeehouses and truffles mean more to me than you'll know. You're the greatest!

Finally, I dedicate this story to my parents Jesse and Edna Mae Walker. I thank God for you and love you both with all my heart.

—Diann Hunt

Prayers, Paws & Providence

Chapter One

Frosted rooftops glistened in the twilight and tiny icicles dripped from frozen trees as Alice Howard drove through the heart of Acorn Hill past quaint little shops with their charming window displays. The streets had been cleared though the beauty of the late February ice storm remained. While townsfolk settled down to family dinner, nearby street lamps cast an amber glow upon the now quiet roads and sidewalks, creating a scene reminiscent of a Currier & Ives print.

Alice loved Pennsylvania winters—the cold, crisp air, the startlingly clear blue skies and, yes, the frequent snows. In her sixty-plus years, she had enjoyed all the vagaries of northeastern winters. As she rounded a corner, she saw ahead Grace Chapel Inn, the Victorian bed-and-breakfast she owned with her two sisters.

The iced branches of the old maple tree in the front yard were silhouetted against the darkening sky. Lamplight spilled from the windows onto the frozen front yard. A sigh of pleasure escaped her. The first day of the week was always busy at the hospital, and so she was particularly glad to arrive at her welcoming home.

As she eased into the parking area, her breath caught in her throat. "What in the world!" Her foot hit the brake, forcing the car to a skidding stop.

The headlights shone on a black Labrador retriever sitting in the middle of the driveway. Alice pulled a hand to her chest and tried to catch her breath. Her foot still on the brake, she locked eyes with the dog, which looked only mildly inconvenienced by her intrusion.

Rolling down her window, Alice called out, "If it wouldn't put you out too much, would you kindly move? Please?"

The animal looked at her a moment, yawned hugely, then rose and sauntered out of the way.

Alice rolled up the window, pulled the car into place and waited a moment, wondering if she should get out. The dog looked harmless enough. Still, she knew she should exercise care with strange animals . . . especially *big* strange animals.

She looked into his dark, melting eyes. "Oh, the poor thing," she said aloud, looking at the forlorn creature who had once again plopped his derriere onto the frosty ground and was shivering pitifully. He turned a pathetic look her way. Alice heaved a long sigh. There was no use fighting it. The dog knew how to tug at her heartstrings. Alice shifted into park and turned off the ignition. Dropping her keys into her purse, she lifted up a stack of files and reached for the door handle.

When the door opened, the dog came over, wagging his long tail furiously. He leapt for Alice, throwing his strong, friendly paws onto her lap, nudging his cold nose playfully into her free hand.

"Oh dear," she said with a laugh, wishing she had on her gloves. "You're cold, aren't you?" She stroked the dog's glossy black head, causing him to lean in and nuzzle his face into her. The sheen of his coat, his healthy size and his friendly manner all attested to this dog being a well-cared-for pet.

Alice reached next to her for her handbag and her book. When she turned back to her new friend, she noticed that his red reflector collar had an empty ring, slightly opened, where his tag should have been. "I see that you lost your ID. After you've had a little snack, I'll see what I can do about finding out who you are and how to get you home," she told him, as she climbed out of the car.

The cold stung sharply as Alice and the dog made their way to the back door. She looked toward the west and reveled in the remnants of the dazzling sunset that had spread color across the horizon.

Looking down, Alice whispered in a conspiratorial tone, "You'll get me into trouble with my sisters, you know." The dog glanced up and cocked his head to one side. "Okay, those huge brown eyes of yours have convinced me you're worth it," she said with a chuckle. At this the canine resumed his happy trot beside her.

A gust of wind whipped a strand of her reddish brown hair across her face. Alice quickened her pace up the steps to the back porch, the dog following behind.

"Well, boy, let me go see if I can sneak you a scrap or two," Alice whispered. "Stay," she commanded with authority. The dog played the perfect partner in crime and sat down with a thump.

Alice moved from the back porch into the warm kitchen that smelled of cinnamon and apples. Jane, the youngest of the three Howard sisters, stood at the sink, washing apple peelings into the disposal. A blue and white checkered apron covered the front of her jeans and long-sleeved denim shirt. Her long brown ponytail swished to and fro as she moved around her cooking area with energy. She was a pretty woman who looked much younger than her fifty years.

"Hello, Alice." Jane smiled fondly as her sister entered the room.

"Looks like you've had a busy day," Alice said, glancing at the three pies lined up on the butcher block countertop. "What's the occasion?"

"I baked an apple pie for dinner and made a couple more to freeze."

"Good idea." Alice stole a glance toward the back door hoping the dog had stayed put.

"We have a little time before dinner will be ready. Would you like some tea?" Jane asked as she slipped two of the pies into freezer containers.

Before answering, Alice glanced around the room, wondering what she could offer her furry friend to eat without raising suspicion.

"All right, what's up?" Jane asked, her right fist

perched on her hip, her eyes twinkling with amusement.

"What?" Alice feigned innocence.

"I've seen that look far too many times, Alice Howard," Jane said. "What are you hiding and where?"

Alice sighed. "I'm that obvious, huh?"

Jane laughed. "Yes, you are. You'll have to do better than that if you want to keep anything from Louise."

"Keep what from Louise?" their eldest sister asked as she stepped through the swinging door from the dining room into the kitchen. Her right eyebrow arched questioningly. Dressed in a beige wool skirt and pale blue sweater with pearls around her neck, Louise stood waiting for an answer.

"Okay, I admit it. I'm guilty," Alice said, laughing.

"Guilty of what?" Louise wanted to know. She walked across the black and white checkered floor to the stove and lifted the teakettle. She turned to Jane. "Do we have time for tea before dinner?"

Jane nodded. "In fact, I was getting ready to make some."

"Let me do it, you've been busy all day."

"Thank you."

Putting water into the kettle, Louise said without looking back, "Well, Alice, I'm still waiting to learn what it is you're hiding from me." Louise placed the kettle on the stove and turned to Alice.

As if on cue, the dog whimpered from the back porch.

Terrific, Alice thought.

"What is that?" Louise asked as her eyes turned toward the door.

Jane tried to hide her amusement by busying herself at the stove.

Then understanding lit Louise's expression. She frowned at her sister. "Alice Howard, have you brought home another stray?" Though her voice held a reprimand, Louise wasn't angry. Alice knew her sisters had grown accustomed to her weakness for animals.

"I didn't bring him home. He was actually waiting in the driveway when I got here."

"Smart dog," Jane said, walking toward the counter on which some plastic containers sat. "It so happens that I just cleaned out the refrigerator. There's some leftover meat that I was going to toss. It's perfectly good, just a little dry. You can give it to your friend." Jane handed a container to Alice and winked.

"Thanks, Jane."

Louise pulled some cups and saucers from the cabinet. Before Alice could escape, Louise said, "Alice, I believe if you had your way we would run an inn for stray animals rather than people." Despite her chiding, Louise wore an amused smile.

Alice sighed. "What can I say? I love animals."

"I think you missed your calling. You should've been a veterinarian instead of a nurse," Jane said.

Alice shrugged. "Perhaps."

Louise and Jane followed Alice to the back door where the Lab sat patiently. At the sight of them, he wagged his tail happily, banging it against the floor. As Alice walked closer with the beef scraps, he sniffed, rose and began to prance about and whine until Alice lowered the container in front of him.

"Okay, boy, here you go."

The animal started eating with enthusiasm.

"He sure is hungry," Jane said. "But he looks well cared for."

"That he does," Alice agreed. "After he eats, I'll make some calls to see if anyone knows who he is."

The teakettle whistled and the three made their way back into the kitchen. No sooner had Louise filled the cups than the back door opened.

"Land's sake, what are you doing here?" a startled voice called.

The sisters shared a look of alarm and rose to their feet at the sound of Ethel Buckley's voice. Their aunt Ethel lived in the carriage house next to the inn and frequently used the back door when popping in on her nieces.

"Oh, oh!" Ethel said.

Alice and Jane arrived just as the dog pushed past their aunt and went down the stairs out into the dark. Alice raced after him. "Here boy," she called, but the black dog had become invisible in the night. She turned and went back in the house.

"Well, what was that all about?" Ethel asked.

Alice shivered from the cold and secured the back door. "Let's talk about it over tea in the warmth of the kitchen," Jane said, giving Alice a chance to catch her breath.

Ethel brushed any possible dog hairs from her coat sleeves, then composed herself and followed the sisters into the kitchen. "Alice Howard, what on earth was that dog doing sitting there as big as you please near the back door?"

Alice knew that it was only natural that Ethel would assume this was Alice's doing. She took a deep breath before explaining the dog's presence.

Ethel shook her head. "*Tsk, tsk.* I declare, Alice, you have the softest heart of anyone I know, but you can't take in every stray that happens into our town."

Alice sighed and slipped back into her chair, already worrying about the dog.

After a moment or two, Ethel surprised everyone by giggling. "I can't say for sure who was surprised more, me or that clumsy dog," she said.

The sisters exchanged glances and joined her in laughter.

"He really seemed to be a sweet animal," Alice said thoughtfully. "I hope he finds his way back home. It's awfully cold out there."

Jane patted Alice's arm. "At least you filled his stomach before he took off."

Alice gave Jane a warning look, and Jane clamped her hand over her mouth, realizing that she'd said the wrong thing.

"You fed him?" Ethel put her hand to her chest. "Alice Howard, you can't be giving away perfectly good food to these animals. Why, when I was young—"

"Aunt Ethel, Alice gave the dog meat scraps that Jane was going to throw away anyway, so there's no harm done," Louise said, coming to the rescue.

"But you'll never get rid of him."

"Would you like some tea, Auntie?" Jane asked before her aunt could go on about the stray.

Ethel blinked. "Well, yes. Thank you, Jane." Though Ethel could quickly get into a snit, she could just as easily forget about whatever it was that twisted her out of sorts—a fact for which they were all thankful.

While Louise, Jane and Ethel engaged in conversation about the cold weather, Alice's mind drifted to the animal that had run away. Surely he would find his way to a warm home. The red collar and evidence that he once had a dog tag assured her he had a home. He would find his way back there. At least she hoped he would.

After dinner, the sisters gathered in the living room. The wind moaned an icy ballad across

Acorn Hill. "Sounds like the predicted storm is blowing in," Louise said, clicking her knitting needles as she spoke.

Jane looked up from her magazine. "I hope the Sandersons make it here safely."

"It certainly isn't a good time of year to visit Pennsylvania, I'm afraid." Concern tinged Louise's voice.

"When are they due to arrive?" Alice asked.

Louise peered over the rims of her glasses. "They said that they'd be here sometime tomorrow afternoon."

"It makes you wonder why people come here from the South in the middle of winter," Jane said.

Alice shrugged. "I guess they're lured by the snow as we are by warm weather."

"Well, I'd choose sunny and warm over snow any day," Jane said with a laugh, turning the page of her magazine. "Snow keeps you cooped up inside the house all the time, and you both know how I feel about that," Jane said.

Alice smiled, thinking of Jane's endless supply of energy and desire to be on the go. She understood her sister's preference for warmth to winter's chill. Still, the sight of snow continued to fill Alice with excitement . . . except when she was driving.

"Do you miss San Francisco?" Louise kept her knitting needles in motion.

"Sometimes," Jane confessed. "But I wouldn't want to go back. Besides, it could get pretty cold there too. Remember what Mark Twain supposedly said? The coldest winter he ever saw was the summer he spent in San Francisco."

"It's a good thing you don't want to go back, because we wouldn't let you go," Alice said. "Without you, Louise and I would have to order breakfast for our guests from the bakery. You can imagine how that would cut into our profits."

Louise nodded enthusiastically.

"I used to miss my work at the Blue Fish Grille," Jane said, referring to the restaurant in San Francisco where she had served as head chef before returning home, "but Grace Chapel Inn satisfies my desire to work in the culinary arts." She smiled fondly at her sisters.

"What about you, Louise, do you miss Philadelphia?"

Louise stilled her needles and thought a moment. "Oh, I missed it at first, but with Elliot gone and Cynthia working in Boston, well, there seemed little point in staying when I could be with my sisters. Besides, somebody has to keep you two in line."

Alice chuckled. "True enough. You know, when Father died, I realized how big and lonely this house would seem without someone to share it. Except for being in Philadelphia for nursing school, I've lived only in Acorn Hill. This house, Grace Chapel, this town, they're as much a part of me as the Howard blood that runs through my veins. I'm thankful that I could stay here and that you two could join me."

Just then Wendell, their black and gray tabby, jumped up on Alice's lap, kneading her long sweater between his paws in an effort to get comfortable. Alice laughed. "Okay, okay, I'm glad you're here too."

The sisters laughed.

Alice watched Louise's skillful hands working with the green yarn. "Louise, you're coming right along on those shamrock coasters. I really appreciate your making all those for the ANGELs," Alice said, referring to the group of junior high girls she worked with at Grace Chapel. "They'll enjoy the gift, and the coasters will help illustrate St. Patrick's teaching of the Trinity using the shamrock."

Louise continued to work the tiny loops and shrugged. "Well, you know how I like to have projects to work on in the wintertime."

A gust of wind rattled the windowpane. Inside the room the fireplace crackled with dancing flames as the Howard sisters enjoyed the warmth of the evening and the pleasure of one another's company.

Alice thought of the Acorn Hill folks tonight. She could imagine her best friend, Vera Humbert, and Vera's husband Fred snug in their living room, eating popcorn and watching TV. She pictured the owner of the town's bookstore, Viola Reed, on her sofa reading, oblivious with her feline friends curled next to her. Alice pictured other good citizens of her beloved community in their warm homes tonight visiting with their families. Perhaps they were talking about the latest happenings in the *Acorn Nutshell*, their town paper, or maybe they were just enjoying the pleasure of each other's company as much as Alice was enjoying the company of her sisters.

Acorn Hill. There was no other place in the entire world where she would rather be.

Chapter Two

Never a dull moment, Alice thought the next morning, as she glanced over her "To Do" list at the Potterston Hospital. Not that she minded being busy. She'd much rather that than watching the clock. And honestly, she couldn't complain. Her flexible schedule afforded her ample time at Grace Chapel Inn to do the things she enjoyed.

After penning a note to talk with a doctor about a patient's medications, Alice stuck the reminder under a paperweight. She stood, adjusted her stethoscope and made her way down the hall.

Stepping inside a room, Alice smiled at the young woman whose copper curls were scattered about her pillow like soft feathers, and whose slight form barely disturbed the bedclothes. As

Alice walked closer, the woman gave her a weak smile.

"I'm Alice Howard. I'm your attending nurse today," Alice said smiling. "I understand you took a nasty fall last night."

"So I've heard."

Alice picked up the blood pressure cuff and wrapped it around her patient's arm. Inflating the black band, Alice used her stethoscope to listen carefully. "It appears you're going to be all right, though," she said finally, while releasing the cuff from the woman's arm. Once the instrument hung in its place by the bed, Alice picked up the chart. After making a notation of the readings, Alice looked once more toward her charge. "The doctor just wanted to keep you here for observation. It's more of a safety precaution than anything."

The woman nodded.

Alice asked her some medical questions and jotted down another note. When she finished, Alice slipped the brown plastic clipboard back into the opening at the foot of the bed.

"May I get you anything, Ms. Middleton?"

"No, thank you, I'm fine. And please, call me Paula."

Alice smiled again. "Paula it is." Lifting the plastic pitcher from Paula's bedside stand, Alice walked over to the sink and filled it with water, then replaced it.

"It's a beautiful day today. Well, the sun is

shining even if it is cold. Would you like me to open the blinds?"

"Sure."

Alice walked over and twirled the handle for the blinds, allowing a blaze of sunshine to burst into the room.

"Do you know when I get to go home?"

"The doctor should be in soon. He may keep you one more night. Do you have a family member nearby who can take you home this afternoon if he releases you?"

She shook her head. "I live alone."

Alice was surprised by that bit of information. "How did you get help yesterday?"

Paula swallowed as if she did not want to answer. "A neighbor needed some sugar. When she knocked, I called out to her. The door was unlocked, so she came in and helped me."

Oh dear. Alice found the story disturbing. Living alone, the woman was fortunate she hadn't suffered something far worse than a concussion.

Paula studied Alice a moment. "I know what you're thinking, but I'm fine. I've had these seizures since I was a kid. Normally, I don't hurt myself. I try to take care in how I do things in case one hits."

Alice wasn't at all happy with this information. "Well, I'm sorry it happened." She tucked in the bed sheets, then she patted Paula's foot. "If you need anything, dear, you just let me know," she said with a smile that hid her concern. She left the room and headed for the nurse's station.

While completing some paperwork, Alice found it difficult to concentrate. After her father had died, Alice had thought for a time that she would grow old alone. The idea had frightened her. Knowing how vulnerable she had felt then made her want to reach out to this woman. There had to be some way of getting help for her. Perhaps the neighbor would keep a closer watch on her. Alice normally didn't get too involved with her patients. Still, the patient lived alone. How could Alice knowingly let someone return to a possibly dangerous situation?

Alice had little time to consider it further as her day at the hospital filled with activity. The doctor decided to keep Paula Middleton another night, which gave Alice a little more time to think about what she could do to help the woman.

There had to be something someone could do.

Later that evening, the sisters were cleaning up the dinner dishes when Ethel arrived.

"Jane," she said, "I wanted to return this cookbook to you before it got mixed in with my collection." Ethel handed the book to Jane.

"Thanks, Auntie. May I get you something?" she called over her shoulder, as she returned the cookbook to its place.

"Oh, no thank you. I've just had dinner."

Jane wondered how to approach the subject that

was on her mind and decided it was best to dive right in.

"You know, I'm glad you stopped by, Auntie." Jane exchanged a quick glance with her sisters.

"Oh?"

"Do you have a minute to sit down?" Jane asked, pointing to a kitchen chair.

"Well, I suppose I have a moment, although my favorite TV show will be coming on in about half an hour. Will this take long?"

Jane smiled. "Not long at all."

Ethel nodded and settled into a chair. Alice and Louise continued to tidy the kitchen.

"You remember I told you I had agreed to teach that bread-making course for the adult education program at the high school starting on Thursday of next week?"

Ethel nodded.

"Well, as you know, Sylvia Songer slipped on the ice and broke her arm and is in need of a lot of help."

"*Tsk, tsk,* yes, I'd heard that," Ethel said.

"She has someone to help her in the mornings, and I would like to be able to help her in the after- noons. But we have a guest coming who will be eating all her meals with us, so I will be very busy." Jane took extra care with her next words. "You are such a great cook and . . ." she cleared her throat, "I wondered if you would consider teaching the class."

All eyes turned to Ethel who looked startled. She uttered a gasp followed by "Land's sake!"

Jane hurried on. "One of us would drive you there and come back to get you afterward. The class will meet twice a week, Tuesday and Thursday nights from six-thirty to eight-thirty, and there are only five classes. I can give you the class schedule. You just teach them about the ins and outs of baking bread. That'd be a snap for you." Jane paused, allowing the idea to sink in.

"You had mentioned the other day that you wished you had something worthwhile to do with your time," Alice said. "This could be just the thing." She poured some dishwashing liquid into the washer, snapped the door closed and turned on the machine.

Louise joined the sales pitch. "Baking is your specialty, Aunt Ethel. The students would benefit from your experience."

A sense of pride seemed to settle upon Ethel. She thought a moment. "I might be able to do it. I've never taught a class before, though."

"It really would be no different from your offering advice to me here in the kitchen," Jane said, trying not to smile. Ethel generously handed out her advice with little or no encouragement. "Those people want to be in class, and they're eager to learn. You'd be just the one who could teach them."

"Well, give me the details, and I'll give the

matter some thought," Ethel said, though Jane suspected Ethel Buckley was already planning what steps she would take to improve the culinary arts of her students.

After Ethel left, the sisters gathered in the living room. A beeswax candle flickered from a nearby stand, perfuming the air with sweetness.

"Oh, I almost forgot," Alice said. "You received a note in the mail today, Louise. I'll be right back."

Louise nodded without looking up. With her glasses perched on the end of her nose, she concentrated on her knitting.

Alice stepped into the foyer and retrieved the mail from the reception desk. She reentered the living room and handed the note to her sister.

Louise put her knitting aside and looked at the note. "It's from Martha Spangler." Louise tore open the envelope as quickly and neatly as she could.

Jane and Alice waited in silence as Louise read her note, watching her expression and then hearing her gasp.

"Is everything all right?" Jane asked.

"Oh my!" Louise exclaimed, holding her hand to her throat.

"Louise, what is it?" Alice asked.

"Hmm?" Louise commented absently. She reread the letter, then lifted her gaze to her sisters.

"You remember my friend Martha from the Philadelphia Conservatory?"

Jane and Alice nodded.

"She knows how I love the music of pianist Eduardo Fink. It seems he's scheduled to perform a concert at the Conservatory in a few weeks. She's invited me to attend the concert and afterward spend the night as a guest in her home." Louise's eyes sparkled.

"Louise, that's wonderful," Alice said, remembering the CDs of this famous pianist's works that Louise often played.

"I can hardly believe it. I've never had the opportunity to hear him in person. What a privilege."

Alice and Jane smiled at their sister's atypical excitement.

"I must call Martha at once and let her know I'll be there." Louise rose and went to call her friend.

"Well, that certainly made her evening," Alice said with a laugh.

Jane agreed.

The sisters discussed what a wonderful opportunity this would be for Louise and how she deserved to get out more and to enjoy the musical events that she so longed to attend.

"Still no sign of our guests," Alice commented after a time of comfortable silence.

"You know, I'm a little worried about them," Jane said. "I'd think that they would call if they were delayed."

Alice looked at her watch. "They are a couple of hours late. They probably know that there is no shortage of rooms at this time of year."

"Maybe." Jane did not look convinced.

Louise returned and announced, "It's all set."

"That's wonderful," Alice said.

The phone rang.

"That may be our guests calling," Jane said, jumping up from the sofa. She dashed out to the hall to answer the telephone.

"I have no idea where she gets her energy," Louise said.

Alice chuckled, thinking of Jane's energy and that of the dog who had greeted her after work yesterday. "She's like an excited puppy."

"She is at that." Louise picked up her knitting needles and set to work once again.

"Mr. and Mrs. Sanderson will be here in another hour," Jane said, taking her seat. "They had some car trouble."

"That's too bad," Louise said. "I do hope they arrive without further trouble."

"They'll be fine. Mr. Sanderson said they had the car worked on and everything is now in tip-top shape." Jane sat on the sofa and tucked her feet under her before she returned to her magazine.

"You know, I've a matter I wanted to share with you before our guests get here," Alice said.

Louise's needles stopped moving, and she laid her work aside.

Jane closed her magazine and looked at Alice. "What's up?"

Alice explained the events of the day with her patient, Paula Middleton, and Alice's concerns about the woman living alone.

"I don't see what you can do about the matter, Alice. It seems quite out of your hands," Louise said.

Alice's gaze lifted toward the window as her mind clicked with possible solutions. "I suppose, but still . . ."

"What are you thinking, Alice? What could we do to help?" Jane asked.

Alice waited a moment more, then turned to her sisters. "Oh, I don't know. I'm not sure there is anything we can do. It's just that I can't stop thinking of her need."

"Would it help if we took some meals over to her this week while she is recovering? I mean, provided she doesn't live too far away?" Jane, ever the hostess, asked.

Alice brightened. "That's a wonderful idea, Jane. I found out that she lives at the south edge of town in Bill and Carolyn Morris' old farmhouse."

Jane nodded.

"They're still renting that out?" Louise asked.

"Evidently. The Morrises bought that new place in town. Carolyn told me they just couldn't part with the old farmhouse yet. They raised all their kids there. It holds too many memories."

Louise nodded.

"Anyway," Alice continued, "I might call a few friends and see if we can put together a schedule of meals for Paula, at least for a few days."

"Is she going home tomorrow?" Louise asked.

"Yes, I'm almost certain she will."

"I'll plan her dinner for tomorrow. Do you think that would be all right?" Jane asked.

"Yes. That'll give me time to contact some other people and get her taken care of." Alice settled back into her chair. "I'm glad you thought of that, Jane. I feel much better that we're helping in some way."

Before they could talk further about Paula, a knock sounded.

"That must be our guests," Jane said, moving quickly to the front door. Louise and Alice locked eyes. Louise shook her head and Alice laughed. "As I said, an excited puppy."

Chapter Three

A nd how are you this fine Wednesday morning, Paula?" Alice greeted her patient as she entered her room.

The woman smiled cheerfully. "I'm fine. I get to go home today."

"So I'm told," Alice said, wondering how to approach the matter of the meals. "You know, Paula, I live in Acorn Hill, and I—"

"You do?" Her eyes brightened. "I love living

there," she said. "I've been there only a few months, but it's a wonderful little town."

Alice smiled. "Where did you live before you moved to Acorn Hill?"

"I lived here in Potterston. After my mother died, I had no family left. We knew the Morris family, and they told me about their farmhouse. The change of scenery was just what I needed."

Alice nodded, feeling her heart warm toward this young woman who was all alone in the world and dealing with a serious illness.

"I especially love that big old Victorian home next to Grace Chapel. It's the one they've made into a bed-and-breakfast," Paula chattered on.

"As a matter of fact, my sisters and I run that bed-and-breakfast," Alice said with amusement.

Paula's eyes widened. "You do? It's a beautiful place."

"Would you like to come for a tour sometime? We'd love to have you."

"I'd like that," she said. "I admit I get a little lonely sometimes in that big old farmhouse. The Morrises and my neighbor are about the only people I've gotten to know since I've moved there."

Alice glanced through Paula's chart and made a few notations. "Well, that's about to change."

Paula looked confused.

"My sisters and I were wondering if you would mind, *um,* what I mean to say is, well, we were hoping to have a few people bring meals to your house for the next couple of days."

"Oh no," she said, shaking her head. "I couldn't ask anyone to do that."

"You haven't asked. We've offered. You'll have to get used to it. That's the way things are in Acorn Hill. Neighbors help neighbors." Alice smiled. "Acorn Hill is a truly caring community," she added with a dash of pride.

"Well . . ." Paula bit her lip and seemed to consider the matter.

"My sister has already volunteered, and she's the chef for our bed-and-breakfast. Trust me, you don't want to miss out on her cooking."

Paula looked up and smiled. "It's really nice of you. It would be wonderful."

"Good. It's settled then. You'll be home before dinner tonight, I'm sure. Your doctor normally dismisses his patients by around two o'clock. We'll bring dinner by, say, around six o'clock. Will that work for you?"

Paula's eyes lit up. "That would be great. Thank you, Alice."

"You're welcome. We'll see you tonight."

Alice stepped into the hospital hallway and actually felt a little bounce to her step. It could be the rubber-soled shoes, but she didn't think so. With a two-step and a muffled giggle, she made her way through the now-deserted hallway back to the nurses' station.

· · ·

"Are you sure you have time to go with me, Alice? I don't want to make you late for your ANGELs meeting tonight," Jane said as she carefully wrapped the chicken pot pie with a square of red and white checked gingham and nestled it into a basket.

"No problem, Jane. It's only five-thirty now. I've plenty of time."

Jane picked up the basket. "I guess we're all set then."

"I'll go tell Louise we're leaving so she can listen for the door. Then I'll come back, get the salad and bring it to the car," Alice said.

Jane nodded.

Alice tiptoed up to the parlor door that stood ajar. She could hear Louise's student plunking at the piano keys. The child hit a wrong note, causing Alice to cringe slightly. Louise had to have nerves of steel. The playing stopped momentarily, giving Alice the opportunity she needed to let Louise know they were leaving.

She tapped softly on the door.

"Yes?"

Alice opened the door farther and poked her head inside. "Jane and I are going to Paula's house now. We wanted to let you know so you could listen for the door."

"Thank you, Alice. Would you mind leaving the door open? I'll have a better chance of hearing someone coming in. I believe the Sandersons went out to dinner."

"Sure," Alice said, pushing the door fully open.

Alice shrugged on her coat and made her way to the kitchen. Picking up the covered salad bowl, she headed outside to Jane's car.

The frigid air pricked her cheeks like tiny needles. She hurriedly got inside the car. "My goodness, it's cold." She yanked the door closed and strapped on her seat belt. The warmth of the car chased away the sting of cold from her face.

Alice gave Jane directions and in no time they had arrived in front of the two-story farmhouse. Jane glanced around.

"It doesn't look like her neighbor is all that close," she said, pointing down the road toward the nearest house.

Alice frowned. "That's precisely why I'm concerned about her. Had her neighbor not needed sugar, who knows how long it would have taken her to get help."

Jane sighed. "Well, there's not much we can do about it now, but we *can* feed her."

Alice brightened. "That we can," she said, happy that there was something they could do, though not convinced her work with Paula was finished. There had to be something out there for people with epilepsy. Alice just had to find out what it was. Perhaps she'd do some research on the options available. By the time she and Jane thumped across the wooden porch in their boots and arrived at the door, Alice had decided that was exactly what she'd do.

The door squeaked open and Paula appeared. "Hello. Please, come in," she said.

They stepped onto a thick beige carpet that covered the living room area. Toward the front of the room in one corner stood a black television set. On the opposite side, an earth-toned sofa faced the TV, as did a taupe recliner with tiny rust-colored designs. With a basket of books near its base, a large oak rocking chair perched near the fireplace that was set in the center of the wall opposite the front door. A fire crackled pleasantly and filled the room with warmth. A computer and desk at the other end completed the furnishings.

"It's simple, but I call it home," Paula said as Alice and Jane glanced around the room.

"It's charming," Alice said.

"Very," Jane added.

Paula shrugged. "It's kind of big for just one person, but I love living out here. I grew up on a farm."

The sisters smiled.

"Paula, this is my sister Jane. Jane, this is Paula Middleton."

They exchanged greetings.

"If you want to follow me into the kitchen, we can bring your food in there," Paula said.

They stepped into a large country kitchen. Cedar

cabinets lined the walls, offering an abundance of storage space, and butcher block countertops provided ample workspace. Cheery bright yellow curtains framed the windows over the deep porcelain sink. Baskets dangled from cedar beams in the ceiling.

"Oh my, this room is wonderful," Jane exclaimed.

Paula followed their gaze with a smile. "It's my favorite place," she announced.

Jane handed her the basket. "Do you like to cook?"

Paula placed the basket on the counter. "I love to, though I'm not a fancy cook, just good old-fashioned home cooking." She paused, a frown shadowing her face. "I don't do much of it anymore, I'm afraid. Mother loved for me to cook, but with her gone . . ." Her voice trailed off.

A moment of silence and understanding hovered among them.

"Well, I hope you'll like what I've prepared for your dinner. Chicken pot pie," Jane said.

Paula clapped her hands together. "Oh, it's one of my favorites. Thank you so much. I'll never be able to eat it all myself, won't you join me?"

Alice shook her head. "Thank you, Paula, but no. I have to get back to a meeting, and Jane has things to do as well."

"Besides, what you can't eat you can save for leftovers," Jane said with a smile.

"Vera Humbert will be bringing you dinner tomorrow around six o'clock, if that works for you," Alice said.

"That'll be fine." A delicate blush crept up Paula's face. "You really shouldn't go to all the trouble."

Alice took Paula's hand. "No trouble at all. It's our pleasure. That's what being a good neighbor is all about."

"A rented neighbor, not a planted citizen," Paula said with a chuckle.

"Rented or otherwise, as long as you live in Acorn Hill, you're a neighbor."

Jane smiled in agreement and led the way back toward the front door.

"Well, thank you again, Alice and Jane."

"Remember, Paula, you're supposed to come to the inn soon and take a tour," Alice reminded her.

Paula perked up. "I'm really looking forward to that, Alice."

"Good. How about one day next week?" Jane asked.

"Sounds good to me."

"Maybe on Monday evening?" Alice suggested. She looked at Jane. "I think we're all scheduled to be home then."

Jane nodded.

Alice turned back to Paula. "Will that work for you?"

"Yes."

"Great. It's settled then." Alice and Jane turned to go.

"Thanks again. I really feel—"

Her words stopped short, causing Alice and Jane to turn around just as Paula crumpled into a heap on the carpet.

"I can't imagine what is triggering these attacks," Paula said a few minutes later as she sipped some water.

"Do you know what has caused them in the past?" Alice sat beside her on the sofa.

"Mostly genetic, they tell me. Epilepsy runs in my mother's side of the family. I'm thankful that my seizures have never been too severe. But I do find that sometimes stress can aggravate the problem. I haven't felt all that stressed lately, though, so I don't know why I'm having more seizures than usual."

Alice wondered if the woman still struggled with the death of her mother. "What is normal for you?"

"Oh, I normally have about a seizure a week."

"And lately?"

"Maybe one every day or two."

"How curious," Alice said.

"I'm sorry you missed your meeting, Alice. I feel terrible about that," Paula said abruptly, as if wanting to talk about something else.

Alice waved her hand. "That's no problem. I had everything ready, and Jane was happy to handle it for me. All she really had to do was to make sure that the girls did their jobs. They really are a great bunch of kids."

"What kind of group is it?"

Alice suspected Paula asked the question to keep the discussion away from her health. "They're junior high girls who meet weekly for a Bible lesson. We make some kind of craft or food at our meetings after the lesson, usually for other people, and send them out anonymously most of the time."

"That's really nice."

"It's a good way for them to learn Scripture." Alice smiled. "I look forward to our gatherings."

Paula nodded, though her mind seemed elsewhere. "How long was I out, do you know?"

Just as Alice thought, the young woman was more concerned than she let on. "I'd say about twenty seconds," Alice answered. "Is that normal for you?"

"It seems to be. I don't know for sure, because I don't always see the time just before it happens. Sometimes I get a feeling, a warning sign, but most of the time, I have no warning." Paula hesitated. "To tell you the truth, I don't really know what I do when I have a seizure." She thought a minute. "When I was younger, Mom told me I just fell to the floor. I didn't really do anything like jerk or whatever." She looked up at Alice. "Did I just fall to the floor this time?"

"Yes. Has your doctor told you that you have a tonic, or what is sometimes called drop, seizures?"

Paula nodded.

"Basically, that's when your muscles relax involuntarily, causing you to go down."

"Most children grow out of the drop seizures," Paula said rather mournfully. "I guess I haven't grown up yet." She attempted to smile.

Alice wanted to sympathize, but did not want Paula to interpret her words as pity. She kept silent.

"I know it could be much worse. I'm thankful that it isn't."

Alice looked at her. "I have to admit, I'm worried about your living out here so far from help."

Paula straightened and steadied herself as she stood up. "It's not so far out, Alice. Besides, my seizures don't last long. I've never really hurt myself before . . . that is, until the concussion."

"What about your stairs?"

Paula lifted her chin a notch, though her eyes betrayed her worry. "I've managed this long, I'm sure I'll be fine. I can't let fear control my life. I have to live," she said with a hint of finality.

"I understand," Alice said, sensing the woman's independent spirit.

We'll think of something, Alice thought. *We have to . . . and soon.*

Chapter Four

Alice was not in the mood to socialize, but Jane had asked Mary and David Sanderson to join the sisters in the living room for dessert later that evening.

"This peach crisp is wonderful, Jane," Mary said.

"Thanks. That recipe is one of my favorites. Especially in the dead of winter like this," Jane said. "Real comfort food."

"Well, I don't think I have ever tasted better," David said. He lifted his coffee in the air as a toast to Jane's baking.

The ladies smiled.

Louise turned to David. "You said that you're retired?"

David nodded. "I used to build homes. Now I volunteer my services to Habitat for Humanity. I think I'm busier now than I was when I worked full-time," he said with a chuckle.

Mary agreed. "And he loves every minute of it."

Alice studied him. Though his thinning white hair gave away his age, his body looked firm and strong, no doubt from years of manual labor. The rough, calloused hands gave testimony to hard work.

Mary looked relaxed and quite comfortable beside him. Dressed in a nice pair of gray wool slacks and a sweater with a pattern of gray and white diamonds, she was an attractive woman with pretty, reddish colored hair cut in a chin-length bob.

"I do enjoy the work. I suppose that's why I have devoted my life to it." David took a sip from his cup of coffee.

"We have two daughters. The older one married and moved away two years ago. The younger one just got married this past summer, leaving me to figure out what I'm going to do when I grow up," Mary said with a laugh.

"Oh, empty nesters, huh?" Alice smiled.

Mary nodded. Alice thought she detected a shimmer of tears in Mary's eyes. The woman coughed, then reached for her purse and pulled out a tissue. For people used to having kids in the house, Alice supposed the empty nest would take some adjustment.

"Oh my, I love your purse," Jane said with such enthusiasm, her comment drew everyone's attention.

Glancing at the navy quilted handbag on her lap, Mary asked with surprise, "This?"

"Yes. I've never seen anything quite like it," Jane said.

Mary chuckled. "Well, I suppose that's because I made it."

"You made it?" Jane asked.

Alice recognized that wide-eyed appreciation in

Jane. She lit up like that when she marveled at the creative work of another. Everyone looked at Mary.

"What's wrong?" Mary asked.

"Do you make them to sell?" Jane asked.

"Oh goodness, no," Mary said. "I love to sew and I love quilts, so I decided to put the two together." She shrugged.

"Don't let her modesty fool you. Several people have stopped her on the streets back home asking where she purchased her bag," her husband bragged. "She also makes big ones, the kind you use when traveling. She brought a couple of her bags on our trip."

Mary rolled her eyes. "It's not a big deal, really."

"Could we see your other bags sometime?" Jane asked eagerly.

Mary smiled, obviously pleased. "Well, sure, if you want to."

"You don't need to get them now," Jane said. "Just sometime before you leave."

Mary nodded. Her face flushed with the attention.

"By the way, you sure do have a smart dog," David said.

The sisters looked at him in surprise.

"Did I say something wrong?" David asked when he saw their reaction.

"Well, we don't have a dog," Alice said, trying to act nonchalant and avoiding her sisters' eyes.

"What did he look like?" Alice had a feeling that Jane's scraps had been a little too good. The hungry dog most likely had returned for more.

"A Lab. Beautiful dog, actually. Sleek black hair. Had a red collar," David said, looking from sister to sister. "Not your dog?"

Jane shook her head and smiled.

"Sore subject?"

Louise sighed. "It's not a sore subject, really. It is just that, well, Alice loves to help strays. Sometimes it takes a while to convince them to go home."

"I've got to say that I am glad that stray was here last night," David said.

Alice perked up a little. "How so?"

"Well, Mary and I were discussing your maple tree in the front yard, not really paying attention to where we were going." David looked at Mary and encouraged her to continue the story.

"I was looking at the tree and didn't notice that a tree branch had fallen partly on the sidewalk. Just as I was about to step on the branch, which surely would have caused me to fall, your dog—or somebody's dog—just shot out of nowhere. I mean, we hadn't seen him before that moment. He jumped in front of me, causing me to stop short. No harm done. We felt so very thankful he happened along when he did."

"Indeed," Louise said.

Jane smiled. "I love stories in which the Lord protects us in unusual ways."

Mary agreed.

"Did you learn who he belongs to?" David asked.

Alice shook her head and explained how she had found the dog when she came home Monday and that they had fed him, but that he had run off before they could try to locate his owner.

"I do hope he finds his way home," Louise said, "and before he gets a glimpse of Wendell." Louise glanced at their tabby sitting in a chair as though he owned it. He raised his head at the mention of his name, looking a tad annoyed at being disturbed from his nap.

Alice frowned. "I hadn't thought of that."

"Oh, I doubt that Wendell'd feel threatened in the least," Jane said with a laugh.

"You know, those Labs are good dogs. They're used a lot as medical assistance dogs," David said.

"Medical assistance dogs?" Louise asked.

"You haven't heard of them?" Mary asked.

"I'm sure that I must have heard the term, but I don't know much about them."

"Oh my, they are amazing," David said. "These dogs are trained to help people who have all sorts of disabilities. We saw a special on public television about them a couple of months ago."

"Really," Louise said. "Are they like Seeing Eye dogs?"

"Along the same lines," Mary said. "These dogs are called different things: medical assistance dogs, seizure dogs, facility dogs, depending on the need they fill. Medical assistance dogs, I think, are for disabled people. Let's see, seizure dogs are, of course, for people who deal with seizures—that type of thing. People who have physical problems that could prevent them from getting help, like breathing problems, or maybe because they are wheelchair-bound, find these dogs helpful and comforting."

Alice kept silent, taking in everything.

"They had one dog on the program," David said, "whose owner suffered some kind of an attack and fell to the floor. The dog ran to a special device similar to a phone and hit his paw three times on the preprogrammed numbers. Immediately, a 911 dispatcher answered and the dog barked. Having been notified ahead of time of the routine, the dispatcher knew to get an ambulance to the owner's place as soon as possible." David settled back into his chair. "Saved the man's life."

Alice scooted to the edge of her seat. "It sounds as if a device like that and a trained dog would be just the thing for an ailing person living alone."

"I know where you are going with this," Jane said with a grin, and then explained about Paula to Mary and David.

"You have to admit it's worth a try," Alice said.

Louise sighed. "I learned long ago that when Alice decides to help someone, she'll let nothing stand in her way."

Alice smiled, thinking she would call her veterinarian friend Mark Graves first thing in the morning and see what he knew about seizure dogs.

"Mark, I'm so sorry to bother you this early. Do you have a minute?" Alice asked.

"Alice, I always have time for you. How are you? Is everything all right?" he asked.

"Everything is fine, thanks."

"Aren't you headed off for work this morning?"

"Yes, in a few minutes," Alice said. "That's why I called you this early. I wanted to talk to you before we both started our days." Glancing at her watch, she hurried on. "Have you ever heard of assistance or seizure dogs?"

"Sure. Why?"

She explained the situation with Paula Middleton and the discussion with the Sandersons the night before.

"I see. So you want to see about getting a dog for her?"

"Well, I thought it was worth checking out at least."

"How does she feel about it?"

"Well," Alice stalled a moment, making a design on the floor with the toe of her shoe, "I haven't talked to her about it. I thought I'd see what was involved before I got her hopes up." She had a suspicion that Paula might object to the idea at first, but Alice felt sure that she could convince her to consider it.

"The bad news is that the dogs are very hard to come by. Patients are put on waiting lists, and it could take quite some time to get one. Sometimes they don't go by strict order of names received. They try to match the dog's skills to the patient's needs."

Alice's spirits dipped. She reminded herself of Paula's words, "I've made it this long without help, and I'll be fine. I can't live in fear." The words brought Alice little comfort. Paula also said her seizures were coming more often.

"Alice, are you still there?"

"Yes, I'm here."

"I haven't told you the good news yet," he said. Alice could hear amusement in his voice.

"Oh?"

"I have a friend who trains assistance/seizure dogs. Maybe he can pull some strings and get her one a little quicker. I can't make any promises, though."

"Oh Mark, that would be wonderful." Her mind raced. She would have to talk Paula into it, then she would have to see what was involved in getting the dog. Then she would—

"Now, Alice, I will tell you, the dogs are not cheap."

She glanced at her watch. She had to get to work. "Mark, I can see this is more involved than I had anticipated. Could you please check with your friend about the availability of dogs and then perhaps come here for dinner tomorrow night so we can discuss it further?"

He paused a moment. Alice assumed he was mentally going through his schedule. "Yeah, I think I can manage that. I look forward to seeing you."

Alice could feel the warmth creep up her cheeks. "I look forward to your visit too, Mark."

"I'll do what I can about the dog. See you tomorrow night."

"Good-bye." Alice put the phone in its cradle. Louise happened by on her way to the kitchen. "Who were you talking to this early in the morning?"

Alice followed her. "Mark Graves."

Louise stopped and turned to her. "Indeed?"

"I wanted to discuss the seizure dogs with him."

"Alice, aren't you getting too involved with this patient?" Louise asked.

"Indeed," Alice repeated with a mischievous smile.

Louise shook her head and put her arm around Alice's waist as they made their way to the kitchen.

"This looks wonderful, Jane," Louise said as they sat down to dinner that evening. "What kind of sandwich is this?"

"It's apple wood smoked bacon, basil marinated tomatoes, lettuce and warm goat cheese on grilled Italian bread." Jane flipped her napkin on her lap. "In layman's terms it's a BLT." She laughed.

Louise shook her head. "Whatever you call it, I know it'll be delicious."

"Thanks, Louise." Jane glanced at Alice. "Are you all right?"

"I'm fine," Alice said, sounding anything but fine.

"I'm not convinced," Jane said.

"Alice?" Louise said.

She looked up to the worried eyes of her sisters. She knew she owed them an explanation. "I went to Paula's house tonight."

"Isn't she well?" Louise asked.

"She is fine . . . for now." Alice pushed her plate away from her, her appetite clearly gone. "You know, I thought I had the answer for her. The seizure dog seemed just the thing." She explained about her conversation with Mark and the possibility of getting a dog a little sooner than usual. "It all seemed perfect, until I went to Paula's house. I was going to tell her about the dog, but thought better of it. The timing didn't seem right. She seems a little, well, stubborn. She wants her independence, and she does not want anyone to think she can't make it on her own." Alice gave a frustrated sigh. "I'm not sure how to approach the subject with her."

"I think you'll know when the time is right, Alice. If she doesn't like the idea at first, maybe she'll warm up to it after giving it some thought," Jane said.

"What about the dog in the meantime? I don't want to turn down a dog if we can get one sooner. It could take quite some time to get another one," Alice said.

"Well, remember, Alice," Louise said, "our obstacles are nothing for God. He cares about Paula more than we can imagine, and He will take care of her."

"I don't doubt His care for her. I just hope she'll listen to His promptings."

"Let's pray about it," Jane suggested. "We'll ask the Lord to give you direction about presenting the idea to Paula. Let's pray before we clear off the dishes. That way, you'll feel like eating," Jane said, nodding toward Alice's full plate.

Alice smiled. "Thank you, Jane."

The sisters held hands around the table and lifted the matter before the Lord. Once they felt the situation was safely in His hands, they went back to their meal.

"I don't know what I would do without you two." Alice looked at Jane and then Louise.

"Nor we without you," Louise said.

Jane nodded her head. After a moment or two she said, "They're predicting a good foot of snow by morning. I'd better check my supplies in case I need to make a grocery run tonight."

"Oh dear," Alice said. "I wonder if Paula has everything she needs."

"Remember, Vera Humbert brought her dinner tonight," Jane said, referring to Alice's teacher friend. "Paula should have plenty of leftovers from all the food coming her way."

"That's true." Alice thought a moment. "I hope she has enough medicine."

"Now, Alice, you cannot worry about her all the time. Remember, we just placed her in the Lord's hands," Louise reminded her.

Alice smiled. "You're right," she said.

Chapter Five

A lice was awakened by bright sunlight slanting through her bedroom window. She stretched luxuriously in her bed, enjoying the soft warmth of her plump pillows and thick comforter. She was thankful that she did not have to go to work. Mentally, she began to go through her agenda for the day. When she remembered that Mark Graves was coming to dinner, her heart gave a little skip, making her feel foolish for reacting like a college girl.

Sitting up, she dangled her legs over the side of her bed and wiggled her toes, then eased her feet into the fuzzy pink slippers that Jane had given her for Christmas. Then she walked over to the window to see how much snow had fallen during the night. A sparkling winter wonderland stretched across the grounds of Grace Chapel Inn and the street beyond. The thrill of a fresh, new day set Alice into motion. She headed for the shower and in no time at all, she was dressed and down the stairs, ready for breakfast. She stopped at the reception desk to call Paula. Unfortunately, the phones were out, probably because the heavy snow had downed the lines somewhere. She entered the dining room.

"Good morning," the Sandersons greeted her, all smiles.

"Good morning." She gave them a bright smile in return, then said to Louise, "Did you know the phones were out?"

Louise nodded. "I had the radio on a while ago and the newsman reported the problem. He said the phone company had workers out trying to get downed lines reconnected."

Alice looked at the Sandersons. "I trust you didn't have big plans today," she said with a nod toward the window.

"Oh, a little snowstorm won't stop us from having a good time," David said, shaking off her concern.

"David thinks it's an adventure," Mary said with a hint of excitement in her voice.

"Something tells me you folks like the winter season," Louise said.

"That we do," David said.

Alice smiled. "Well, have fun but stay out of the ditches."

"Oh, Alice?" Mary said.

Alice turned around. "Yes?"

"I brought my bags down for Jane to look at when she has the time."

Alice glanced at Mary's hand to see her holding the thick cloth handles of a luggage-sized quilted bag and a quilted book bag, both in a navy paisley print. "I don't know if she's interested, but I have these as well." Mary unzipped the luggage bag and pulled out a quilted eyeglass case, a billfold and a curling iron holder.

"Oh my," Alice exclaimed. "Jane will definitely want to see these."

Just then Jane stepped through the swinging door from the kitchen into the dining room. "Jane will want to see what?" she asked, carrying breakfast dishes to the table. "Oh, they are terrific," she said after one glance at the bags. She placed the dishes on the table and examined the bags carefully, exclaiming over each one. "Are you sure you've never thought of selling these, Mary?"

"Not really."

Jane looked at her. "You said that you've been looking for something to do with your time. You might consider making these to sell."

Mary stared at her, seeming at a loss for words.

David nudged her side, "See, I told you they were good enough."

"They're wonderful," Jane agreed. "In fact, my friend Sylvia owns the fabric store, Sylvia's Buttons, down the road, and I would like to show these to her. She often carries specialty items, as well as sewing supplies. Maybe you could go with me to see her?"

She looked first at David. He smiled. She turned back to Jane and grinned. "Why not?"

Before they could say anything else, David rubbed his hands together. "Great. Now, let's eat."

Everyone laughed.

Jane returned to the kitchen to get a serving spoon for the apple butter. Alice followed her.

"I feel I should check on Paula this morning," Alice said, as she retrieved a cup and saucer from the cabinet.

"Are you sure it's wise to drive right now before the roads are fully plowed? I've been hearing reports on the radio of people getting stuck along the roadway. They don't have all the rural roads cleared yet," Jane said.

Alice didn't relish driving on snow-covered roads, but she couldn't get past the need to check on Paula, especially with the phones out.

"You know, Samuel Bellwood just stopped by. He was on his way to the general store and asked if I needed anything. I decided that we could use more cream, so he's stopping back with it."

Alice nodded, wondering what that had to do with her.

"Well, he's riding his snowmobile. He told me if we needed to go anywhere, he would be glad to take us."

Alice looked up with a start, beginning to get the idea.

Jane was smiling. "You thinking what I'm thinking?"

"I sure am," Alice said, although the thought raced through her mind that she was too old for such an adventure. It was quickly replaced by the conviction that she needed to do this for Paula.

"He should be back in about fifteen minutes. You'd better get bundled up if you want to go with him."

"You're a genius, Jane," Alice said, already making her way to her room.

Jane was chatting with Samuel when Alice walked into the kitchen looking like a cocoon with a hat.

Samuel and Alice said their good-byes and headed outside.

"Be careful with my sister," Jane called out as Alice climbed rather awkwardly onto the snowmobile.

Alice could only pray that Louise was not watching, lest she think that Alice had taken leave of her senses.

Samuel started the motor and turned his head

sideways. "Here, put this on," he said, handing her a helmet.

She put it on, feeling quite sure she must look like she was ready to take her first step on Mars.

"Okay, now hang on tight, because these things can be a bit tricky, and I don't want to lose you on a turn."

Alice felt a rush of excitement—or was it fear—zoom through her. Slowly, Samuel pulled out of the drive. Alice had seen him zipping across his property on this machine and realized that he was taking extra precautions because of her.

They swished over the snow-covered streets. The cold air stung her face—the only exposed skin on her body—in an exhilarating way. In fact, she might have felt liberated had she not been bound like a mummy. Growing more confident as the ride wore on, Alice felt herself relax. She admitted to herself that she felt a flush of pride at her daring. Not too many people of her age would take on such an adventure. She felt, well, brave. A giggle bubbled up as she thought of the picture she must be making.

The snowmobile veered toward the right and she leaned into the turn as Samuel had instructed. By the time they had arrived at Paula's house, Alice felt almost sure she could handle the machine by herself. *Perhaps I should check into renting one some day,* she thought. Suddenly, Louise's disapproving expression came to mind. *Then again, maybe not.*

· · ·

Alice climbed off the snowmobile, her body still tingling from the ride, and turned to see Samuel waving at Paula's distant neighbor. "Hey, Alice, if you don't mind, I'll just mosey down there and pay a visit while you see to your friend. Pick you up in a few minutes, okay?"

"That's fine, Samuel. Thank you." Alice smiled as she watched him glide down the road. She turned and headed up Paula's porch. Now that she was there, Alice began to feel a little foolish. Would Paula think Alice was a snoop or, at the very least, a fussy old lady? Neither image appealed to Alice.

She lifted her hand to knock on the door, then hesitated. Was she doing the right thing? Maybe Louise was right, Alice shouldn't have interfered. After her moment of indecision passed, Alice decided that since she was already there, she had to go through with her mission. She knocked. No answer. She knocked again. This time she heard footsteps. The door finally creaked open.

Paula's pasty skin tone emphasized the dark circles under her eyes. Her hair was uncombed. Alice feared she had disturbed the woman from her sleep. "I'm sorry to bother you, Paula. The phones are out, and I was concerned about you."

"Please, come in, Alice."

Alice stepped inside. "I don't mean to be a nuisance," Alice said, hoping Paula would understand.

Paula motioned Alice to come over to the sofa. Alice quickly saw that Paula was limping, but waited for her to explain.

After Alice removed her coat and hat, they both sat down. "I want to tell you I'm totally fine, and I don't need you to check on me." Paula twisted her hands. "But the truth is I'm not fine."

Alice leaned toward her friend.

"I fell down some stairs a while ago."

Alice gasped.

Paula raised a hand. "I'm okay. Just a little beat up. I only fell down the last four or five steps. But that and the snow made me do some thinking."

Alice watched the woman as she seemed to search for just the right words.

"I've always been independent," she said with the tiniest lift of her chin.

Alice nodded.

"I don't like depending on anyone. I like my privacy. I want to come and go as I please without answering to another. That's one of the reasons I haven't married yet." She looked at Alice. "Does that make sense?"

"It makes perfect sense."

Paula gave a weak smile. "But I fear all of that is about to change. My seizures are happening more often, and I must admit I'm a bit afraid."

"Paula, have you talked with your doctor about the increased seizures?"

"Yes. I'm going in tomorrow to see him about changing my medications."

Alice said a silent prayer for the right words, sensing the Lord was directing the conversation. "I may have an option for you as far as your living alone is concerned," Alice ventured.

Paula wore a sorrowful expression as if her whole world was about to change, and Alice supposed in some ways that was true. "Have you ever heard of seizure response dogs?"

Paula blinked. "Seizure response dogs?" she repeated.

Alice nodded.

"Yes, I have. But it's been a while since I've discussed them with anyone."

"I've just learned about them myself, but this is what I know about them." Alice proceeded to recite the speech she had mentally gone over so many times to prepare for this moment with Paula.

Paula opened her mouth to speak, but Alice plowed ahead. If she let Paula interrupt now, Alice felt that she might forget some valuable point that she wanted to make. She continued on, sharing all the things Mark had told her about the dogs. She said that she would be talking with Mark later that night and would let Paula know anything she found out.

After Alice finished talking, Paula smiled. "As a matter of fact, I was about to tell you that I've already applied for a dog." Paula stared blankly toward the window. "To tell you the truth, I had forgotten about that until now. I guess I pushed it out of my mind, thinking I didn't really need one."

"You're on a list somewhere?"

Paula nodded.

"Well, that's wonderful."

Paula thought a moment. "That was some time ago. I didn't really want to get a dog at that time but felt somewhat pressured into signing up for one, at the insistence of a good friend." She looked up. "Someone like you." She smiled.

Alice grinned in return. "Perhaps we could check on the status of that application?" Alice suggested.

"I'll have to dig out the information. I think I know where I put it. They came over to my house at the time, not here, and interviewed me."

"Well, I'll still let Mark talk to his friend in case you can't find the information," Alice said.

Paula let out a sigh.

Sensing her reluctance, Alice patted Paula's arm. "I know it's not an easy decision, Paula, but it's truly for your own good."

"I know you're right," she said, still holding back somewhat.

By the time they had finished their discussion, Paula admitted that a seizure response dog was what she needed. Then, they heard Samuel's snowmobile pull up at the front of the house.

Alice stood to leave. "You're sure you're all right?"

"Yes, I'll be fine. I just bruised my pride," she said with a rueful grin. "Oh well, a dog might be fun."

"That's the spirit." Alice reached over to give Paula a quick hug. "You have enough medication for now? Food?"

"Yes."

Alice talked as she put on her coat and hat. "You look for your information, and I'll let you know what I find out. In the meantime, you might want to give your neighbor a key to your house just in case."

"Thank you," Paula said shyly, "*um,* for caring about me."

"You're welcome," Alice said, giving her hand a squeeze. As she made her way to the snowmobile, she remembered her sisters' prayer. Alice felt sure God was at work in Paula's situation. *Funny how He works in ways we don't always expect,* she thought. She had presumed Paula needed a roommate, never imagining the roommate could be a canine. Of course, no one knew how things would turn out. God could surprise them with a different answer altogether. Still, Alice knew they could trust it all to Him.

"You ready?" Samuel asked.

Charged with the excitement of knowing God was working in the situation, Alice put on her helmet and hopped on the back like a pro. "Ready," she said. Before she could blink, the vehicle jerked into gear and off they went onto the snowy streets of Acorn Hill.

Alice stepped inside the back door and peeled off her outer wraps. She felt invigorated by the cold and her time spent with Paula—and the snowmobile ride.

Jane turned upon hearing Alice enter the room. "Well, don't you look chipper," she said. "All pink-cheeked and sparkly-eyed."

Alice laughed. "I have to admit, the ride was fun."

Jane sat down at the table. "By the way, the phones are fixed. Mark called to say that the main roads are clear and that he still plans to come here tonight."

"Oh, good."

"Now, tell me about your visit with Paula," Jane said.

Just then Louise came into the room. "Alice, was that you on the snowmobile?" she asked incredulously.

Alice smiled and nodded.

"What were you thinking? Why, you could have hurt yourself," Louise admonished, taking her place at the table.

"I had so many layers on me, Louise, that if I had fallen, I wouldn't have felt a thing. Besides, sometimes we have to take risks to help a friend."

"I just want you to be careful." Louise gave her

a motherly look. "You are in your sixties, after all." Louise started to chuckle. "Oh my. What a sight, you on the back of that snowmobile."

"You did appear pretty, well, stiff when Samuel pulled away from our house. Like one of those stand-up dolls that don't bend," Jane said. "So, tell us what happened with Paula."

Alice told them everything about her visit. The sisters agreed the situation held hope.

Jane turned her attention to Louise. "I forgot to ask you about your phone call from Pastor Ken last night," Jane said, referring to Rev. Kenneth Thompson, minister at Grace Chapel. "What was that about?"

"Oh, he has been asked to be one of the speakers at a one-day seminar for pastors in Philadelphia. In fact, he has been asked to speak the same evening that I will be at the concert. He wondered if we might brainstorm some ideas together. With all the church responsibilities of late, he has struggled to get to it before now."

"You are just the person to help him," Jane said.

"It's true, Louise," Alice said. "I think Pastor Ken really respects your insights."

"I don't know about all that, but I do look forward to working with him. I am going to the church tomorrow afternoon to discuss some ideas."

"Pastor Ken is a wonderful speaker. His messages always challenge me to grow," Jane said.

"You will have to let us know what you come up with, Louise," Alice said, then glanced at her watch. "Oh my goodness, I have to get dressed. Mark will be here before we know it." With her thoughts already turned to what she would wear for dinner, Alice hardly noticed when her sisters shared a glance and a smile.

Chapter Six

That was a fine dinner, Jane," Mark said as he stood and pushed his chair up to the table.

Alice got up and began to clear their dishes.

Jane frowned and shook her head. "You two have some things to discuss. You go on into the parlor. Louise and I will clear the table. We'll be in shortly."

Mark smiled and followed Alice into the parlor. Being so familiar with her surroundings, Alice sometimes failed to stop and take notice of their home. She glanced at the antique glass vases and porcelain doll collection on the walnut table. Everything looked warm and inviting. The scent of burning wood from the fireplace offered a cozy ambience the moment they entered the room. They settled onto the Victorian settee.

"With all the snow, I was worried that you might not be able to come," Alice said.

Mark shrugged. "The street crews have been out working, so the main roads were not that bad. I took you up on your offer, though, and brought some clothes with me to stay overnight. I'll get an early start in the morning."

"Good. That way I won't worry about you sliding around the roads tonight."

Mark placed his hand on hers and gave it a gentle pat. "Ever the concerned nurse," he said.

Alice stared into the fire a moment, then looked toward Mark. His gaze was still fixed on her. "How have you been, Alice?" He lifted his hand from hers and shifted in his chair.

"I've been fine, thanks. I've been busy at the hospital with the usual influx of winter injuries plus some flu cases. How are things for you?" she asked.

Mark stared into the flames. She noticed the sharp crease of his khaki pants, the crisp blue button-down shirt. His hair, though peppered with gray, still held traces of black from his youth. "Going pretty well," he said, "though we did have a bear with an abscessed tooth that presented some problems."

"And I think some of *my* patients are ornery," Alice said with a laugh.

They fell into an easy conversation that covered their common interest in medicine—human and animal—as well as news from Acorn Hill and Philadelphia.

At last, Jane and Louise entered the room carrying a tray holding mugs filled with steaming hot tea and a plate with a variety of homemade cookies. "The perfect ending to a wonderful meal, Jane," Mark said. "Those lamb kabobs were great and so are these cookies, I suspect."

Alice noticed he still kept fit and trim, just as he had in his college days.

"So, Alice, about the assistance dogs . . ."

She looked at him expectantly.

"I called Andy Turner, the friend I told you about who heads up a training center for them. He tells me that he could get a dog for you." He took a drink. "That's the good news."

Alice leaned forward.

"The bad news is they are expensive, and it will take some time. You would need to talk to him about the price. It varies, but I know they can run up to several thousand dollars."

Alice frowned as she wondered if Paula could come up with that kind of money.

"There are ways to work out the finances," he said when he saw her expression. "I'm telling you, Alice, these dogs are truly amazing. They can be taught to lie beside the patient until the seizure is over or they can run for help, whatever suits that particular patient."

"It's almost unbelievable what they can do," Alice said. She then explained that Paula had already applied for a dog somewhere. "I'm trusting she will be able to find the paperwork, and we can check into the matter."

Mark thought a moment. "Didn't you tell me Paula lives out in the country?"

"Yes," Alice said.

"It might be a good idea to get one of those telephone devices that contacts 911 in case she gets into trouble. The dog could activate it with his paw and alert the medical personnel. She would have help in no time."

"How amazing," Louise said.

"It really is," Mark agreed.

"Her seizures only last about twenty to thirty seconds, so probably if the dog just settled beside her that would be good enough," Alice said. "Of course, it would be great to train it to get help if needed. Though by the time help got there, her seizure would be over. Still, if she fell and hurt herself . . ."

"It would probably be a good idea to have one, just for that kind of situation," Mark said.

"Do you think Paula has the funds to pay for such an animal, Alice?" Jane asked.

Alice thought a moment. "I'm sure she doesn't. She works out of her home as a consultant of some type, but I don't think she makes all that much money." Her mind searched for ideas. "I'm not sure how we could help her. We certainly don't have the means to do so."

Everyone grew quiet, lost in thought. The bluish-yellow flames danced about in the fireplace.

"Didn't you say she attends the community church in Potterston, Alice?" Louise asked.

"Yes, well, she did before she moved here. She doesn't drive because of her seizures, so she can't get there now."

Louise looked surprised. "How does she get her groceries and run her errands?"

"She told me her neighbor takes her when she needs to go. If the weather is nice, she'll walk, though it's quite a distance."

"Poor thing." Louise thought a moment longer. "Perhaps the community church would still be willing to help her."

Alice shook her head. "I doubt it. She told me they recently had a fire. It damaged the kitchen in the fellowship center. They have some insurance issues, so the church is hard pressed financially at present."

"Oh dear," Louise said.

"What about the outreach fund that Grace Chapel has?" Jane asked. "Could it be used for something like this?"

Alice hesitated. "You know, Jane, you might be onto something there. I'll ask at the board meeting this week."

Mark pulled out his Palm Pilot and poked his stylus a few times on the tiny screen. He looked up at Alice. "If you could get something to write on, I'll give you Andy's number so you can contact him directly."

Alice got a pen and paper, and Mark gave her the number. Soon it was bedtime. After saying their good nights, the sisters cleared the dishes and Mark made his way to the Symphony Room. He would head back to Philadelphia first thing in the morning.

When Alice finally got settled into her bed, she couldn't fall asleep. Thoughts of helping Paula get the dog filled her mind. Then, of course, her evening in Mark's company also distracted her from slumber. Finally, she drifted off, her dreams populated by dogs, patients and a special friend.

The next afternoon, Mary Sanderson and Jane stepped into the warmth of Sylvia's Buttons. The fresh smell of fabric mingling with the floral pot-pourri on the counter gave the room a muted springtime scent.

Jane glanced about the room. Bolts of colored fabric lined shelves that stretched from the floor to the ceiling. Notions were arranged in one corner. Sewing and quilting books filled a nearby black wire rack.

"This is a quaint little shop," Mary said.

"It is nice," Jane agreed. Looking around and seeing no one, Jane guessed Sylvia to be in the back room. "Let's go back here and see if Sylvia is in her workroom." Mary followed Jane. Sylvia sat at the worktable maneuvering a piece of fabric around using her good right hand and holding the edge of the fabric with the cast on her left arm.

"Knock, knock, anybody home?" Jane asked with a smile.

Sylvia looked up with a start. "Oh hi, Jane. I'm sorry. I didn't hear you come in." A pale crimson crept up her cheeks. "Hello," she said when she saw Mary.

"Sylvia, this is Mary Sanderson. Mary is a guest at our inn," Jane said.

"The woman who makes the bags?" Sylvia asked with a smile.

"Yes, I guess that's me," Mary said. "That doesn't look like much fun," she added, pointing to Sylvia's cast.

"Oddly enough, I'm getting used to it." She settled back into her chair and reached up with her good hand to tuck a strand of strawberry blond hair behind her ear.

"We brought lunch," Jane said, placing a picnic basket on Sylvia's worktable.

"You didn't need to," Sylvia said, "though I'm glad you did. What do we have?"

"Chicken salad sandwiches, assorted raw veggies, apples and angel food cake. I thought it might be fun for all of us to have lunch together," Jane said, pulling the food from the basket.

"I feel terrible that you are going to this much trouble for me." Sylvia peeled the plastic wrap from her sandwich.

"That's what friends are for." Jane placed matching paper plates, napkins and cups on the table.

Sylvia laughed. "I should have known you would have everything coordinated."

"I'm hopeless, what can I say?" Once she got everything situated, Jane said the prayer for their meal.

After their prayer, Sylvia looked at Mary. "Jane has been telling me about your bags. I can't wait to see them," Sylvia picked up her sandwich and bit into it.

Mary reached into the shopping bag she had placed on the floor and lifted out the quilted bags one by one and put them onto the worktable.

Sylvia placed her sandwich back on the plate, wiped her hand on her napkin and examined the bags. "Oh, Jane you were so right. These are wonderful, Mary." She opened pockets and zippers and examined the stitching. "Would you allow me to display these? If anyone is interested, they could place an order."

Mary bit her lip and thought a moment. "Well, I suppose it'd be fine. I doubt that anyone will be interested."

"Oh ye of little faith," Jane said with a laugh. "We're pretty good judges of what sells here in Acorn Hill, and I think you should trust us on this one."

Mary's face glowed with excitement. "What have I got to lose?"

"Exactly." Jane filled each of their cups with raspberry tea from her thermos.

They sat in silence a moment, each enjoying her lunch.

"So, how are you managing, Sylvia?" Jane asked.

"Oh, all right. It's a bit difficult to cut fabric for customers. With practice, I'm learning how to grip it with my cast as I cut with my right hand. Your help has been a godsend, I can tell you that."

Jane smiled. "I'm glad I'm able to help. We only have a couple of guests currently, so it's not a problem getting away now and then."

Sylvia chewed on a carrot. "I'm working on a new quilt—or at least I was before I broke my arm," she said. "I'm looking forward to getting back at it once I get my cast off."

"When do you get it removed?"

Sylvia frowned. "Not for a while."

Jane nodded and took a sip of her tea.

"Did your aunt Ethel decide if she would teach the bread-making class?" Sylvia asked.

"She hasn't told me for sure," Jane answered, "but I think she will. She looked excited when I mentioned it—well, after the shock of the idea wore off."

They both laughed. Jane turned to Mary and explained about the class. "Auntie will do a good job, and it'll be good for her," Jane said.

"Sometimes we just need a little push in the right direction." She gave Sylvia a mischievous grin.

Sylvia smiled in return.

Just then, they heard the front door to the store open. Jane lifted a hand as Sylvia started to get up. "You stay put. I'll go check on it." Before Sylvia could argue, Jane had stepped into the front room.

A woman stood there with a rosy-cheeked toddler all bundled in winter wraps.

"Hello, may I help you?"

"I'd like to look through your quilting books," the woman said.

"Sure, that's fine. Help yourself," Jane answered, pointing to the books. "I'm Jane. If you need any help, please call me." She stepped back into the room with Sylvia.

"Who is it?" Sylvia asked.

Jane shook her head. "I didn't recognize her. Must be from out of town."

Sylvia stood. "I think I'll just go in and welcome her."

Jane nodded, before picking up her sandwich once again. She could hear the women chatting softly in the other room. Jane and Mary entered into conversation about Mary's daughters. They were discussing Mary's younger daughter's wedding when they heard a sharp cry coming from the other room.

Jane and Mary jumped up from the table and ran into the room.

"My baby, where's my baby?" the customer was saying frantically as she looked around the shop. The woman's eyes were wide with panic. She darted around the room, looking under draped fabric. She called out, "Emma, Emma!" between gasps of breath. "She was just here beside me when I was thumbing through these books. Where could she have gone?"

Then Jane noticed the front door ajar and alarm seized her. The mother followed Jane's gaze and a cry escaped her.

"It's okay, ma'am," Jane said, already pulling on her coat and gloves. "She hasn't been gone long. She couldn't be far." Jane dashed out the door while the mother followed close behind her. Looking to the left and then to the right, Jane noticed the flash of something dark just turning the corner. Running until the cold bit into her lungs, she reached the end of the street and turned to see the little girl standing with the stray dog that had visited the inn.

Jane heard the crunch of footsteps in the snow just behind her. Tears streaming down her face, the mother fell to her knees in front of the little girl. She held her daughter tight against her. "Emma, don't you ever leave Mommy like that again, do you hear me?"

With her shiny red cheeks and wide blue eyes, the toddler looked like a doll. "I sorry, Mommy. See doggie?" she asked, pointing to the black Lab standing nearby between the little girl and the street.

"I see the doggie." The mother appeared apprehensive at first, but then she reached up to stroke the Lab. "Thank you." Tears trickled down her face. "If you hadn't distracted Emma, who knows where she might have gone?"

"You know, I thought the same thing," Jane said.

Somewhat out of breath, Sylvia and Mary caught up with them. "Oh good," Sylvia said, her right hand pressed against her chest as she struggled to breathe, "you found her."

Jane turned and smiled at them, noting how the left arm of Sylvia's coat hung limply at her side, her cast tucked safely within the folds of the coat. Jane walked toward the dog to get a look at his tags, but just as she reached for him, he darted away.

"Doggie," Emma said, pointing. They turned to see the stray run across the street and disappear between the shops. "Doggie go?" she asked.

The mother stooped down to squeeze her daughter tight against her. "Doggie had to go home, sweetheart," she said. Once she rose to her feet, they all headed back to the store. They talked about the mysterious dog and how thankful they were he showed up when he did.

As they made their way back to Sylvia's Buttons, Jane wondered where home was for the mysterious canine.

Chapter Seven

Alice met Vera Humbert at the Coffee Shop for lunch and the two of them slipped into a booth, the red faux leather seats creaking beneath them.

Vera unbuttoned her red coat and settled in for a friendly chat. "Alice, I can tell you that I'll be glad when spring break comes," she said with a laugh.

Alice thought of Vera's job as a fifth grade teacher and smiled. She pulled off her blue and green plaid coat and green scarf and said, "I'm sure the children are getting restless."

Vera sighed. "Restless is a mild word for it. I have a boy in my classroom who is making me crazy. No matter how many times I make him clean the blackboard, write pages of sentences or stay in from recess, he still will not stop pestering the girls."

Alice chuckled. "Some boys do like the girls' attention, negative or otherwise."

"He wants their attention all right."

"Just think how he'll be when he's twenty." Alice laughed again.

Vera shrugged. "At this rate, he'll probably still be in my class." Vera looked at her menu. "This time of year, it's hard to teach. I mean, the kids haven't had much of a break since Christmas, and they're ready, believe me." She laughed. "Then again, I can't blame them. I'm ready too."

Hope Collins stepped up to their booth. "Hello, ladies," she said.

"How have you been, Hope?" Vera asked.

"Oh pretty good. Business is slow. Not many folks want to go out in this weather." Hope pulled the pencil from behind her ear. "What can I get you?"

"I think I'll take a bowl of chili," Vera said.

"*Hmm,* make that two," Alice said.

"Good choice for a cold afternoon. Two bowls of chili coming up." Hope turned toward the kitchen.

Once Hope left, Vera leaned across the table. "I'm dying to hear more about Paula."

Alice nodded. She proceeded to tell Vera about her discussion with Paula and then with Mark the night before. "I called his friend who runs the training center for assistance and seizure dogs, but he wasn't there. I left a message. Guess I'll have to wait till I hear from him."

Just then, a cold wind whooshed through the open door as Clara Horn came in. She spotted Vera and Alice and with great enthusiasm waved a greeting. Alice felt a surge of disappointment as the older woman headed their way. Clara was a nice person, but Alice really wanted some one-on-one time with Vera.

Clara was Ethel's friend. Two peas in a pod, Alice called them. Actually, the two of them were also friends with Florence Simpson, a member of the church board and town busybody. The three of them together could stir up more ruckus than a swarm of bees at a garden party.

Dressed in a heavy black coat, a multicolored stocking cap with a fuzzy ball at the tip and big fluffy red mittens, Clara clopped across the floor in her snow boots.

"Hello, Vera, Alice," she said. "Mind if I join you?" Before they could respond, she scooted into the seat beside Alice and commenced taking off her coat, hat and mittens, scattering wet snow on the seat. "Oh," she said shivering, "I feel like I live at the North Pole, I tell you."

Vera and Alice exchanged amused glances.

Clara turned to Alice. "Now, what's this I hear about you wanting a guide dog or some such thing?"

The sisters had brought Ethel up to date on Paula's situation, and obviously Ethel had shared the information with Clara. Alice explained what she knew about the dogs and how she hoped a dog would help Paula.

"Interesting," the older woman said. "May I have a hot chocolate, Hope," she said as the waitress approached their table. Then she launched into her preferred topic of conversation.

"Well, as you know, my Daisy," she said, referring to her Vietnamese potbellied pig, "is quite smart." Squaring her shoulders, Clara sat up straighter in the booth and seemed to grow two inches on the spot. "In fact," she leaned in for effect, "I'm considering allowing her to work with the Acorn Hill Police Department."

Alice glanced atVera, who rolled her eyes slightly. "Doing what for the police, Clara?" Vera asked.

"Well," she said as someone in the know, "pot-bellied pigs are quite useful in sniffing out drugs. I saw one being used that way on television. It set me to thinking how Daisy could probably handle the job if she had a mind to."

Alice pursed her lips to keep from laughing at the thought of Daisy sniffing out drugs. Clara normally dressed Daisy in, well, girlie clothes. There was nothing funnier than seeing a snorting, grunting pig dressed in frills, ruffles and bonnets. Sometimes poor Daisy could be spotted on the streets of Acorn Hill riding in a baby carriage. The idea of Daisy participating in a drug bust dressed to kill was almost more than Alice could handle. She envisioned the pig as an undercover cop, sporting a leather jacket and silver chains, and she had to duck her head to cover her grin.

"Alice, what are you smirking about?" Clara asked, as she stirred the hot chocolate that Hope had just placed in front of her.

"I'm sorry, Clara, I was just thinking about something."

Clara stared at Alice a moment, then resumed her

speech about how smart potbellied pigs were and how the citizens of Acorn Hill should be pleased as punch that she had brought her Daisy into their midst.

Vera finished her chili, then dabbed her mouth with her napkin. "Well, Clara, there are other ways to employ a pig. As you know, our school has fundraisers from time to time. One year, the kids were rewarded for their efforts when a lady in Potterston came to our school with her pig dressed in a tutu. And you know what? Right there in front of the entire student body, that pig kissed the principal smack on his face."

Wide-eyed, Clara whispered, "No."

"Honest truth," Vera said, crossing her heart.

"Well, I'll be," Clara said. Then she sat up and with an air of dignity said, "Well, I don't believe I'll have Daisy prancing about town in a tutu. And kissing principals? My, my." She shook her head. "After all, Daisy's got her pride."

"I see your point," Vera finally said, trying to look serious.

The door opened again and in walked Florence Simpson.

"Oh, yoo-hoo," Clara called out, waving her arm, as if they could not be seen otherwise.

Alice thought that Florence might join them too, but Vera came to the rescue. "You know, Alice, I probably need to get going."

Clara started collecting her things.

"Hello, all," Florence said when she approached the table.

"How about I join you?" Clara asked. "These ladies are about to leave."

"That would be fine. I am ready for some coffee. The cold is beastly," she said, shivering in her coat dramatically.

Before Florence could visit any more, Clara lifted her things and nodded toward a booth where they could visit. They said their good-byes, leaving Vera and Alice alone.

"Whew," was all Vera said.

"My sentiments exactly."

Alice and Vera looked at each other and erupted into quiet laughter.

"Good morning, Louise," Pastor Thompson said as he approached her the next morning after church.

"Hello, Pastor Ken. Wonderful message this morning."

"Thank you. I've always liked the story of Balaam's donkey. That God would use a donkey to deliver a message to Balaam shows that you never know what marvelous ways God will choose to speak to His people," he said with a smile.

"Well, I thought it interesting that though Balaam mistreated his donkey, the animal still tried to protect him. I am not surprised that when God finally opened the creature's mouth so he could talk, he got Balaam's attention. I am quite sure that it would get mine," Louise said with a chuckle. "Makes me glad we take good care of Wendell."

Pastor Thompson laughed along with her.

"And it is so true, the point you brought out, that the Lord many times works in ways we cannot comprehend." They continued to follow the crowd as they left the church. "I know I expect Him to do things a certain way and often He surprises me," Louise said.

"Great message, Pastor," Jane said as she and Alice approached them.

"Yes, just wonderful," Alice agreed.

"Thank you, ladies." He turned to Louise. "Louise, I would like to talk to you again sometime tomorrow or Tuesday, if possible, about the seminar, if you have the time."

"I have some time this afternoon," Louise offered.

Jane jumped in, "Why don't you join us for lunch today, Pastor? Then after lunch you and Louise can discuss your seminar."

He looked at the sisters. "Well, I don't want to intrude."

Jane waved her hand to brush the matter aside. "No intrusion whatsoever. We would love to have you."

He smiled and shrugged. "How can I refuse?"

"We'll eat in about forty-five minutes. Come over any time before then," Jane said.

"I'll be there."

It seemed no time at all before the Howard sisters and Pastor Thompson gathered around the dining room table and settled in for a Sunday meal of marinated steak tips, whole artichokes, buttered new potatoes, bread sticks and a salad of apple and pear wedges with provolone cheese. Their conversation ranged over a variety of topics, including various church programs and the health of some of the older members.

When the main course was finished, Jane turned to Louise. "Alice and I will take care of clearing. Why don't you and Pastor Ken go into the parlor? That way you can go ahead with your meeting, and we won't disturb you. When you are finished, I'll serve dessert in there. By the way, we're having double-chocolate torte."

"Oh my." Pastor Thompson's eyebrows rose.

"Unless, of course, you don't have any room for it," Jane said.

He smiled. "I'll always make room for your torte."

Pastor Thompson and Louise settled into the parlor. Louise had turned on the CD player, and Eduardo Fink's Piano Rhapsodies swirled around the room.

"Nice music," Pastor Thompson commented.

"Eduardo Fink is one of my favorite pianists," Louise said. "In fact, he is performing at the concert I'm attending in Philadelphia."

Pastor Thompson's gaze lifted questioningly.

"I have a friend who works at the Philadelphia Conservatory. She oversees the scheduling of artists performing at the Conservatory. Eduardo Fink—" Louise pointed toward the CD player "—will be in concert the night of your seminar. My friend has invited me to come for a visit and to attend the event with her."

"I am sure it will be quite a treat for you to attend," Pastor Thompson said. "And I'm glad one of my prayer partners will be nearby."

"You still seem a bit concerned about your speech."

"This seminar is important, Louise. I mean, well, it is an honor to speak to the clergy." He clasped his fingers together and stared at them. "I have to admit that I feel somewhat intimidated speaking before a group of pastors, some of whom have years more experience than I have. My struggle is to present the right message and not let myself get in the way.

"There is a temptation to try to deliver an impressive message rather than waiting for God's direction about what He would have me share. Please pray that I'll be sensitive to His leading and not let my human emotions get in the way."

"Of course." Louise smiled fondly at the sensitive pastor.

"I'm praying that somehow God will use this message, whatever He might lay upon my heart, to strengthen and encourage the clergy that we might be more effective in our world."

"I will continue to pray about the matter, and I know my sisters will as well, Pastor Ken. I am quite sure the Lord will supply."

Pastor Thompson smiled. "Yes, I know that He will. Would you pray with me now for guidance?"

Together they bowed their heads and sent their prayer to the Lord. Once they were finished, Louise felt certain that God's message would soon be revealed to the pastor. In the meantime, they would continue to pray, search the Scriptures and listen for His voice.

In light of the morning's sermon, Louise could only hope He would not have to use a donkey as His messenger.

Chapter Eight

The following day the sisters had no sooner cleared the breakfast dishes when Ethel came through the back door.

"Good morning, Aunt Ethel. I'm sorry to run off so soon, but I have to get to work," Alice said.

Ethel looked as though she had not heard Alice. Taking off her coat, she glanced around the kitchen. Alice looked at Jane and Louise, shrugged and left for work.

"I'm afraid I have some errands to run," Louise said.

Ethel did not respond.

Jane and Louise shared a puzzled glance.

"Are you feeling well this morning?" Louise asked her aunt.

Ethel was silent for a moment, and then as if Louise's question had just registered, she answered, "Oh, fine, fine."

Louise raised her eyebrows, turned to Jane and said good-bye, leaving Jane alone to unravel the mystery of Ethel's strange behavior.

Jane took one more swipe across the counter with her sponge, while Ethel flitted around the kitchen like a bird out of its cage.

"Auntie, are you sure you're all right?" Jane asked.

"I'm fine, why?" Ethel asked, as she poured herself a glass of water, took the tiniest of sips and poured the rest into the sink.

"You seem to have something on your mind."

Ethel bit her lower lip. "Well, there is something bothering me," she finally said, wringing her hands together.

"What is the matter, Auntie?" Jane asked, gently patting Ethel's back.

"Well, you know I believe a body can do anything they set their mind to," Ethel said.

Jane nodded, trying to encourage her to continue.

"It's just that I told you I would teach the class, and well, I've been thinking it over. I've never"— she swallowed hard—"taught a class before."

A twinge of guilt pricked Jane's conscience for asking this favor of her aunt. She put her arm around Ethel's shoulders. "Oh Auntie, you'll do just fine. I would've never asked you if I hadn't been sure that you'd be great." Jane studied Ethel, noting the circles under her eyes. Obviously Ethel had lost some sleep over the matter.

"You are a wonderful cook," Jane assured her. "I thought you'd enjoy doing something different and sharing your talents."

"It's just that I haven't baked bread from scratch recently," she said. "Land's sake, I have a bread-making machine that practically bakes the bread by itself." Her voice had an edge of panic.

Jane considered how she might lessen her aunt's concerns. The teakettle whistled. Lost in thought, Jane set the tea to brew and placed cups and saucers on the table. She and Ethel settled into their chairs. Suddenly, inspiration struck her.

"I have an idea," Jane said. "How about we have a trial run?"

Ethel gave her a questioning glance.

"I was going to bake some bread for dinner tonight. If you don't have plans this morning, how about you do it for me? Give yourself sort of a practice run, and we can talk about the aspects of baking, just as you would do in front of your class. Also, if you'd like, I can sit in on your first class."

For the first time since she had arrived, the worry left Ethel's face.

"You don't mind helping me, Jane, and going to the first class?"

"I would be happy to help you. Why, we'll have fun doing it together," she encouraged. "We can go over your class plans too. I had meant to give you my notes on the class syllabus, but I forgot. I'm sorry." Jane walked over to the counter, lifted a cookbook from the shelf and pulled out her notes. She turned to Ethel. "Do you have time to start it now?"

A look of relief washed over Ethel, and she nodded with enthusiasm.

"You look these notes over, and I'll get the cookbook." Jane gave Ethel the notes, then walked back to the cupboard, thinking about her schedule for the day. If they got started right now, she would still be able to go to Sylvia's shop after lunch.

"Here we go," she said, pulling the thin book off the shelf. "This deals with the types of flours that work best for different kinds of bread."

They sat down and studied the recipes. Ethel made notes and together they filled out a class schedule Ethel could handle.

Ethel breathed a sigh of relief. "I can't tell you how much this helps me, Jane. Thank you."

"You're welcome. Now let's pick a basic recipe so we can get started on that bread," Jane said.

Together, Ethel and Jane sat at the table and looked through the book until they came upon a recipe for wheat bread. "This seems to be a good one for basic wheat bread, what do you think, Auntie?" Jane scooted the book closer to Ethel so she could get a better look.

After reading through the recipe, Ethel said, "I'm sure I can handle this."

"While you're getting familiar with the directions, I'll gather the supplies we need to get started," Jane said.

Ethel reached out and touched Jane's arm. "Are you sure you don't have plans to do something else this morning, Jane?"

"It's no problem at all, Auntie. Remember that by teaching this class, you are freeing me to help Sylvia at her shop and to be able to take care of our new guest. So I want to do what I can to get you started." Jane bent over and gave Ethel a squeeze.

When Jane pulled away, Ethel's hand reached up and gently brushed Jane's face. "I wish your mother could have known you, Jane," Ethel said, her voice unusually warm and sentimental.

Madeleine Howard had died giving birth to Jane. Though Jane had worked through the ache of never knowing her mother, it still startled her when someone mentioned Madeleine in conversation.

"I know she would be proud of you," Ethel said.

Jane choked back the knot in her throat. She did not know which touched her more, thoughts of making her mother proud or her aunt's rare display of emotion. "Thank you, Auntie."

Before Jane could drop the first tear, Ethel's no-

nonsense manner returned. Mischief replaced the softness in her eyes with a sparkle as she said, "Let's get this show on the road."

Jane rose to her feet. With a smile on her face, she walked to the pantry to gather the necessary supplies while Ethel buried her nose in the recipe book.

During her morning break, Alice decided to try calling Andy Turner again. She had missed his earlier call, so they were playing phone tag. "Hello. Is this Andy Turner?" she asked when the deep voice answered on the other end of the line.

"Yes, this is Andy."

"Hi, Andy. My name is Alice Howard—"

Before she could say more, he cut in with a friendly manner. "Alice, finally we meet," he said. "Mark Graves has told me a lot about you."

For some reason, the very idea of Mark talking about her to someone else made her face feel warm. For the next fifteen minutes they discussed Paula's situation and how the process worked for obtaining a seizure response dog.

"If you would like to come to our facility, I would be happy to talk to you about the dogs in more detail. We don't actually train the dogs at our center. The animals are paired with their trainers and go to live with them while being educated in the assistance program. It's possible I could schedule you in to one of the homes, but I'm not sure. I don't want to disrupt the training process."

"I'm sure it's fascinating, but that's not necessary," Alice said, all the while thinking how interesting it would be to see the actual training in progress. "I would, however, like to come and talk to you in more detail."

"Certainly," he said. Alice could hear him flipping through some pages, most likely of his calendar. "How about we meet tomorrow?"

"Great," she said. They worked out the details of the meeting, and by the time they had ended their conversation, Alice felt like a woman on a mission. It thrilled her that she was able to make a difference, if only one step, one phone call, one task, at a time.

Alice glanced at her watch. Seeing that she had a few minutes left on her break, she picked up the phone again and called Paula.

"Hello?"

"Hi, Paula. This is Alice."

"Oh Alice, hello."

Alice could hear the genuine enthusiasm in Paula's voice. "How are things going?"

"I'm doing all right. My doctor increased my medication dosage and so far my seizures seem to have stabilized."

Alice hoped this would not keep Paula from checking into the service dog program. "Did you talk to your doctor about getting a seizure response dog?"

"Yes, I did. He highly recommended that I consider getting one."

Alice relaxed. "Good. In fact, that's one of the reasons why I called you. I wanted to check and see if you found anything on your prior application."

"As a matter of fact, I did. I called them this morning. Guess what, they wanted to know if I could come for a training program beginning tomorrow at Caring Canines in Philadelphia."

"Oh Paula, we have our answer to prayer," Alice said, wondering why she was always amazed when God came through for her.

"Well, before you get too excited, Alice, I'm afraid there is a hitch."

"What is that?"

"When I applied before, I qualified financially because my church had offered to help me get the dog, but you know much of my church was damaged in a fire . . ." Her words trailed off. "I haven't told the people at Caring Canines yet. I wasn't sure what to do."

Alice felt a catch in her throat. She could not answer for Grace Chapel's board, but she prayed that her friend would get the help she needed. "I understand. I have an idea about that, Paula. Don't give up just yet. I'm working on it."

"Well, I have the savings to cover my two weeks' training, and I can stay with a friend while I'm there, so that will cut costs. But I couldn't accept—"

Alice interrupted her. "You wouldn't want to interfere with the Lord's work, would you?"

"I . . . I suppose not."

"Well, we'll just have to wait and see what He has in mind. I'll keep you posted."

"Thanks, Alice."

"You're welcome," Alice said. "Now, I wanted to make sure that you are still coming for dinner tonight, as we planned. Will you have time?"

"Oh my, I'd completely forgotten about that. I've been so busy with my job and trying to get my health situation under control."

"Would you rather we do it another time?"

"Oh no, I've already started packing for Philadelphia and should be done before long. I would love to come if it still works out for you and your sisters."

"I'll pick you up around six-thirty."

"I'll be ready," Paula said.

"By the way, how are you getting to Philadelphia?"

"My friend from Philly is coming to get me."

"Great. Well, I'll see you tonight." Alice hung up the phone, walked down the hall, and remembered something she needed to pick up from the nurses' station on the next floor. Deciding to take the stairs, she walked to the nearest door. A glance at the steps reminded her of the hill she had yet to climb.

The Grace Chapel Board.

Chapter Nine

I feel much better about the bread-making now, Jane," Ethel said as she sat in the living room with her niece. "Thank you for helping me."

"It was a fun way to spend our morning. I'm glad we could do it," Jane said. "The dough should be just about ready to put into the oven by now. We'll check on it in a minute."

"Is Sylvia getting along all right?" Ethel asked.

"She's adjusting fairly well."

"Do you have to go over and help her at the shop this afternoon?"

"Yes, I'm planning to go for a little while, then come back to put the finishing touches on dinner before Paula gets here."

"Thanks, Jane, for helping me make up a schedule for my classes. That's the thing that was really bothering me. But by talking about the different flours and yeasts available, the baking pans, the process of shaping the bread, the variety of recipes, and so on, I think I'll fill up the class time just fine."

"Will you actually bake the bread there?"

"Well, not as a class. The class is over by eight-thirty. We have to wrap the dough and take it home to bake."

"Shall we check on the bread dough?" Jane asked, feeling a little proud of herself for coming up with this idea.

"Sure."

Together they headed for the kitchen. One glance at the dough stopped them in their tracks. Not only had the dough risen, but it had spilled over the side of the bowl and was creeping toward the edge of the countertop. The scene reminded Jane of an old horror movie.

"Land's sake!"

"Auntie, how much yeast did you put in?"

Ethel thought a moment. "Oh dear, we were talking, and I'm not sure what I did."

Jane walked to the trash can. Two empty packets of yeast lay on top. "I think I've found the culprit." She waved the evidence. Wiggling her eyebrows she said, "Too much yeast and your dough can take over Acorn Hill." She gave a maniacal laugh.

Ethel sighed.

For a moment, Jane wasn't sure if Ethel would laugh or cry. Then, the shadow disappeared from Ethel's face, and she began to chuckle. Pretty soon tears of laughter were running down her face.

Just watching her aunt caused Jane to giggle. Before they knew it, they were hugging, laughing and crying together.

"Oh dear, I haven't laughed that hard in ages," Ethel said as she wiped away her tears.

"Me either. It felt good."

Then, as one, they turned toward the growing blob. "What are we to do about dinner? You have Paula coming over," Ethel said.

"I'll just go down to the bakery and get some dinner rolls."

"I'll go. This is my fault."

"Don't worry about it. I'll just stop by on my way home from Sylvia's shop." She looked at her watch. "In fact, I'm supposed to be there shortly."

Ethel got her coat. "Thank you again, Jane, for all your help."

"You're welcome. Now don't forget to join us for dinner."

Ethel looked at her and grinned. "Oh, I never forget a meal."

Jane put on her coat. "Why don't you hop in the car with me, and I'll drop you off next door on my way."

"I don't do well with hopping these days. Besides, it's just as easy for me to walk home. See you tonight," she said as they made their way into the brisk noonday air.

At dinnertime, Alice arrived with Paula Middleton, and the sisters, Ethel and Paula gathered around the dining room table ready to eat.

Alice offered the blessing for the meal and soon they were enjoying Jane's delicious roasted chicken, piped potatoes, broccoli sautéed in a rich sauce of garlic butter and seasoning, and field greens with a raspberry vinaigrette.

"So Paula, please tell us about yourself," Jane said.

Paula smoothed the cloth napkin in her lap. "Well, let's see. I'm thirty-two years old. I've never been married. My parents are both deceased. I grew up in Philadelphia, and later we moved to Potterston. I prefer small-town living. After my mother died and my landlord in Potterston sold his house, I had to find another place to live. I always enjoyed my visits to Acorn Hill and thought it would be nice to live here. I know Bill and Carolyn Morris, so when they mentioned their farmhouse was for rent, I jumped at the chance to move in. The rest I think you know."

"So what about this dog you're wanting?" Ethel asked, changing the subject abruptly.

Not knowing how Ethel stood on the idea of the dog, the sisters exchanged nervous glances.

Oblivious to the sisters' reaction, Ethel took a bite of chicken and looked to Paula for a response.

Paula hesitated, as if trying to think how to answer. "Well—"

"Aunt Ethel, right now Paula is merely looking into the matter," Alice interrupted. "I'll be able to tell you more about the dogs after tomorrow."

Ethel turned to her. "Oh? Why is that?"

"I'm going over to a dog-training facility to learn about these dogs."

"I thought you had to work tomorrow," Ethel said with a frown.

"No, my schedule has changed this week."

"Land's sake, I can't keep up with you and that

flexible schedule of yours." Ethel took a moment to chew and swallow another bite of food. "I just wondered how that worked with a dog taking you everywhere . . ."

When Ethel paused to sip her water, Jane jumped in, "May I get anything more for anyone?"

Ethel thought about Jane's offer, declined it, then took another bite of chicken, her question to Paula forgotten.

Everyone else agreed that they had eaten enough.

"Acorn Hill is a lovely place in which to live," Louise commented, getting back to the original conversation. "My sister Jane and I have only recently moved back." Louise then explained how after their father had died, the sisters needed to make a decision about the house and that's when they came up with the idea to convert it into a bed-and-breakfast.

"Oh, that explains it. I didn't think it was a bed-and-breakfast when I had driven by it the first time I visited Acorn Hill. Your home is absolutely beautiful."

"Thank you," Louise said.

"It's been home to you for a long time, then?" Paula asked Alice.

"Yes. It's a little different now, however, but it still has the same charm it had while I was growing up."

"It sounds as if your parents would be very

happy with what you've done. In a way, you're sort of continuing your father's legacy," Paula said.

"That's an interesting way to put it," Jane said.

"Well, you said he was pastor at Grace Chapel. He offered food for the soul. You offer soul food too with the beautiful surroundings and warm fellowship that you extend to all who enter Grace Chapel Inn. I've heard people talking around town, and now I've experienced your generosity firsthand."

"Goodness, there'll be no living with us if you keep this up," Alice admonished light-heartedly.

"These rolls are delicious, Jane," Paula said, splitting one open and spreading butter on it.

Jane and Ethel exchanged a glance. Ethel straightened in her chair. "I can't take credit for them," Jane said. "That's another great thing about this town—it has a fabulous bakery."

Jane looked over at her aunt, and they shared a conspiratorial smile.

"If everyone is finished," Jane said, "I'll bring in the dessert. I hope you all have saved room for butterscotch pie."

"Oh dear, Jane, how you do spoil us," Louise said.

"I'll just clear the table first."

"I'll help you, Jane," Louise offered.

"Great. Alice, why don't you show Paula around," Jane suggested.

Alice looked at Paula, who said. "I'd love a tour."

"Would you give us a hand, Aunt Ethel?" Louise asked.

"Oh yes, I can do that," Ethel said, though her gaze followed Alice and Paula.

Dear Auntie, Jane thought. *She does love being where the action is.* "We will meet in the parlor when you are finished," Jane said, while clearing dishes from the dining room table. "Enjoy your tour."

Alice led Paula into the living room where a fire crackled on the hearth.

"I tried to take this in when I came through here before dinner. It's just beautiful," Paula said, her gaze sweeping across the room. "I love that antique rocker," she said, pointing toward the corner.

"Oh, that was Mother's," Alice said with fond remembrance.

They crossed the foyer and went into Daniel's study, then peeked into the sunroom now closed off for the winter, the wicker furniture looking stiff and cold without its colorful cushions. From there they went to the staircase. "You'll see the parlor when we gather for dessert," Alice said, nodding toward the parlor door.

Alice placed her hand on the wooden banister and Paula climbed the steps beside her.

"Underneath the staircase we have a reception area where we have a desk, phone, answering machine, that kind of thing. We don't have phones in the guest rooms, so our guests go there to make calls."

"I think the lack of phones is quaint." Paula said.

"It allows our guests to truly get away from it all. We have four guest rooms, only one of which is in use right now," Alice said when they reached the second floor. "My bedroom and my sisters' bedrooms are on the third floor."

Alice took Paula through the unoccupied rooms, enjoying the woman's expression with the opening of each door. Whenever someone new visited the inn, it seemed to bring the sisters a fresh look at their home, reminding them how blessed they were to live there.

After they had finished the tour, Alice and Paula returned to the parlor, where Jane, Ethel and Louise waited for them—and for dessert.

The evening passed pleasantly, and soon it was time for Alice to take Paula home. When Alice returned, the lower floor of the inn was shrouded in darkness except for the lights on the front porch and in the foyer. She glanced toward her sisters' rooms to see squares of lamplight shining from their windows. They had retired for the evening.

Alice trudged up the steps toward the porch. It had been a long day, but a good one. She was glad

Paula had joined them for dinner. Alice hoped that she would be able to get her seizure response dog. The young woman's paleness tonight had not escaped Alice's trained eye.

Chapter Ten

Alice arrived at the training center in Vintage, a town just south of Lancaster, the next morning. The weather had cooperated and she had sunshine the entire way, with only a smattering of clouds dotting the azure blue sky. She drove the car into the parking lot and cut the engine.

Pulling out her keys and dropping them into her purse, she looked up at the front of the small, tan building. A couple of shrubs flanked the entrance area and a white sign out front read "Mission Dogs."

Alice followed the sun-drenched sidewalk to the door, read the "Come In" sign and stepped inside. Organized stacks of paper, a Rolodex, several files and a telephone were on top of the large gray metal desk that faced the door. A steaming mug of coffee suggested someone had just left the desk and would return shortly.

To Alice's right were several brown metal chairs and a coffee table holding a selection of magazines, many having to do with dogs. The pictures on the walls gave testimony to the work of the company.

Alice settled onto a chair, picked up a magazine and began to flip through it absently.

"Oh, I'm sorry, I didn't hear you come in," a thirty-something woman said, walking toward Alice. "Welcome to Mission Dogs. I assume you are Miss Howard to see Mr. Turner?"

"Yes, that's right," Alice said.

"My name is Heidi Pickett. I'll let Mr. Turner know you're here." She picked up the phone and pressed a couple of numbers. "Mr. Turner, Miss Howard is here to see you. Okay, thank you." She turned to Alice. "Mr. Turner will be right with you."

"Thank you."

The phone on the desk rang. "Mission Dogs, this is Heidi, may I help you?"

Before Alice could hear anything further, a paunchy middle-aged man with gray, thinning hair entered the room. "Miss Howard?"

"Yes."

A wide smile lit his face. "I'm Andy Turner. It's certainly a pleasure to meet you."

"It's nice to meet you."

"If you'll just follow me to my office," he said, turning and walking back down the hall. The room they entered had a desk and a couple of worn chairs, standard not-for-profit equipment.

"Please sit down." He took a chair opposite hers and smiled. "So you're a friend of Mark Graves?"

"Yes, Mark and I became acquainted during my college days."

He studied her a moment, making her a tad uncomfortable. "Mark is a good man. I've known him for years. A remarkable veterinarian."

Her earlier tension left. "Yes, he is."

"So, you're interested in seizure response dogs?" he asked brightly, clearly delighted with the topic.

"Yes." She explained that she was a nurse and told how she had met Paula Middleton. She described Paula's physical problems and where she stood currently in her dog application process. She also mentioned that she hoped to gather enough information about the dog to present to the church board in an effort to help Paula financially.

When Alice had finished talking, Andy Turner thought a moment. "It does sound like your friend would be a good candidate. You say she is already on a list somewhere?"

Alice nodded. "Actually, she's started training with Caring Canines in Philadelphia, but we thought it best to check out all options in case that doesn't work out."

"That's a good idea. Though they have a nice program at Caring Canines and a great staff of trainers."

The information made Alice feel better.

"Well, let me tell you a little about our program. Our dogs must complete a minimum of one hundred and twenty hours of training over a period of no less than six months. During that time, they live with their trainers.

"Trainers, by the way, are paid staff. Most work around thirty-five hours a week, Monday through Friday. Of course, that can vary, depending on their duties. For instance, some trainers and mobility instructors drive long distances to visit dogs and their owners.

"This is a very active job. There is a lot of walking and outdoor work in all kinds of weather."

"It sounds like a big job. What are the trainers' qualifications?"

"Entrants need to be at least eighteen years old and have a driver's license. Some organizations require academic training, training with dog behavior and development, others do not. Depends on where you go. Getting into this work is extremely competitive, and applicants must have experience both working with dogs, particularly in training, and working with people, preferably in a caring role. The organizations also like the trainer to be experienced with the particular disability issues involved, as in your case with seizures."

"I had no idea there was so much involved."

Andy smiled. "Most people don't. Then there are the volunteers who house the dogs while they complete their initial stage of training. There's always that added concern about keeping a dog in your home for the six months' training, getting emotionally attached to it, and then having to give it up to its new master. This is a job you almost have to feel called to do."

"Tell me a little about the training the trainer goes through."

"Again, depends on the organization and the type of assistance dog, but training can last up to three years, starting with kennel work and moving on to learning to train dogs under supervision and to working with owners. In some organizations, the training covers canine anatomy and physiology."

He took a drink of coffee. "Getting back to the dogs' training, when we train the dogs, thirty hours are devoted to regularly scheduled field trips and public exposure to help the dog get acclimated to public settings, crowds, the various street noises and so on.

"The dog must be able to perform obedience skills, both on and off the leash, with voice and/or hand signals. Such commands might include 'sit,' 'stay,' 'come,' 'down,' those kinds of things. The dogs must exhibit absolute control on and off their leash."

"Can any dog be trained to do this or is there a certain breed that works best?" Alice asked.

"Dogs that are easily trained as companion animals can probably be trained to respond to a seizure. My experience has been that golden retrievers and Labrador retrievers make the best assistance dogs. Though there are other breeds that serve this purpose as well."

"Why those dogs?"

"There are several reasons. Small dogs can't pick up big objects or pull wheelchairs. Really large dogs are too cumbersome in a restaurant or traveling on a bus or plane. Field dogs tend to be more interested in their environment than people. A good service dog is people-oriented, not overly active, and confident but not aggressive in behavior."

"How do you get your dogs?"

"Sometimes people who can no longer have a dog bring their dogs in to see if they can be trained. Also, we breed our own dogs."

"Retrievers?"

He nodded.

"How do you decide which ones to train—or how they are selected?" she asked.

"We test them and of the many we test, only a few are chosen." Andy leaned forward. "The dogs are trained in social behaviors. For example, there must be no inappropriate barking, no biting, jumping on strangers, begging, sniffing, that kind of thing."

"What if a dog is found incompatible with his master?"

"Well, that's one of the reasons for the training sessions between the dog and his new owner. If, after time, a problem develops and the dog is not able to meet the needs of the owner, we may work with the dog to help another individual."

"When are the dogs retired?"

"Normally, when the dog develops a physical problem or becomes too old to help with his owner's disability."

"What exactly is the dog trained to do when the person has a seizure?"

"They may bark in order to summon help, have physical contact with someone, or activate an emergency medical alert system. It depends on the individual's need. If the seizures are not severe, the dog may lie down beside its owner and wait until it's over. I have heard amazing accounts of dogs saving their owners' lives."

"How wonderful." Alice shook her head in amazement. "When the training is over, is there any follow-up?" she asked.

"That's another good question, and the answer is yes. The recipient does a follow-up progress report once a month for the first six months. Within about eighteen months of graduation and annually there-after, a personal contact is made by a qualified staff or program volunteer. Some organizations send staff or volunteer personnel out more often."

Andy reached into the left drawer of his desk, pulled out a picture and laid it on top of his desk. "As you can see here, our dogs wear harnesses that say 'Mission Dog' so they are easily identifiable to the public as service dogs."

Alice looked at the picture of the man and his dog, noting the harness. "I assume the dogs are examined by a veterinarian before they are given to their charges?" she asked.

"Absolutely. They are either spayed or neutered and receive a thorough medical evaluation, ensuring the dog is in the best of health."

"What a wonderful program. I'm sure it is a god-send to many people."

He smiled in the way of someone who was proud of his work. "I could not agree more."

Alice rose to leave. "I appreciate so much the valuable information you have given me."

"One more thing," he said, rising to stand next to her. "Do you know that there are two different types of seizure assistance dogs?"

Alice shook her head.

He smiled. "There is a response dog. This is a dog that supports the patient during the seizure. It might lie beside the person until the seizure is over and lick his or her face until the owner is fully conscious. It might run over to a nearby medical device and hit its paw against the machine, which will, in turn, contact the 911 personnel. When 911 answers, the dog will respond with barking, alerting the medical people to go to the patient's house. The patient contacts the emergency medical personnel ahead of time, so that they know the patient's problems and where the patient lives."

"And the other type of dog?" Alice asked.

"The other dog is an alert dog. These dogs are rare, and we don't know if we have an alert dog until the dog has lived with the patient for quite some time and has grown accustomed to the patient's seizures." He leaned against his desk. "You can't believe these dogs, Alice. They can detect that their owner is about to have a seizure *before* the person actually has one."

"How does the dog do that?"

"We're not sure. It could be a scent the person emits before a seizure or some behavior that gives the signal to the dog. We don't know. We only know that these dogs are able to alert the patient that a seizure is about to commence so that the patient can protect himself from falling."

"That is amazing."

"Isn't it?" He went on to discuss the cost of the dogs.

Alice understood now why they were expensive.

"These animals are more than just pets. They give their owners a chance for a normal life, one that they could never hope for without the help of such dogs."

Alice glanced at her watch. "Oh my, I have kept you far too long," she said, realizing it was past the lunch hour.

"Not at all," he said. "People can't shut me up when I start talking about our dogs. I love being a small part of helping disabled people get what they need to make their lives more manageable."

"You have been very helpful. Thank you again for taking the time to educate me. Your information will help me to enlighten our church board."

Andy shook her hand. "I hope your board will consider helping your friend. It sounds as though a seizure dog could be the thing she needs to enjoy a fairly normal life."

Andy followed Alice out of his office to the outside door. "Let me know how it works out for your friend, will you?"

"I will be happy to," Alice said.

The visit had convinced Alice that an assistance dog was the answer to her prayers. Now, if she could just get the board to share her belief when she presented her plan that evening.

Chapter Eleven

Alice had attempted to get to Grace Chapel before the board meeting so that she might have time for prayer, but the cars in the parking lot told her that June Carter and Florence Simpson had already arrived. The others would soon follow.

She stepped through the double front doors of the church. She would go downstairs and join the others soon, but for now she needed time to herself. She took a deep breath and drank in the quiet. Closing her eyes tight, Alice said a prayer for Paula and her future. She prayed for the Grace Chapel Board and whatever role they might play in helping her friend.

The door creaked open behind her. Her eyes

opened and she turned. "Oh hello, Pastor Ken," she said.

"Good evening, Alice. How are you tonight?"

"Fine, thank you," she said, noticing how the cold air had given him rosy cheeks. "You are working late tonight."

"Yes. I suppose Louise told you about the upcoming seminar?"

Alice nodded.

"I'm still trying to decide what message to present. Thought I might study for a while in my office."

They talked about his dilemma for a short while. Then Alice decided she had better get downstairs for the meeting, and they parted ways.

The board members enjoyed a time of fellowship, catching up on children, grandchildren, illnesses and the latest Acorn Hill happenings. Then the meeting came to order. With a short agenda for the evening, they quickly covered the various items, finally coming to the one weighing most on Alice's heart.

Fred Humbert, the board chairman, asked Alice to present her case.

Looking around the room, she felt her throat constrict. Florence Simpson had pulled herself to full attention. The stout woman's lips squeezed together in a thin line.

Alice took a deep breath. "Well, as you know we have considerable funds in our outreach program."

"Yes, and we've worked hard to put that money there," Florence said in a frosty voice. With a frown, she reached down and massaged her right foot through her shoe. That could only mean one thing. Florence's bunion was bothering her. Pain did nothing for her temperament. Alice groaned inwardly. She had her work cut out for her tonight. Florence was hardly Miss Congeniality on a good day.

"I understand that, Florence," Alice said. "I understand, too, those funds are set aside for special needs cases, and I believe I have one." She glanced over and saw Florence lock eyes with Ethel. This usually was not a good sign.

"Recently, I cared for a patient at the hospital, Paula Middleton. Paula lives alone, just south of Acorn Hill in Bill and Carolyn Morris' farmhouse. Paula suffers from a disorder known as drop seizures. They can occur at any time, anywhere, without warning." Alice heard someone murmur sympathetically. She continued.

"Her seizures render her unconscious for fifteen to thirty seconds."

"That's not very long," Florence said, scowling as she continued to knead her foot.

"True," Alice said, "but if you happen to be on a stairway, crossing an intersection, lighting a fire or doing a number of other seemingly ordinary things, the consequences of a seizure could be devastating."

"What would you have us do, Alice? Provide nursing care?" Fred asked.

"No, Fred, nothing like that." She proceeded to tell them what she had learned from Andy Turner. "So you see, a special phone device and a dog that is trained to get help is just the thing for someone like Paula."

Florence stopped working her bunion. "You want us to use the money to buy a phone device and a *dog?*" Florence asked incredulously.

Alice's heart sank. She could imagine where the discussion was heading.

"That's exactly what she's asking," Ethel said.

Alice feared this would be the beginning of the end. If Ethel and Florence got their hackles up, there would be no hope for Paula. Alice shot up a prayer, took another deep breath and braced herself for the worst.

"I think it's a wonderful idea," Ethel said. "The poor girl is in Philadelphia right now training with that dog."

"Well, if she can't afford the dog, what is she doing training with it?" Florence wanted to know.

Surprised by Ethel's display of compassion, it took Alice a moment to find her voice. "She's checking out her options," Alice said, "though she doesn't know how she will manage the financial aspect of the dog." Alice didn't mention that she had given Paula the idea that things would work out. Indeed, Alice believed things would work out, she just didn't know how or when.

Then before Alice could continue, Ethel took up the speech. One would have thought Ethel was on a campaign. She told the group what a lovely young Christian woman Paula was and how she needed someone, something, to be with her in her "delicate moments," as Ethel put it. By the time Ethel had finished, the board members were murmuring, nodding, smiling.

Indecision flickered across Florence's face before her expression finally settled into firm determination. "Well, I suppose it's our Christian duty to help this young woman," she said, as if the whole thing was her idea from the start.

Alice was speechless.

Fred asked for a motion to provide money for the purchase of a seizure response dog for Paula Middleton and also to look into a medical device system. Ethel made the motion and Florence seconded it. It passed with a unanimous vote.

The meeting closed in prayer, and Alice left the board meeting shaking her head in wonder. When she had prayed for a miracle on Paula's behalf, she never once considered that God might use Ethel to provide the answer.

"It's a miracle!" Alice exclaimed when she walked in through the back door after the board meeting.

"Alice," Louise turned, her hand tight against her chest, "you nearly scared the life out of me."

"Oh, I'm sorry, Louise."

"You're home early. What's up?" Jane asked.

Alice pulled off her hat, scarf and gloves. "First, I want to thank you for your prayers. The board meeting went wonderfully." She unbuttoned her coat and took it off. "Just a minute." She walked to the coat closet, put her things away and reentered the kitchen, fluffing her hair into place. "As I was saying, the board meeting went well. After I explained Paula's need, everyone was more than happy to contribute toward the seizure dog. I'm still amazed it went off without a hitch," Alice said, sitting down at the kitchen table.

"You look positively radiant, Alice," Jane said with a smile.

"Because of the board meeting?" Louise asked.

"Yes, and here's the real surprise," Alice said in a hushed tone as if the board members might hear her. "Florence Simpson agreed with the plan despite an aching bunion."

"No," Jane said.

"Yes. Well, she did need a bit of persuasion. As you know, Florence likes to look at things from every angle."

"Yes, indeed," Louise said. "And then she likes to look at them all over again."

"And Auntie behaved herself?" Jane asked.

"She not only behaved herself, but she actually

took over my cause, saying what a lovely young woman Paula was and how could we stand by as a church and not reach out to her when we had the ability to do so. I don't know if they would have approved giving the money had it not been for Aunt Ethel."

"Go Auntie," Jane cheered. "No wonder Florence was agreeable. Birds of a feather and all that." Jane rinsed off the last pan and sprayed away the suds from her sink. She wiped the pan dry, then placed it in the cabinet.

"Well, I appreciate what Aunt Ethel did, and I'm just thankful it's over," Alice said.

Jane wiped her hands on a red and white checked towel and hung it to dry. "So what happens now?" She walked over and joined her sisters at the table.

"I have to wait for Paula to call me so that I can tell her. I don't know how to reach her until she gets back," Alice said. "We'll go from there."

"How wonderful that you made it this far, Alice. At one point, you weren't so sure about things," Louise commented.

"You haven't even had a chance to tell us what you learned yesterday about these dogs," Jane said.

Alice told them about her fascinating discussion with Andy Turner. "Isn't it wonderful?" she finished. "I'm praying that the Lord will bless the board for its generosity."

Jane looked at her watch. "Oh, we can't forget

the little celebration that Mr. Sanderson spoke to me about. They should be home soon."

"Let's go into the parlor to relax while we wait for them. I could stand the warmth of the fireplace," Alice said.

The sisters headed for the parlor. Just as they entered the foyer, the front door swished open. David and Mary Sanderson walked into the inn, bringing the winter's chill with them.

"Sorry for letting the cold air in," David said as he applied some strength to the door to close it against the wind.

"You're just in time to join us for dessert in the parlor," Jane said with a smile.

David looked at Mary. She nodded. "Just let us get out of our coats and we'll be right down," he said.

"Great."

Jane and Alice went back into the kitchen to get the cake plates and cups for coffee and tea ready, then brought the tray to the parlor door. They could hear Eduardo Fink's music from the CD player. Alice peeked in to make sure the Sandersons were in the room. She turned and nodded to Jane. Once she walked inside, she waited until every eye turned to her.

Then, on the count of three, the sisters called out, "Happy Anniversary!"

David looked at his bride. "Happy anniversary, honey," he said, pulling her into an embrace.

"Oh darling," Mary said, "What a wonderful surprise!"

Everyone commented on the exquisite cake Jane had created. It was a white heart-shaped cake sitting atop a white sheet cake. "Happy Anniversary" was written across the top of the heart cake in pink icing, while pink roses with green leaves brought color to the creation. The cakes sides were double-ruffled piped with pink on the edges.

"Unbelievable," Mary said with a gasp. "Jane, this had to take you forever."

"I enjoyed it. It's an art form for me," Jane said, lifting a knife to cut into it.

"Wait," David called out. "Let me get a picture of it first, and then you can cut it."

The room grew silent as David took the picture. Afterward, Jane and her sisters passed out cake, tea and coffee.

"I asked Jane to make an anniversary cake for us, Mary. I hope you don't mind. I know you've been watching your weight and all, but I thought this would be a nice way of sharing our joy with our new friends," David said.

Mary leaned into him. "Of course I don't mind. How could I mind such a thoughtful gesture? Jane, I appreciate all the trouble you have gone through to make this a memorable anniversary for us. Thank you so much."

Jane smiled. "It was my pleasure, really."

Mary tasted her cake. "Oh my, this tastes as delectable as it looks, Jane."

Everyone agreed.

Alice surveyed the lifelike flowers and the intricate ruffles, and thought of the time it took Jane to make such a display. Alice knew she would never have the patience for such a thing.

The room grew quiet as they enjoyed their dessert.

"I have some news to share," Jane said, looking at Mary.

Mary raised her eyebrows quizzically.

"I spoke with Sylvia today, and she says that two people placed orders for your bags."

Mary brought a hand to her chest. "Truly?"

David reached over and squeezed her arm. "I told you, honey, those bags are very nice."

"But I never thought . . ."

"Well, sounds like you had better start thinking and sewing," Jane said with a laugh. "You were wondering what you could do to keep busy. It looks to me like you've found something."

The sisters and their guests spent the next hour chatting about the bags, the possibilities of selling them on the Internet and of Mary's eventually opening her own shop. They spoke of the Sandersons' twenty-eight-year marriage, and the bumps and joys along the way.

At last it was time to say good night.

In her room preparing for bed, Alice thought

about how the smallest event could change a person's life. Alice and Paula's meeting in the hospital was leading to Paula's getting a service dog and having a more worry-free life. Mary's stay at the inn had opened up a career opportunity.

Yes, Alice thought, *every day is an adventure all its own.*

Chapter Twelve

"Thank you for meeting me this morning, Louise," Pastor Thompson said as they settled comfortably into a booth at the Coffee Shop.

"My pleasure, Pastor Ken." Louise removed her hat, coat and gloves.

"Good morning, Louise," Hope Collins said. "Morning, Pastor Thompson."

"Hello, Hope," they replied cheerily.

"What can I get for you two this morning?" Hope pulled a pad and pencil from the pocket of her white uniform and flipped the pad open.

"Louise?" Pastor Thompson asked.

"I'll have a decaf."

"Make that two, please," Pastor Thompson said.

"Okay, two decafs coming up." Hope smiled, tucking the pad and pencil back into her pocket. "Be back in a jif."

Louise adjusted her purse on the booth beside her. "So, have you come up with any ideas for your message yet?"

Pastor Thompson ran his fingers through his hair. "You know, I haven't."

Louise regarded the pastor with maternal concern. Fatigue replaced the sparkle in his eyes. Clearly the matter was causing him considerable worry.

"I don't know what my problem is. Normally, ideas for messages come easily enough. I think my trouble is knowing this one is so important," he said.

"How so?"

"I want to make sure it's the right message. There may be someone there who needs to hear something special, maybe a pastor who is burned out, ready to give up, or someone who is struggling with health issues, whatever."

"Don't you feel that way every Sunday?"

"Yes, that's true, but this situation is more complicated since I will be speaking to my colleagues."

Louise thought a moment. "Perhaps you are concentrating too hard on what you feel you should teach rather than listening." At the flicker that crossed his face, Louise wondered if she had overstepped her bounds.

"How do you mean?"

"Well," she said carefully, "you told me that you did not want to get in the way of what God might want you to say. Maybe you are concentrating too hard on not getting in the way."

He considered this. Before he could say anything, Hope arrived with steaming mugs of coffee. Another customer stepped into the shop. "Be right with you," Hope said, placing the cups in front of Pastor Thompson and Louise and hurrying off.

Louise took a sip of coffee, hoping she had not said too much. The pastor looked at her. "How did you get so smart?"

His comment surprised her, and she felt herself relax. "Remember, I've been on earth a long time."

He smiled. "I think you isolated my problem." His gaze drifted out the window. "I just had not considered that. Makes me sound a bit self-absorbed, I'm afraid."

"Not at all. God knows your motives. Sometimes when we try hard not to focus on ourselves, we end up doing exactly that. Kind of like dieting. We want to eat less, but find ourselves thinking about food more, so it's hard to cut back."

"True enough." He studied his fingers clasped around his mug. "Still, I hope something comes to me pretty soon. I'm getting a little nervous as the date draws near."

"I can understand that. Sometimes, though, I think He lets us get to the point where we know it's out of our hands and in His capable ones."

He looked at her with surprise. "I think you should be the pastor."

Louise laughed. "No, thank you. I know your job

is not an easy one. I have my hands full just teaching piano."

They paused to drink their coffee. Louise looked out the window. "It surely is cold."

Pastor Thompson sighed. "I don't mind telling you I am getting a little weary of this weather. I should be used to it by now, but I must say I'm looking forward to spring."

"I agree. Though it's a beautiful sight to see Acorn Hill blanketed with snow."

"Spoken like someone who tries to see the good in everything."

Louise laughed. "No, that would be Alice."

That made him laugh too. Then worry seemed to settle on his face once again.

"You know, Pastor Ken, I could search through my father's old sermon notes to look for some ideas for you."

He brightened. "That might be helpful. At this point, I am willing to do anything. Yet, I know the right thing to do is keep praying and wait for inspiration."

"Exactly."

The pastor and Louise continued to enjoy a friendly conversation over their coffee, talking of church happenings, the weather and Louise's piano lessons.

Hope approached their table holding a carafe of hot coffee in her hand. "Would you like more?"

"No, thank you," Louise said.

"I believe I'm finished as well," Pastor Thompson said.

Louise glanced at her watch. "Oh dear. I had better get back. I have a student coming in twenty minutes." She wrapped her scarf around her neck and put on her coat, hat and gloves. "Thank you for the coffee."

"You're welcome. I appreciate your friendship and your prayers, Louise," he said, donning his coat. "Let me know if you come up with any-thing."

He walked her to the parking lot and they settled into their cars. Louise waved good-bye to the pastor as he pulled out of the lot. She turned the car engine on and shifted into gear, wondering just how the Lord might answer the prayers of Grace Chapel's pastor.

As she drove toward the intersection, Louise noticed an elderly man standing on the corner waiting to cross the street. He was a stranger, at least to her. The car in front of her was ready to turn when all of a sudden the man stepped off the curb into traffic. Louise gasped.

Suddenly, a big, black dog appeared, placing itself between the man and the car in front of Louise. The man stopped in his tracks. The driver screeched his car to a halt. Louise hit her brakes.

Before she could catch her breath, people had already started coming out of the shops to see about the commotion. Louise pulled over to the side of the street and got out with the others to check on the man.

"I'm telling you, if it hadn't been for that dog, I would have been hurt," he was saying when Louise walked up. "The sun was so bright, it blinded me and I didn't see that car turning."

"Whose dog is it?" someone asked.

"I think he's a stray. Hope over at the Coffee Shop has been feeding him scraps," someone else said.

"I think Fred at the hardware store has been feeding him too," another in the crowd joined in.

"Hey, there he goes!" a voice shouted.

The dog ran past Louise, the sun's rays flashing on the reflective strips on his red collar. *Alice's mystery dog! How peculiar,* she thought.

"Louise, are you all right?" Jane asked when her sister came into the kitchen.

Caught up in her thoughts, Louise looked up with a start. "What? Oh, yes . . . yes, I'm fine. Why do you ask?"

Jane studied her. "Well, you look pale, which seems strange since you've been out in the cold."

"Let me get my coat off, and I'll tell you what happened." They settled at the kitchen table. Louise shared what had occurred with Alice's mystery dog while Jane listened intently.

"Goodness, Louise, do you think that dog acted intentionally?"

128

Louise shook her head. "I don't know what to think, to tell you the truth. It's strange how he always shows up at just the right time."

"It sure is. I'm glad that the man was all right. Thank goodness the dog showed up, intentionally or not."

"Indeed."

Just then, Wendell sauntered into the kitchen. He looked around and, spotting nothing of real interest, padded over to Jane and jumped up on her lap. "Oh Wendell. It's just a good thing I'm not cooking now or you would be in big trouble for jumping up on me." Wendell looked up at her as if he couldn't be any less concerned about the matter and turned his attention to a paw that obviously needed a good washing.

Jane scratched Wendell behind the ear and he forgot about his paw, settling in to enjoy a thoroughly pleasurable rub.

"You know, all these dog stories have set me to thinking," Jane said.

Louise groaned. "Every time you start thinking, I want to run and hide."

Jane made a face. "If dogs can learn tricks, why can't cats?"

"What? You mean Wendell?"

"Sure. Wendell's smart." Wendell covered his face with his paw.

Louise's eyebrow arched. "There you are," she said, pointing to Wendell, whose snout had completely disappeared between his paws. "I believe he would prefer not to be bothered. Besides, you know the adage, 'You can't teach an old dog new tricks.' "

"Wendell is not a dog," Jane said, as if the suggestion was insulting.

"Well, all I can say is 'good luck' if you want to teach that cat a trick." With that, Louise stood and straightened her sweater. "I have a student arriving soon."

Louise turned and walked out of the kitchen, leaving Wendell at Jane's mercy.

Later that afternoon, Louise sat on the sofa in the living room, working on the coasters for Alice's ANGELs group while classical music floated from the CD player. Jane had gone to help Sylvia, and Alice was at work. Outside the sky was clear, but the air was cold.

Louise had settled into a steady rhythm of knit, purl, knit, purl, when she heard footsteps coming down the stairway. She glanced up when the steps stopped at the living room.

"Oh, you're ready to leave?" she asked when she saw David and Mary standing with luggage in hand at the doorway.

"I'm afraid so," David said.

Louise laid aside her knitting, stood and walked toward the reception desk. They followed behind.

Once Louise completed the paperwork, the

Sandersons turned in their keys and prepared to leave.

"I know my sisters will be sorry to have missed you," Louise said.

"I'm sorry that we aren't able to say good-bye to them, but we're already making a late start," Mary said. "Please let Jane know I will keep her posted on the progress of my bags on the Internet." Mary chuckled. "Who would have ever thought I would end up doing something like this?" She shook her head.

"I tried to tell you," David said with a teasing grin.

"I just never took you seriously, I suppose," she said.

"Well, I know that Jane and Sylvia are very excited about the possibilities. Sylvia is glad you left the two bags with her so she can take orders. She feels when the weather clears, she'll have more people coming into the store, which will increase your sales," Louise said.

David looked down at his wife. "It sounds to me like you're going to have more work than you know what to do with."

"I hope you're right. I need to keep busy." She reached over and hugged Louise. "Thank you for our most wonderful stay. Your home is beautiful, the food was delicious and your friendship will last us a lifetime."

"We'll be back, that's for sure," David said.

Louise followed them to the door and waved good-bye. "We'll look forward to seeing you again soon," she called after them. They nodded and waved.

When she closed the door, she thought about Mary and her newly created business. It's so exciting when life offers one a change. Louise knew all about that. After all, a few years ago she would never have thought that one day she would be running a bed-and-breakfast with her sisters.

Chapter Thirteen

The next day Louise went to the Nine Lives Bookstore to browse through the section of religious books. Entering the shop, she breathed deeply, taking in the odor of musty old bindings and new paper. She pulled a book from the shelf and flipped quietly through the pages.

"Good morning, Louise." The voice came from behind her.

Louise turned to see Viola Reed, the bookstore owner and Louise's good friend. "Hello, Viola."

"I was in the back room and didn't hear you come in. Have you found what you want?" Viola asked.

"I'm just browsing," Louise said. "I was so tired of staying inside, I had to get out."

"I know exactly what you mean," Viola said. "Business is slow. Hardly anyone is venturing out." She turned. "Harry, get off that table," she said to her orange marmalade cat.

Turning back around, Viola adjusted her bifocals. "Since I have had nary a customer in two days, why don't we go over to the Coffee Shop for some lunch?" Viola asked.

"That's a wonderful idea, Viola. I feel that we haven't really conversed in ages." Louise replaced the book on the shelf. "May I use your phone? I should let Jane know not to expect me home for lunch."

"Go right ahead," Viola said. "I'll get my coat."

Louise made her phone call and walked toward the front door and waited. Viola was short of breath by the time she reached Louise.

"Ready?"

Louise nodded.

Viola turned the "Closed" sign around on the window and pulled the door shut, causing the bell to jangle behind her.

They walked across the street to the Coffee Shop. Once inside, Louise and Viola took their places at a booth and began pulling off their winter wraps. Viola shivered.

"I tell you, if people would stop assaulting the earth's atmosphere, we wouldn't have all this bizarre weather."

"The earth's atmosphere?"

"Oh, the depletion of the ozone layer, atomic testing . . ." Viola said waving her hand. "We're probably even doing damage by sending men off into space. If God had wanted man to fly, He would have given him wings." She pulled open the menu on the table.

Louise didn't wish to engage in a discussion of the earth's atmosphere. "What new books are on your 'recommend' list?"

Viola's frown softened into a smile. To put Viola into a better frame of mind, all one had to do was mention books or cats.

"The spring lists aren't out yet, but I understand that there will be some excellent books published soon."

June Carter, the owner of the Coffee Shop, approached their table.

"Hello, Louise. Viola," June said. "What can I get you, ladies?"

"I will take a bowl of stew, please," Louise said, "and water with lemon."

"*Mmm,* that does sound good. I believe I'll have the same," Viola announced, "only make my beverage black coffee."

"I'll be back in a moment." June turned and left the two friends to catch up on things.

"Let's see, where was I? Oh, I was going to tell you about my last trip to Philadelphia. I found some wonderful old books, including one dated 1860 that is a series of sermons for children."

"Oh, that sounds like a treasure," Louise said. She enjoyed the mere thought of poring over old books, especially those dealing with religious matters.

The front door of the shop opened, allowing in a cold gust of wind that ruffled loose napkins and straw papers and chilled ankles. Florence Simpson entered.

"Well, look what the wind blew in," Viola said behind a cupped hand, though her efforts did little to muffle her voice. Florence looked their way and limped over to their table.

"Is your bunion bothering you again, Florence?" Viola asked.

The abrupt comment seemed to catch Florence off guard. "Yes, it is," she said, her cranky voice attesting to the pain in her foot. Without as much as a by-your-leave, she edged her way into the seat beside Viola, causing the bookseller considerable effort to move her ample frame across the booth. Viola didn't bother to hide her irritation. Florence seemed oblivious or perhaps chose to ignore her.

"I suppose you heard about the board's decision on that dog for Alice's friend?" Florence asked.

Louise sighed. She did not wish to discuss the church's affairs in front of Viola, who had a different take on spiritual matters. By the look on Florence's face, Louise could tell they were indeed in for a discussion. "Yes, I did."

"Well, Louise, I hate to be the bearer of bad news, but I happened to overhear—"

At this, Viola grunted.

Florence looked at Viola.

Louise wished June would hurry up with that stew.

Florence continued. "As I was saying, I overheard that some folks are upset about the decision."

The comment surprised Louise. "Why?"

Florence settled into her seat. Now that she had an audience, she was going to make the most of it. "It seems they don't like the idea of an animal being in public places. Now, you know I've approved of this dog for the girl, I'm just telling you what others are saying."

"Oh, hogwash," Viola said. "Service animals have as much right to be in public places as we do."

Louise said a silent thank you when June showed up just then with their orders. She took Florence's order and cast Louise a glance of sympathy.

"Like I said, I'm only telling you what I've heard," Florence said while smoothing a paper napkin on the table into ever smaller squares.

"I don't understand why people would be concerned, Florence, but I'll make sure Alice knows," Louise said.

"It's beyond me why anyone would make a fuss," Florence said, still smoothing her napkin, "but then you know how people are." She folded her hands on the table and smiled sweetly.

Viola rolled her eyes. "Yes, indeed we do."

Florence looked at Viola sharply, sensing an offense.

Quickly changing the subject, Louise complimented Florence on her sweater, which led to a discussion of the high cost of clothes and a comment from Florence along the lines of "the things young women are wearing these days make a person wonder why more of them don't catch their death of pneumonia." Louise realized that any subject would bring up some complaint, but she felt that she was making headway if she could at least get Florence and Viola to complain about the same thing.

After some considerable discussion, the ladies said their good-byes, and Louise drove to the inn. As she entered the foyer, Jane was headed to the second floor. She turned on the stairway. "Hi, Louise. I'm just going to freshen the Garden Room for our next guest."

Pulling off her scarf and gloves, Louise said, "As soon as I get out of these, I'll come and help you."

Jane smiled. "Thank you."

Louise placed her coat and accessories in the closet, then joined Jane upstairs.

"Did you have a nice lunch with Viola?" Jane asked.

Louise sighed and told of her visit with Viola and Florence.

Jane laughed. "Good old Florence. Always offering an encouraging word."

"And Viola always has something to add to that good word," Louise said wryly.

"Well, at least you didn't have Aunt Ethel in the mix or you could have been there all day, listening to their solutions for every problem known to mankind."

"That is so true."

Once they were in the Garden Room, Jane said, "The bed linens are changed, but I thought I would dust and run the vacuum, since no one has been in here in a while." She added, "If you wouldn't mind, you can do the dusting, and I'll vacuum, and we can be done in no time."

"That would be fine," Louise agreed.

They quickly set to cleaning the room, and within a short time, they were finished.

With her hands on her hips, Louise surveyed the room. It smelled of furniture polish and bathroom cleaner. "Some potpourri might be nice."

"Good idea. I have some downstairs." She glanced around. "Other than that, I think we're ready." She turned to Louise. "And I think we've earned a rest. Do you have the time to relax in the living room?"

Louise glanced at her watch. "I have time. My first student comes immediately after school, another hour from now."

"Great. Let's go," Jane said as they exited the room.

Louise and Jane walked into the living room

and settled into their comfortable seats. "I wonder if Alice has heard anything from Paula," Jane said.

"I haven't heard her mention anything. I hope things work out for Paula. She seems like such a nice young woman." Louise's thoughts drifted. "Life can be so hard sometimes."

Jane studied her. "You okay?"

"I'm fine." Louise looked up. "I know we have all discussed many times how thankful we are to be running this inn together, but truly some days I can't stop thinking how blessed we are to be together. We have our health—but even if we didn't, we have each other."

Jane nodded, growing a bit pensive herself. "I don't know how I'd have gotten over my divorce without you and Alice. You helped me to move past that failure and realize my life is not over." She glanced out the window a moment, then turned back to Louise. "In other words, God isn't finished with me yet."

Louise smiled. "He isn't finished with any of us as long as there's breath in our lungs."

Wendell strolled lazily into the room. "Well, look who decided to join us. King Wendell," Jane said with a laugh. Wendell glanced her way, then found a shaft of afternoon sunlight to lie in. Jane's eyes narrowed. "You know, I haven't given up on the idea of Wendell learning a trick or two." Wendell's ears twitched. He looked over at Louise as if she should come to his defense. Wendell rose and snaked around Louise's legs.

Louise chuckled. "Oh dear, I think Wendell is a bit too old to learn new tricks."

"No, Louise, we discussed that, remember? The saying refers to dogs. Wendell is not a dog and he's not old."

"Oh dear, I can see that you are serious about this."

Jane looked over to Wendell, who was now leaving the room with all the dignity of an aristocrat, or more accurately, as an aristocat. "I believe I can accomplish anything I set my mind to."

"It's not your mind I'm worried about. It is Wendell's."

"Jane, it's so sweet of you to drive me to class and come in to observe," Ethel said.

"Are you sure that my presence won't make you nervous?" Jane asked.

"Oh my, no. I'll feel better having you there for moral support."

"I'm glad, Auntie. So, what's on the agenda tonight?"

"We are going to prepare a basic bread dough, and I'll talk about the different types of yeasts."

"Sounds good." Jane pulled into the lighted parking lot, cut the engine and retrieved the supplies from the back seat.

They walked to the brick building, where Ethel

unlocked the door and led the way down a dimly lit hallway and into a room. She flicked on the lights.

Jane gasped. "Oh my, they didn't have things like this when I was in school." She looked at the demonstration table in the middle of the room and the six kitchen cubicles forming a U-shape against the walls so that the teacher could see into each area. Each lab contained a table with six chairs, a stove, sink, microwave and a couple of cabinets.

"Wow, basically, each student has his or her own little kitchen."

Ethel nodded. "Isn't it something?"

Jane put a sack of ingredients on the table. "It sure is."

Ethel pulled the items from the bag and began to arrange them on her demonstration table.

Jane wandered around the room. She shook her head. "I just can't get over this. They're sure to glean some chefs from this type of learning center. I get excited just thinking of the possibilities." Jane turned to Ethel and smiled.

"Let's just hope they get excited about this class."

"I'm sure they will, Auntie. They wouldn't have taken the course if they hadn't wanted to learn how to make better breads. And you are the perfect instructor." She walked over and patted Ethel on the shoulder.

"Oh you," she said, "You'll make my head swell like that bread dough I made at your house."

They both laughed.

"What can I help you do to get ready?" Jane asked.

"Nothing, really. I'm pretty much set up."

Just then footsteps sounded outside of the classroom and they looked up to see a middle-aged woman step through the door.

"Hello," Ethel said.

The woman smiled. "Hello." Her gaze went to Jane. "Hi."

"My name is Ethel Buckley. I am the class instructor. This is my niece, Jane Howard."

"My name is Marilyn Bennett."

"Jane used to be a chef at a very nice restaurant in San Francisco. Now she's a chef at the bed-and-breakfast she runs with her sisters," Ethel said.

The woman's eyebrows rose, obviously impressed. "Wow, a real chef. I'm merely the chef of our family, but I love to cook."

"That's half the battle, enjoying it," Jane said.

Before long, the other students entered the room and chatted until Ethel called the room to order. She introduced herself and Jane to the class, then requested that the students give their names and tell a little about themselves. Most were there because they loved to cook. One student was hoping to own a bakery one day.

The students first cleaned their work areas and

washed their hands. Then Ethel explained the process of making the basic bread dough. The class soon got to work on their dough.

"As you may know, you will work your dough on a flour-dusted surface on your tables," Ethel said. "To turn out a smooth and satiny dough, you must knead it for approximately eight to ten minutes, so I hope you have the strength to whip your dough into shape." Ethel laughed at herself. "Before Jane and I come around to see how you're doing, I want to remind you that fresh-baked breads should be used within a few days, since bread will dry out and become moldy if kept too long. To retain moisture, wrap breads tightly in foil or plastic wrap, or place in airtight containers and store in a cool dry place."

One student raised a hand. "Miss Buckley, does it help to store bread in the refrigerator?"

"It does retard the mold growth, but the bread will become stale more quickly than when it's kept at room temperature," Ethel advised. "For longer storage, it's best to keep it in the freezer."

Jane was truly impressed with how Ethel handled the class like a true teacher.

"One thing I should mention about freezing bread is that your bread should be cooled to room temperature. Don't frost or decorate your bread before freezing. Wrap it in foil, heavy-duty plastic wrap or airtight plastic bags. Press all air from the package. You can freeze it for up to three months.

After that, the bread may lose some flavor," Ethel said.

"Do we leave it wrapped to thaw it out, Mrs. Buckley?"

"If it's a soft-crusted bread, leave it wrapped. If it's crisp-crusted, unwrap it to thaw, then use it right away. Any more questions?"

There were no more questions, so Ethel and Jane walked from table to table to check each student's progress. Suddenly, Marilyn Bennett, on the other side of the room, called out, "Oh my!"

They turned to her. "Is everything all right?" Ethel asked.

"Well, um, I think you should see this," Marilyn said, pointing to the blob of dough sprawled out before her.

Jane and Ethel walked over. The dough had picked up some ink from the table. The word *doughboy* paraded across Marilyn's dough. Backward, of course. Jane stifled a giggle.

"Well, that certainly is interesting," Ethel said.

"The oil must have picked that up," Jane commented.

The trio giggled. "I suppose if you don't want the ABCs scattered all around your loaf of bread, you had better pluck that piece of dough out of there," Ethel advised.

"Yes, you *knead* to get rid of that," Jane said.

"You won't get a *rise* out of me," Marilyn responded.

They all groaned and laughed, then Ethel and Jane continued on around the room.

While waiting for the dough to rise, Ethel discussed how yeast works through dough and how to dress up plain dough with raisins and a drizzle of confectioner's sugar to make a very tempting treat. Jane spoke of sprinkling cinnamon and sugar over a rectangular dough and rolling it into a loaf. The finished product would produce a bread with a pretty swirl of cinnamon at its center.

Once class was over, the students gathered their filled loaf pans and took them home to bake. They would discuss the results at the next session.

After the last student had left, Jane and Ethel made their way back to the car. "You know, I can't remember when I've had such fun, Auntie. Thanks for letting me tag along."

Ethel chuckled. "I think they liked having a real chef in their midst. It made me feel a lot better too."

Chapter Fourteen

After the morning dishes had been washed and put away, Louise and Jane straightened the main level of the house, dusting and vacuuming where needed. When they had finished, they went into the living room for their morning break.

The wind howled. Jane looked out the window to see the bare tree branches wave wildly. "I wonder if spring will ever come."

"Seems like I wonder that every year at this time, but somehow spring's warmth manages to thaw winter's freeze." Louise cleared the throw pillows from her seat, and then settled onto the burgundy sofa. Reaching over the side, she picked up her knitting.

Jane plopped onto the matching overstuffed chair and opened the cookbook she held. "Boy, it feels good to sit," she said, pushing a strand of dark hair from her face.

"Yes, it does. We had a busy morning," Louise said, without lifting her gaze from the yarn.

"Now for some inspiration," Jane said as she turned to the sandwich section of her book, trying to garner ideas for lunch.

"Tell me about Sylvia."

"She's coming along well. I've been helping her get a handle on her inventory. She's using this slow time to restock so she can be ready when customers start to come in again." Jane smiled.

"That's sensible. Speaking of customers, Catherine Schmidt should be arriving this afternoon," Louise said.

"Yes, I've been planning meals, because she requested full board. I wonder why she's staying with us when she lives in Potterston."

Louise shook her head. "Her daughter explained

that Mrs. Schmidt's sister died about three months ago. Evidently, they were both widowed and had moved in together. The loss of her sister has been hard on her. Her daughter thought perhaps a week here would help her relax. She asked that Mrs. Schmidt be able to eat her meals with us, because she was concerned about her mother going out in bad weather."

"That's understandable," Jane said. "I feel so sorry for her. I can only imagine how I would feel if I lost you or Alice."

"Well, I hope you do not have to face that any time soon," Louise said.

Jane smiled. "Well, we'll just have to do what we can to make Mrs. Schmidt's stay wonderful in every way. How old is she?"

Louise thought a moment. "I have no idea. I only know that she is a retired music teacher."

"A music teacher," Jane repeated. "You and she should have much in common."

Louise looked up. "Yes, indeed. She might even like to sit in on a lesson or two." She glanced at her watch.

"I thought you didn't have a piano student until this afternoon," Jane mentioned.

"I don't. I was just thinking now would be a good time to look through Father's old sermon notes."

"Have fun," Jane said, turning back to her cookbook.

Jane hoped Louise would have better luck at finding a sermon than she was having finding a recipe for lunch.

Louise brought the CD player into the library and started Eduardo's music once again. After gathering Daniel Howard's Bible and a couple of notebooks from the mahogany bookshelves, Louise sat at his desk.

The music lifted her spirits and her heart stirred as she looked through the pages of her father's Bible. Underlined passages with side notes gave her insight into her father's thoughts. She felt almost a bit of a snoop for reading such private writings, but at the same time she was drawn to her father in a powerful way. She had forgotten how much particular Scripture verses had meant to him.

A sigh escaped her as she opened a notebook. Abbreviated sentences and phrases covered the pages. These appeared to be reminders for stories. Her father loved to share anecdotes of life on the farm where he grew up. A short sentence or phrase no doubt conjured up an event in his life to which he could tie a spiritual application.

Louise wished she had her father's clarity of vision, to be able to see God in the details of daily life. She and her sisters tried to have a time of prayer and devotional reading together, but sometimes things were too hectic. On the busier days at the inn, she sometimes forgot about God altogether until she slipped into bed at night. Since it was her practice to read the Scriptures and pray before bed, thoughts of God always came to her then.

Though she felt God understood the busyness of life, she also knew she was the one who suffered when she left Him out of her day.

By the time Louise left the library to prepare for her lesson, she felt good. She had spent some hours surrounded with memories of her father and had gleaned an idea or two to share with Pastor Thompson.

Alice entered the inn, deposited the day's mail on the reception desk and took off her coat. As she hung it up, she caught a whiff of molasses from in the kitchen. She hoped that meant what she thought it did: shoo fly pie. Alice's mouth watered just thinking about the flaky crust, the rich, sweet taste.

Before she could follow her nose to the kitchen, someone entered the front door. Alice turned to see a fragile-looking older woman standing beside a younger woman who appeared to be her daughter.

Alice walked toward them. "Good afternoon. Welcome to Grace Chapel Inn," she said extending her hand. "I'm Alice Howard."

"Hello," the older woman said. Her handshake was weak, her eyes shadowed with . . . what? Illness? Grief?

"Hello," the younger woman said with a warm

smile. "My name is Tricia Burks, and this is my mother, Catherine Schmidt."

"Oh yes," Alice said, "we have been expecting you. If you'll follow me to the desk, I'll sign you in and then show you to your room, Mrs. Schmidt," Alice said.

In no time, the mother and daughter were following Alice up to the Garden Room. Alice opened the door and stepped back so that the ladies could enter.

"Oh my, Mother, this is beautiful," her daughter said, taking in the room with its green walls, floral border and rosewood bedroom set. "It almost makes me believe in spring again."

Her mother nodded. "It is lovely." She turned to Alice. "Thank you," she said in a soft voice.

"Please make yourself comfortable." Alice said, then gave them the times for meals and described the amenities of the inn.

"Mother is a retired music teacher," Tricia mentioned during their conversation.

"Oh, do you play the piano?" Alice asked.

Before Mrs. Schmidt could respond, her daughter jumped in enthusiastically, "She plays beautifully."

"Wonderful. My sister is also a pianist and gives lessons, but if you're interested in playing, I'm sure you can schedule a time around her students' visits," Alice said.

"Thank you," the woman said, though her voice

suggested that she really wasn't interested in doing much of anything.

A look of concern passed between Alice and the daughter. Mrs. Schmidt walked over to a chair and sat down. "I'm afraid you'll have to forgive me. I'm a bit tired."

"Not at all," Alice said. "I'll leave you to rest. You can meet my sisters at dinner." Alice turned to walk out of the room.

"Ma'am, if you could wait just a moment?" Tricia Burks said. She placed her hand on her mother's shoulder. "Mother, I'll call to check on you. If you need anything, you call me, all right?"

Her mother reached a thin hand up and covered her daughter's hand. "I'll be fine, dear."

The daughter dropped a kiss on her mother's head. "I love you." She turned and walked out of the room with Alice.

"Thank you for waiting for me," Mrs. Burks said. "I'm afraid my mother has been through a lot. I mentioned this to your sister, I believe, on the telephone." She then explained about the death of her aunt and how difficult things had been for her mother since then.

By this time they had reached the bottom of the stairs and walked over toward the door. "I assure you we will do everything we can to make her stay at Grace Chapel Inn a positive one," Alice promised.

"Thank you so much. I have heard great things

about your bed-and-breakfast, that's why I brought Mother here."

"Thank you for your kind words," Alice said. "Pray for us, Mrs. Burks, that we will do our part, and then we'll trust God with the rest."

"That's all I could hope for. And please, call me Tricia," she said.

"Tricia." Alice smiled.

Tricia studied Alice a moment. "You know, I feel very good about Mother staying here. Very good indeed." Tricia Burks opened the door and left.

Alice went to the window and watched Tricia walk down the path to her car. Alice prayed that God would give her and her sisters the grace to help their guest with whatever she needed.

Chapter Fifteen

Good morning, Mrs. Schmidt," Jane said, placing a dish on the table.

"Oh my," the older woman exclaimed, looking at the table laden with a chilled pitcher of freshly squeezed orange juice, carafes of steaming coffee and tea, a bowl of fresh fruit salad and a heated tray holding something that looked and smelled delicious. "What is that heavenly dish?" she asked, pointing to the tray.

Jane smiled. "Cinnamon and pecan stuffed French toast. This is my first time serving it. I hope it tastes as good as it looks."

Alice entered the dining room and glanced at the table, noticing the new dish Jane had prepared. "Oh Jane," Alice said, "You've made something new. It looks wonderful. I'll be hard pressed to mind my manners this morning."

After Louise arrived at the table, Jane prepared plates for everyone, and they all took their places at the table, where Louise said grace for the meal.

"I didn't know I would get to eat with you," Mrs. Schmidt commented, pouring praline sauce over her toast.

"I hope you don't mind," Alice said.

"Oh, to the contrary, I was hoping that I wouldn't be eating . . ." she hesitated, "alone."

Jane looked up as Alice turned warm brown eyes to their guest and said. "It is our pleasure to share meals with you."

Jane and Louise smiled in agreement.

"Please tell us about yourself, Mrs. Schmidt," Louise said.

"First, I don't like to be called Mrs. Schmidt." She made a face. "I would much prefer to be called Catherine."

"Catherine it is," Louise said.

Catherine took a sip of milk, then dabbed her mouth with a napkin. "Well, there's not much to tell, really. I was married for thirty years to Wilbur. I taught music at a county school for about forty years. When Wilbur died, I moved in with my sister Helen, who had also lost her husband. We lived together ten years until three months ago when Helen died." Tears sprang to her eyes. She dabbed at them with her napkin. "I'm so sorry. I can't seem to get a grip on my emotions."

Louise placed her hand on Catherine's arm. "I understand completely, dear. It's never easy to let go of someone we love."

Catherine looked up at her and smiled. "Thank you." She straightened in her chair, attempting to control her emotion. "Anyway," she said, taking a deep breath, "my sister, Helen Edgerton, also taught school before retiring."

Jane put down her knife and fork and leaned toward Catherine. "Helen Edgerton? Second grade teacher in Acorn Hill many years ago?"

"That's right, dear." Catherine looked at her questioningly.

Jane reached over and placed her hand on Catherine's. "Mrs. Edgerton was my second grade teacher."

"Truly?" Catherine asked.

Jane nodded. "I have very fond memories of Mrs. Edgerton." She was about to tell her story about how Mrs. Edgerton had helped her through a tough spot, but she decided to wait until she and Catherine were alone.

"She was a wonderful lady and sister," Catherine said. This time her voice held no sadness, but rather love and admiration.

They talked awhile longer about her sister, the

kind of teacher she was and how the schools had changed.

"Well, I guess I had better get things cleaned up or we won't be ready for lunch," Jane said with a smile. "It was so nice talking with you, Catherine. I do hope you enjoy your stay with us."

"Thank you, Jane."

"The fireplace is lit in the living room, if you'd like to find a comfortable spot and read by the fire," Alice said.

"You ladies will spoil me if you're not careful."

"That's precisely what we want to do to our guests," Louise said. She turned to Jane. "Alice and I have some shopping to do. Would you like to come?"

"No thanks. I have a few things already on my agenda. Let me know if you are going to miss lunch," Jane said.

"Not to worry. We won't be gone that long, if I have anything to say about it," Alice said with a laugh. Alice merely tolerated shopping. It was not on her list of favorite things to do.

Jane and her sisters cleared the table and took the dishes into the kitchen. Then Alice and Louise left on their errands. Catherine went upstairs and came back with a book. Jane saw that she made herself comfortable in the overstuffed living room chair, placing a plump pillow under her arm to hold the weight of the book. With the fire snapping and popping in the background, Jane was sure Catherine would be settled in for a good read.

Once the breakfast dishes were in the dishwasher and the kitchen had been restored to its usual sparkle, Jane decided to join Catherine in the living room. She settled onto the sofa with a decorating magazine and began to leaf through the pages.

"You know, it did my heart good to hear you speak so fondly of my sister," Catherine said.

Jane looked up from her magazine. "I didn't want to go into detail, because I'm sure my sisters must get tired of hearing me talk about my never knowing our mother. But I want you to know, Mrs. Edgerton helped me through a tough spot. I remember it clearly, even though I was quite young."

Catherine sat in rapt attention. "Please tell me about it."

Jane curled her stocking feet beneath her on the sofa. "Well, many of the students' mothers were volunteering their time to help out in the classroom and with Brownies, but my mother had died when I was born."

Catherine gave a sympathetic look. "I'm so sorry, dear."

"Thank you." Jane thought for a little bit. "When the other kids' moms came in to help, the mothers' names were put on the blackboard. Beside each mother's name was the name of her child. It seemed like almost everyone had his or her name on the board at one time or another.

"I was feeling left out, and your sister seemed to sense it. She called my father. He brought the matter to Louise's attention, and Louise agreed to come into the classroom periodically to help out and serve as my 'mother.' My name went on the blackboard beside Louise's name. Everyone knew she wasn't my mother, but still I felt special because my name was on the board too."

Catherine smiled.

"I was so thankful that Mrs. Edgerton understood my feelings and called my father. I'll never forget her kindness. It meant so much to me."

" 'Kind' describes Helen perfectly. She loved her students. She prayed for each one by name, every day." A far-away look came to her eyes.

"I should have known," Jane said after a time. "There was always something about her." For a moment Jane visited distant memories, remembering her kind teacher, her gentle ways. She turned back to Catherine and smiled. "The students who went through her classroom were very blessed."

Catherine smiled in kind. "Anyone who knew her was blessed."

Jane bit her lip, wondering if she should say what she was thinking. "Is it hard for you to talk about her?" she ventured.

Catherine's sad eyes met Jane's. "I appreciate

your memory of her. I have so many wonderful memories myself. I'm not ready to let her go. We should still be making memories, my sister and I. But . . ." Her words stopped and her eyes filled with tears. "If you don't mind, Jane, I think I'll go up to my room now."

Jane searched for words to help this woman. She found none. "Certainly, you go ahead." She hesitated. "I hope I haven't made you feel bad."

Catherine looked at her. "No, dear. It's me. It's, well, something I have to work through myself."

Once she heard Catherine's footsteps on the stairway, Jane bowed her head and whispered a prayer for the woman whose grief so consumed her.

"Alice, the phone is for you," Jane said with a teasing glint in her eye.

"Who is it?"

Jane lifted her eyebrows, causing Alice to think that Jane was spending far too much time with Louise. "Why, my dear, it's a gentleman caller, Dr. Mark Graves," she said with a sugary accent.

"Oh, for goodness sakes," Alice said. As she made her way to the phone, Alice could hear Jane laughing. Sometimes her sisters were just a little too . . . too . . . oh, she didn't know what, but too something. "Hello?" she said into the phone's receiver.

"Hi, Alice. This is Mark."

"Hello, Mark. It's nice to hear from you so soon."

"I have a couple of reasons for calling. First, I want to know how your visit went with Andy. Did he help you learn any more about the dogs?"

"Oh yes, Mark, he gave me a lot of information." Alice proceeded to tell Mark all about her visit.

"So he knows your friend is already on a list, right?"

"Actually, she's in Philadelphia right now training with her dog. I told him that." Alice explained what had happened with the board meeting.

"Well, it's great that the church is willing to help her, Alice."

"Isn't it? I was thrilled they were eager to help."

Mark paused a moment.

"Mark? Are you still there?"

"Yes, I'm here. Hey, listen, I know this is last minute, but I found out just awhile ago that I have to go into Potterston this afternoon. I wondered if you'd want to meet me for dinner at Bernardo's Pizza?"

She hesitated, mentally checking her schedule.

"Listen, if that doesn't work for you, I understand," he said with a hint of defeat in his voice.

"No, actually, that'd be fun," Alice said.

"Really?"

She smiled. The truth was that she could hardly wait. "Really. What time do you want to meet?"

"Will six o'clock work for you?"

"It'll work just fine. I'll see you then."

"Great. Thanks, Alice."

She hung up the phone, feeling a tiny kick in her pulse. She smiled and turned from the phone to see her sisters standing there, grinning.

Jane tapped her toe impatiently. "Okay, let's have it. What gives?"

Louise stood beside her, eyebrows raised.

"Now, you two behave yourselves," Alice said. "Mark has to make a trip to Potterston today. He invited me to Bernardo's tonight for pizza. That's all."

The phone rang again, and Alice picked it up. "Grace Chapel Inn. Oh yes, Paula," she said, turning around to see her sisters walk away.

Alice grinned, then turned her attention back to Paula. "I'm so glad to hear from you. How is the training going?"

"I'm doing well, but I've been very busy," Paula said.

"Is the training difficult?"

"It's wonderful, Alice. These dogs are absolutely amazing."

"Do you feel comfortable with your dog?" Alice asked.

"Completely. I feel like I've owned her all my life."

"A female?"

"Yes. Her name is Paws, and she's a two-year-old golden retriever."

"I bet she's beautiful."

"Oh, she is. I hope you get to meet . . . I hope she gets to stay with me . . . I mean—"

"Actually, that's one of the reasons I'm glad you called," Alice broke in. She shared her good news with Paula that the Grace Chapel Board had voted unanimously to help her get the dog.

There was silence on Paula's end, then sniffles. Finally in a shaky voice, Paula said, "I can't believe it, Alice. After being with this dog, I was so afraid this would all be a dream." She sniffled some more. "Thank you so much, and thanks to your church."

"You're welcome. Now," Alice said, "hurry home, so I can meet your new roommate."

"Oh, Alice, our training is going so well, I may even get to leave early. The handler said that some clients just bond quicker with their dogs than others. Paws and I hit it off immediately."

"I'm so happy for you, Paula."

"I owe it all to you, Alice."

"No, the Lord has worked this out. He merely used me to work in the situation."

"I can't believe it. A seizure response dog. Who would have thought that when I was praying for a roommate, the Lord would give me a dog?" Paula laughed. "He certainly does work in mysterious ways."

Alice chuckled along with her. "He does at that."

Chapter Sixteen

Jane headed for her car to go to Sylvia's house. Gray billowy clouds moved slowly across the moonlit sky, while the piercing air nipped at her face and ears. Chilled puffs of air escaped her as she breathed. Despite the thick corduroy trousers and heavy woolen sweater she wore beneath her coat, Jane shivered.

She was looking forward to spending time tonight with Sylvia. Jane had been helping out in the store and taking meals to Sylvia, but for the last few days, Sylvia had been handling things pretty much on her own.

Once Jane pulled up at Sylvia's house, she cut the engine, picked up the DVD and a package of microwave popcorn and then made her way up the shoveled walk to the front door. She lifted her gloved hand and knocked. A gust of wind swirled around her, causing her to burrow into her coat. She could hear footsteps approaching the other side of the door.

"Hi, Jane," Sylvia said enthusiastically.

"Hi." Jane stepped inside. "Let me just put these down for a moment while I take off my coat." Jane placed the movie and popcorn on the entryway table.

"So what are we watching tonight?" Sylvia asked with a smile. She closed the door behind Jane.

"I don't even remember the name. It's a romantic comedy, though," Jane said, gathering the goodies and following Sylvia into the warmth of the kitchen. "It feels so good in here."

Sylvia unwrapped the cellophane from the popcorn and placed it into the microwave. She punched in the appropriate time and set it to humming. Jane retrieved glasses from the cupboard.

"There's diet soda in the refrigerator. I always feel less guilty about eating buttered popcorn if I drink diet soda with it."

Jane reached inside and pulled out two cans. She then plucked some ice cubes from the freezer and dropped them into the glasses. Popping open the cans, she poured the fizzling liquid into the glasses, and the frosty cubes crackled and shifted in response. "As cold as I am, the soda still looks good."

Sylvia nodded.

Jane placed the glasses on a tray. They talked a few minutes about the new colors for spring and about a vintage clothing shop that was opening in Riverton. Then the microwave signaled that the popcorn was done.

As Sylvia opened the bag, a puff of steam escaped. She poured the contents into a big bowl—added a little salt, and they were all set. The smell of buttery corn wafted through the air. She turned to Jane. "Ready?"

Jane nodded. "On with the show."

Halfway through the comedy, they paused the movie to go to the kitchen and refill their glasses.

"You haven't talked about Alice's friend and her assistance dog in a while. How's that going?"

"It's going well. Paula called Alice and said that she should be getting home soon. Looks like things are all set for the dog to come home with her," Jane said, pouring more soda into her glass.

"That's great." Sylvia thought a moment. "Did I ever tell you my amazing dog story?"

Jane's soda fizzed and bubbled in her glass. She took a sip, then looked at Sylvia. "No, you didn't."

Sylvia filled her glass with more ice and soda. "Let's go in there and I'll tell you," she said, motioning toward the living room. Once settled into their seats, Sylvia began.

"Well, when my aunt and uncle were younger, they lived about four blocks apart but didn't know each other. Uncle Al was four years older than Aunt Inge. He lived across the street from a small grocery store that Mom's older brothers frequented. The family dog, Sparky, used to walk to the store with her brothers and then wander off, and they would walk home alone. Sparky would show up sometime later." Sylvia chuckled. "My aunt once admitted that when she was a teenager, she would share her secrets with Sparky. He lived eighteen years."

"Wow, that's a long time for a dog," Jane said.

Sylvia nodded. "Well, one day after my aunt and uncle were married, they were spending an afternoon with Uncle Al's parents, going through photo albums. Aunt Inge came upon a picture of my uncle standing by a kid's swimming pool. There was a dog sitting in the background. My aunt mentioned that the dog looked just like her old dog. Well, Uncle Al's mother laughed and said, 'Oh, that was some stray that used to stop by our house on a weekly, sometimes daily basis.'

"Aunt Inge was stunned. She felt sure that the dog with her future husband was Sparky, and that Sparky knew one day she and Uncle Al would get together." Sylvia sat back in her seat. "Isn't that cool?"

"That's really amazing," Jane agreed.

"Mom always teased Aunt Inge, saying that a dog found her a husband."

Jane laughed. "Do you suppose we ought to get dogs?"

Sylvia laughed. "I think we'd better turn the movie back on," she said, clicking the movie back on the screen.

They laughed their way through the comedy and finally turned off the television.

"I'm glad you came over tonight, Jane. I've been so bored being cooped up in this house and at the store."

"I can only imagine," Jane said. "I'm amazed,

Sylvia, how you've been able to work around the store. I don't know how you do it."

"Same way you do at the inn, sheer determination." She laughed. "I told Mom about how much you're doing for me. She wants you to come to her house for dinner."

"I would like that."

"Good. Maybe once the weather clears, we can drive to Potterston."

"I'll look forward to it." Jane glanced at her watch. "Oh, it's getting late. I'd better get going." She rose from her chair and picked up the dishes. Sylvia followed her.

Once the dishes were rinsed and loaded into the dishwasher, Sylvia retrieved Jane's coat and Jane prepared to go. "Well, I'll see you next week at the store," Jane said.

"Thanks, Jane. I really appreciate your help," Sylvia said.

"Hey, that's what friends are for." Jane put on her coat on. When she finished, Sylvia handed her the movie.

"Here is your DVD. Thanks for bringing it over."

"I had fun," she said as she slipped through the front door.

The wind had subsided, and Jane was wrapped in the crisp, silent night air. She opened the car door, scooted inside and turned on the engine. As she pulled onto the street, she wondered how Alice's evening was going with Mark Graves.

• • •

Alice stepped into the warm haven of Bernardo's Pizza and inhaled the zesty scents of sausage, pepperoni, mixed spices and pizza dough. She looked for Mark and spotted him across the room. The hostess approached her. "Thank you. I see the person I'm meeting," Alice told her, nodding toward Mark.

The waitress smiled and went to the next customer.

Alice made her way through the maze of brown wooden tables and booths until she came to Mark. "Hi," she said.

"Right on time," Mark said as he stood and helped her with her coat, which she placed next to her on the seat across from Mark.

"It smells wonderful in here. I haven't been to Bernardo's in quite some time," said Alice as she automatically unrolled the bundled silverware and placed it into a proper place setting.

"I don't know how you stay away from this retaurant. It's a good thing I don't live nearby, or I'd put on a hundred pounds." He laughed his hearty laugh.

The sound brought a rush of memories to Alice's mind. That laugh had punctuated many a conversation when they were sweethearts during Alice's nursing school days.

The waitress came and took their drink orders, breaking the spell that had overtaken Alice.

"You probably know what you want, but here's the menu in case you're feeling adventurous," Mark said as he handed her the trifold laminated menu.

"I suppose I should look at it, though I suspect I'll stick with my tried and true."

"Deluxe with extra cheese, right?" he asked.

Alice looked up with surprise. "Yes . . . yes, that's right." *We have not shared a pizza in years, how could he have remembered that?* she wondered. In spite of herself, she felt pleased and flattered.

She glanced through the menu but could not concentrate. She quickly closed it. "My suspicion was right. I hear the deluxe calling to me," she said.

"Why change a good thing," Mark said.

The waitress served their beverages, took their orders and left them once again.

"So, Alice, any word on your friend and the dog?" he asked as he slid the paper off a straw.

"Oh Mark, everything is going very well. She called me from Philadelphia where she is doing a short-term training course with her dog, Paws. She sounded so happy on the telephone." Alice could not hide her own enthusiasm.

Mark looked at her and smiled. "That's great. She was lucky she didn't have to wait like most folks."

"Yes. Fortunately for her she had been placed on that list a little over a year ago. It had been so long since the time she applied for the dog, she had forgotten about it. Anyway, they finally matched her with a dog to fit her needs." She shook her head. "That's just like God."

"How do you mean?"

"He takes care of us when we need it. You know, He gives the grace we need when we need it."

Mark smiled. "That's true enough." He paused a moment. "I sure enjoyed my visit to the inn."

"We enjoyed having you."

"I could tell things were going well for you and your sisters. You share a certain camaraderie. That must be why you work so well together."

"Well, we have our days," Alice said with a chuckle. "But for the most part, we do get along beautifully. We all love having people in our home. We each have different gifts to lend to the running of the business, so it works out well," she said.

The waitress brought their pizzas.

"I'll say grace for us," Mark said.

Her heart gave a leap as he reached for her hand. *Was it his touch or his obvious faith that caused her reaction?* she wondered.

Over the next couple of hours, while a dusting of snow fell, Alice and Mark enjoyed their pizza and their comfortable relationship.

Later, Alice glanced out the window. "Oh no, it's snowing. We had better go on our ways before it starts to accumulate."

Mark sighed. "Yes, I guess you're right."

"This has been so nice, Mark. Really. Thank you for inviting me."

He placed his hand on hers. "We need to do this more often, Alice. Philly isn't that far away." He gave her hand a squeeze, then released it.

She smiled and nodded, feeling a rush of warmth spread through her. She got up from the booth, and Mark helped her with her coat. *Always the gentleman,* she thought. That's something she had truly appreciated about Mark.

As he walked her to her car, he asked, "Do you have an ice scraper?"

Alice nodded, opened her car door, and retrieved it.

"Get the car heated up, and I'll scrape the windows for you."

She gave a grateful smile and climbed inside. After starting the engine, she turned on the heat and defrost. Once the windows were clear, Mark came to the driver's side of her car. She rolled down the window, and he gave the ice scraper to her.

"Thanks so much, Mark."

"You take care of yourself, Alice."

"I will. You do the same. I've had a lovely evening."

"Me too." He smiled, then headed for his car.

She rolled up her window and started out of the parking lot. Looking in the rear view mirror to make sure that Mark's car had started, she caught herself smiling. *Yes,* she thought, *it was a lovely evening.*

The snow stopped and a smattering of twinkling stars poked through the night sky as Alice made her way home. The serenity of the country on such a night, and the view of open fields dusted with snow, made the drive back to Acorn Hill pleasant.

When she arrived home, Alice got out of her car and took a deep breath. She lifted her face toward the night sky. "Thank You," she whispered. With a grateful heart, Alice tucked her evening in the place of pleasant memories and smiled while her feet carried her into the house.

Chapter Seventeen

The next morning, the Howard sisters walked with Bibles in hand to Grace Chapel. The wintry sunshine blazed from a sky swept clean by yesterday's winds. Jane looked around, her spirit instantly refreshed. "Finally, we see the sun."

Alice looked up. "It seems right that such a beautiful day is the Sabbath," she said.

Louise agreed.

They entered the double doors of Grace Chapel.

"And how are the Howard sisters this morning?" Pastor Thompson asked, stepping toward them.

The sisters exchanged greetings with him and visited until other people started filing into the church for the service.

Louise took her place at the pipe organ at the back of the chapel, while Alice and Jane took seats in a pew. When they sat down, colors from the stained glass windows dappled their legs and arms.

After a time of worship through music and giving, the pastor stood to preach.

"Today I would like to talk to you about a subject that is rarely talked about these days, the Sabbath. The word comes from the Hebrew and means 'rest.'

"In the rush of our busy days, filled with appointments, meetings, phone calls, faxes, e-mails and more, the very idea of resting seems almost impossible."

Jane thought of how busy their days at the inn could get. Still, the full days at Acorn Hill didn't compare to her hectic days when she worked as a chef in San Francisco.

She turned her thoughts back to the pastor's words.

"The Scripture tells us to keep the Sabbath day holy. Just how do we do that?

"I can remember Sunday afternoons when my family would get in the car and take long rides out in the country. We would go through mile after mile of city streets, through heavy traffic and blaring horns, until we finally entered the open countryside. Almost on cue, Mom would stop nagging Dad to watch out for this or that, and Dad would start to whistle. A gentle peace would settle upon our car. Sometimes Dad pulled over to the side of the road so we could get out and just enjoy the scenery.

"Taking a deep breath, he would look at me and say, 'Do you taste that, Kenneth?' A huge grin would spread across his face. 'That's country air. There's nothing better.'"

Jane and Alice exchanged a smile.

"Those early days taught me about taking time to rest, to enjoy the things we tend to take for granted every day, like the air we breathe, the beauty of a flower, the touch of a friend's hand upon our own. In other words, it taught me to remember to appreciate the gift of life that we are given."

The pastor spoke of the early Christians and their reverence for the Sabbath. He spoke of changing times while emphasizing the need for rest and worship.

"The Bible says, 'Come to me, all you who are weary and burdened, and I will give you rest' (Matthew 11:28). Are you weary? Burdened? He calls us to come to Him."

Jane struggled to keep her thoughts from wandering to springtime, her flower garden and the warmth of the sun.

The pastor's conclusion broke through her mental wandering. "Let me leave you with these points in the form of an acronym for the Sabbath," he said. "*S*—Save some time for the Creator. *A*—Allow yourself moments of rest and reflection.

B—Be kind to your body, physically and emotionally. *B*—Believe God will renew your spirit as you give Him first place in your life. *A*—Accept the gift with joy instead of grumbling. *T*—Take time for yourself. And *H*—Humble yourself before Him that He might bring healing and refreshment to your body and soul."

The pastor was right. Jane agreed that she needed to take time for herself. For a long time, she had wanted to start a journal. She decided today would be the day.

He closed with prayer.

The congregation began to file out in an unusually reverent manner. The sermon had spoken to Jane in a real way. She felt sure that it had also touched the hearts of many others, though the citizens of Acorn Hill were probably better at taking restful moments than the folks who lived in busier places.

"Wonderful sermon, Pastor Ken," Louise said, shaking his hand at the door.

"Thank you, Louise."

"Is it something you are considering . . ." she let her words dangle. Jane knew Louise was referring to the seminar speech.

Understanding lit his eyes. "No, I don't think so, though it is a message dear to my heart."

"Well, one thing I have learned in all my years, Pastor Ken, is that just because we are in a hurry, doesn't mean that God is."

"So true, Louise. So true."

"By the way, I might have an idea for you. Tell me when you'd like to talk about it," she said.

His eyebrows lifted. "That's great. We'll talk soon."

She nodded and moved on ahead, allowing Jane to tell the pastor how much she appreciated his sermon. She then moved on through the door and joined her sisters as they walked toward their home.

Alice was the first to speak. "Well, he certainly gave me a lot to mull over," she said. "I think today after spending some quiet time with the Lord, I'm going to start that new mystery I've been meaning to get to."

Louise smiled. "I always relax when I play the piano. I haven't taken the time to do so in quite a while. I think I will do that today."

"You know, that's exactly what I've been thinking," Jane said. "I've been meaning to start a journal. I bought one in Potterston ages ago. I'm going to crack it open and write in it today."

"Well, it looks as though the pastor's message touched all of us," Alice said.

Catherine was spending the afternoon with her daughter, so the sisters had no other obligations. After lunch, each went to do what she had discussed. Alice took her mystery to the living room and the warmth of a crackling fire. Louise went into the parlor and closed the door, and was soon enveloped in a glorious melody. Jane pulled on warm pants and a bulky sweater and settled onto her bed, journal in hand.

Some time later, Jane and Louise joined Alice in the living room. Alice looked up from her book, placing a marker between the pages. "Did you enjoy your time of rest?" she asked.

Louise nodded and sat on the sofa. Jane smiled before plopping into the overstuffed chair.

"You know, there must be something to this, because you both do look refreshed," Alice said.

"As do you," Louise replied.

"I haven't journaled since I was a kid. I forgot how relaxing it could be just to write down my thoughts," Jane said.

"And you're lucky. You don't have a younger sister trying to snoop in your diary," Alice teased.

Jane winced. "Did I do that?"

Louise lifted her eyebrows and said, "More than once."

Just then a sound at the front door was followed by a familiar, "Yoo-hoo."

"We're in the living room, Aunt Ethel," Jane said.

Ethel stepped into the living room. "Land's sake, it's nice to find you all in the same room. Is it okay if I join you?" She started taking off her coat without waiting for a reply.

"Of course, Aunt Ethel, make yourself at home,"

Alice said, rising to take her aunt's coat and hang it in the closet.

"It looks like you're all taking the pastor's sermon to heart," Ethel said, falling onto the sofa with a thump. "Oh, my bones are stiff from all this cold weather."

"Yes, we did try to spend some time resting and enjoying the Sabbath."

"Me too." She and Louise engaged in conversation about the sermon and how things had changed, and about the good old days when life was slow. Then Ethel asked Alice about the mystery she was reading, which led to further discussion about the questionable material available in today's world.

"I almost forgot the reason I stopped by," Ethel said. "I was walking near Clara Horn's place when I noticed that black dog in front of her house near the street." She looked at Alice. "You know the one." She waggled a wrinkled finger. "The one you fed."

"What happened?" Louise asked.

"Well, I noticed him because he was standing near the road, barking. I was a little nervous about him, so I crossed the road. I thought he might follow me and keep barking, but he didn't. I thought that was kind of odd, so I turned around to see what he was barking at. That's when I noticed Daisy rooting around in her front yard as big as you please."

"Daisy? Clara's potbellied pig?" Alice asked.

Ethel pursed her lips and snapped a nod in one quick motion. She was sitting straight up now, fully into her story. "Well, I knew Clara wouldn't let Daisy out by herself, so I was worried. I walked over to check on her."

"Was she all right?" Louise wanted to know.

"I'll get to that in just a minute," Ethel said, not about to be hurried now that she had their full attention. "I edged closer to the house and the dog came toward me, wagging his tail, so I figured he wasn't going to hurt me. Daisy just ignored me completely." A look of frustration formed on her face. "That's just like a pig."

Jane stifled a giggle.

"I went to the front door and knocked. No answer. So, I pulled open the storm door and knocked again, thinking maybe Clara couldn't hear me." She paused for effect, enjoying every moment of the sisters' interest. "Still no answer. I assumed she was just out and about and didn't know Daisy had gotten loose, so I thought I had better try to get that pig back inside."

Alice didn't even want to think about what that must have looked like.

"What did you do?" Louise asked.

"Well, first I looked around to see how she had gotten loose. The back door was closed, no holes around the foundation near the basement, no sign anywhere of how she had gotten out. I walked up to Daisy, put my hands square on my hips and said, 'Looky here, Miss Piggy, you've got to get back in that house before your mama gets home.' "

Alice let out a laugh in spite of herself. Ethel looked at her, the hint of a smile playing at the corners of her own mouth. "Well, I did."

"And what did Daisy do?" Jane asked with amusement.

"She grunted."

At this everyone laughed.

"Anyway, I've never known Daisy to bite anyone, but I didn't want to be her first victim. I wanted to grab her backside and just sort of drag her to the house, but I figured Daisy would start that high-pitched squealing of hers and scare everyone in the county half to death. So, I tried talking softly to her and reached for her collar. When I did, Daisy still let out a squeak and shot away from me. That's when Clara threw open her window and hollered out. 'Ethel, what are you doing with my pig?' "

Ethel scooted to the edge of the sofa. "Can you imagine? Like I was trying to steal Daisy or something. As if I don't have enough on my hands just trying to keep up with Lloyd."

"What happened next, Auntie?" Jane asked.

"Well, I went over to the window and told Clara what happened. It seems Clara had been putting out some trash in the can by her back door when the phone rang. She left the door open in her rush to get to it. She didn't realize Daisy had sauntered through the kitchen and out the back. After her phone call, Clara closed the door, then went into her room for a nap. Well, she must have heard me trying her doors, because something stirred her from her rest. Then by the time she looked out the window, I was fixing to haul Daisy inside."

"My, my, that's some story," Louise said, picking up her knitting. "Yes, indeed."

"Great story, Auntie," Jane said.

Alice thought for a moment.

"What's the matter, Alice? You look lost in another world," Ethel said.

"Well, I was just thinking that if you hadn't seen our mystery dog, you never would have stopped and who knows what might have happened to Daisy."

"You're right," Ethel said.

"I can see it in the *Acorn Nutshell* now," Jane said as she waved her hand overhead as if writing a caption. "Mystery dog brings home the bacon."

Ethel chuckled. "Wouldn't Clara have a hissy fit over that one?" She scratched her head. "That dog sure is a mystery. He always seems to show up at just the right time. How curious."

"Isn't it, though," Alice commented.

"He could be an angel," Jane said, waggling her eyebrows like Groucho Marx.

"A doggie angel? I've never heard of anything so ridiculous," Ethel said with a chuckle.

Of course, Alice thought, *Jane is being silly. Still* . . . Alice made up her mind right then and there that she was going to capture that dog and find his owner. These coincidences were getting a little too strange.

Chapter Eighteen

Alice was tired when she left work on Monday and more so when she arrived at the inn. She dropped the mail on the reception desk, pulled off her coat and hung it up. A delicious aroma reached her and she followed it to the kitchen.

"Is that roast pork I smell?" Alice asked Jane.

Jane closed the oven door, turned to Alice and smiled. "Good nose." She pulled off her oven mitt.

"Is this in honor of Daisy?"

Jane groaned. "Oh, don't ever say that in front of Clara."

Alice chuckled. "You're right, I shouldn't be so mean."

"So how was your day?" Jane placed the oven mitt on the counter and leaned against the sink.

"Busy," Alice said. She plopped onto a chair and lifted her feet onto another chair. Stretching forward, she rubbed her legs.

"You okay?" Jane asked.

"My legs are sore. Too much standing, I guess." Alice shrugged. "I'm not twenty anymore."

"None of us is." Jane smiled.

The faint sound of piano music filtered into the room. "Louise must be relaxing at the piano," Alice said.

The sound got fuller, richer, stronger. Alice and Jane shared a puzzled glance. Jane pulled off her apron and laid it on the back of a chair. "I don't know how she's doing that, but it's really good."

Alice agreed and together they walked toward the parlor. They stopped short of the open door. "Oh my," Alice said when she saw Catherine at the piano bench with Louise. She and Jane stood there while the music carried them to another place. Once the music came to a stop, they applauded and stepped into the room.

Louise smiled in appreciation. Catherine smiled as well, although she looked a bit embarrassed by the attention.

"That was absolutely marvelous," Jane exclaimed.

"I cannot remember when I've had such fun," Louise said.

"Would you play some more for us after dinner?" Alice asked.

Louise looked at Catherine who nodded her consent.

"Great," Jane said. "Dinner is ready."

After they had gathered at the table and Louise had offered the blessing for the meal, they enjoyed lively conversation and Jane's delicious cooking.

"Did I tell you that Paula may get to come home from her training early?" Alice asked.

They shook their heads.

"She told me that she and her dog were bonding quickly, so the trainer told her it was possible she could go home early. She said she would call me when she got home."

Alice explained to Catherine the program, the different types of assistance dogs and how Paula had come to join it. Catherine listened intently, and Alice noticed a slight frown crease her brow.

They continued to discuss the dog and how Paula's life could only improve. Alice shared how much better she felt knowing that Paula would no longer be alone and that the dog was trained to take care of Paula. Glancing at Catherine, Alice wondered why the woman suddenly had grown quiet.

"If you'll excuse me," Catherine said, "I don't think I will be able to play the piano after dinner."

"Are you all right?" Alice asked.

"I'm fine, just a little tired right now," she said, rising from the table. "Jane, the meal was absolutely delicious. Thank you." She smiled and walked from the room.

"I wonder what that was all about," Louise said.

"I don't know. I had planned to visit Vera this evening, but I wonder if I should stick around in case Catherine isn't feeling well," Alice said.

"You don't need to do that, Alice. We can call

you if there is a problem. You won't be that far away," Jane encouraged.

"How odd." Louise stared into the distance, as if trying to figure out Catherine's strange behavior.

"Well, I suppose it's possible she really was just tired," Alice said.

Louise and Jane both nodded, though Alice suspected they were no more convinced than she was herself.

"Alice, come in," Vera Humbert said, opening the door to her friend.

"It feels wonderful in here," Alice said as she stepped into the warmth of Vera's home.

"I don't doubt it after being out in that cold. Here, let me take your coat for you," Vera offered, already helping Alice to take it off. "Fred went back to the store to finish some paperwork and the tea is brewing, so we're all set to have a good visit," she called over her shoulder as she hung Alice's coat in the closet.

Alice followed Vera to the kitchen. "May I help you get the tea?"

"No, no, you just make yourself at home, and I'll be right with you."

Alice wandered into the living room and admired Vera's home. It was the perfect "sigh" home, as Jane would call it. It was a place where you come home, plop yourself on an overstuffed chair, put your stocking feet on the coffee table, and sigh.

Everything encouraged comfort and relaxation, right down to the flickering pumpkin-scented candles on a nearby stand. Alice took a deep breath, feeling the day's cares slip away. Stepping farther into the room, she admired the quaint window seat that topped ivory-painted drawers decorated with colorful stenciling. Plush pillows nestled against strong insulated windows that revealed the snow scene just beyond.

Alice returned to the buttercream-colored kitchen with bright cherry accessories and felt her spirit lighten. She edged toward the table, where Vera had obviously been grading lessons. School papers covered the table. Alice smiled at the sight.

Vera scooted the papers to one side and brought the tea over. They both sat down and prepared their drinks. "This is so nice, Vera. Thank you. I always enjoy our visits."

Vera stirred sugar into her tea. "So do I, Alice. Tell me, how are things going with the dog and your friend?"

"Just wonderful. She is at a training center right now getting acquainted with her dog, learning the commands, that kind of thing. I can hardly wait until she comes home."

Vera sipped her tea, then looked up at Alice. "You know, Byrdie Hutchison's sister and brother-in-law are visiting her right now."

"Oh?" Alice wondered how the conversation had turned to Byrdie, a widow who lived at the north edge of town. She kept pretty much to herself. She visited Grace Chapel once in a while, but not regularly. Alice overheard the ANGELs saying Byrdie looked mean because she always had a scowl on her face. Alice had to remind them to look for the good inside of people.

"Well, I guess they've heard about Paula's dog, and her brother-in-law said that once you let dogs into public places, pretty soon your restaurants and such get dog hair in them and before you know it, your town is going downhill fast."

"For goodness sakes!" Alice exclaimed, barely able to believe what Vera was saying. "How do you suppose he heard about the dog?"

Vera shrugged. "My guess is Florence might have had something to do with it. She sometimes calls on Byrdie."

"I see." Alice thought a moment. "I would hope Florence didn't get them stirred up about the dog."

"Florence probably just told them about the dog and the brother-in-law took over from there. In any case, I thought you should be forewarned so that you could prepare yourself for any trouble when Paula returns with her dog."

Alice pulled in a long breath. "I can't for the life of me see why people have to go get in a snit over something like this. My goodness, the dog is to help this poor young woman. How would they feel if they needed help?"

Vera held up her hands in surrender. "You don't

have to convince me, Alice. I understand completely. I think it's rather selfish and cruel on their part to complain about it."

"Well, it's the law—the Americans with Disabilities Act. Paula has every right to bring her seizure response dog into a public place. And she most certainly will," Alice said in no uncertain terms.

Vera was taking a sip of tea and almost choked at the edge in Alice's voice. She put her cup down and laughed. "They had better not mess with Alice Howard."

Alice looked up and started to chuckle. "Oh, sometimes people can get me so stirred up, I can't think straight."

"I can see that," Vera teased.

Chapter Nineteen

The next morning, after Alice left for work and Louise settled in the study to read, Jane sat on the sofa in the living room and pulled out her book on teaching cat tricks. Wendell had curled himself on the chair across from her, apparently having no clue whatsoever that he was about to enter the wonderful realm of higher education.

Jane was treading new ground. She promised herself that she would enjoy the process and, if need be, she would prove to be more stubborn than Wendell. If he had known her thoughts, he most surely would have hidden in the farthest reaches of the inn. Jane had enough enthusiasm for the project to take on the most willful of the feline family. This was definitely a plus, because Wendell could very well be named in just such a group.

Opening the book she had purchased at the pet store in Potterston, she flipped through the introduction and advanced to chapter one. Scanning the pages, she learned that cats could be taught tricks, but it would take great patience on the part of the trainer, along with lots of love and rewards. The book went on to say cats couldn't be forced into anything. Jane looked up. "How well I know," she mumbled, looking at Wendell, who slept on.

Quickly skimming through the small book, Jane decided she would teach Wendell how to retrieve his special treats from the pantry. She'd put them on a lower shelf. He could fetch the small package between his teeth and carry them to her.

"Okay," she said, snapping her book closed. Wendell's head popped up and Jane laughed. "Wendell, old boy, we're going to show everyone that you're just as smart as those dogs and pigs out there. We're going to prove that, yes, even you can be taught a trick."

Wendell stared at her a moment, and then proceeded to lick his paws, as though she hadn't uttered a word.

Of course, Jane knew this action was part of their treat-time ritual. About ten o'clock every morning,

Wendell sauntered over to Jane and suddenly became her dearest friend. He'd cuddle into her legs and purr like a well-oiled machine. She'd bend down, scratch him behind the ears and off they'd go to the kitchen pantry. There she'd open his treats, he'd meow his impatience and she'd spill the treasured goodies before his royal paws, thereby making everything right with his world. After he had eaten, Wendell would amble away with barely a glance backward, his undying devotion quickly forgotten until the next snack time.

Jane sat still a moment, waiting on Wendell's next move. She wanted to make sure he was hungry. The book had said the best time to teach a cat is before mealtime.

Wendell stayed firmly in place, staring at Jane. Determination made her stare back, not blinking even once. The hall clock ticked while they came to a Mexican standoff. That Jane found herself caught in a battle of wits with a cat didn't deter her sense of mission. Her stubborn will won out when Wendell finally jumped from his chair and went over to humble himself before her. Jane responded by getting up from the sofa. "Go get your treat, Wendell," she repeated all the way into the kitchen with Wendell right on her heels. "Get your treat, Wendell," Jane said, pointing.

He gave her a look that said, *You're kidding, right?*

"Get your treat, Wendell," Jane cooed. She got a treat packet and crinkled the plastic between her fingers, causing Wendell's ears to perk up. He stood on his hind legs, pawing her knees excitedly. "Get your treat, Wendell," Jane said again. Wendell meowed. Jane was straying from their normal routine and it was obvious Wendell did not approve of it. His meows intensified. He pawed harder against her knees.

Jane opened the package and pulled out a couple of morsels of the dry food. With the food in the palm of her hand, she offered it to Wendell. His scratchy tongue lapped against her hand as he scooped the treats into his mouth. "Get your treat, Wendell," Jane said, shoving the packet toward the tabby. Wendell pawed at the package, giving Jane a sliver of hope. "Good job, Wendell. Good job," she cooed.

Not wanting to push her luck, Jane stood, walked over to Wendell's food bowl and emptied the rest of the treat into his dish. She watched him go at it with a vengeance. Jane walked away, determined about her mission. She just couldn't live with the idea that a potbellied pig could be an upstanding member of the local police department while Wendell languished in lethargic ignorance. No, she would protect Wendell's reputation at all costs.

He would not be outdone by a pig.

In the Coffee Shop that afternoon, Louise sat across from the pastor.

"Well, Louise, I think I've decided on my message for the seminar," Pastor Thompson said.

"Oh? What have you chosen?" she asked before lifting the coffee cup to her lips and taking a sip.

"Many parishioners told me how much they got from the message I gave a few weeks ago about Balaam's donkey, how God sometimes works in ways we might not consider."

She nodded.

"In fact, you mentioned the possibility of my using that message, but I wasn't convinced at the time. Still, this morning in my daily reading I was studying the passage in II Kings dealing with the story of Naaman, the chief military commander of the Aramean army."

Louise listened with interest.

"It is another example of the theme. Here this man was in charge of an army who had battled the Israelites and made slaves of some of them. In fact, he had a young Hebrew slave living in his home. Naaman developed leprosy, and this child encouraged him to seek out the prophet Elisha. Well, you know the story. Upon doing so, the unexpected happened. Elisha sent a messenger, and he told Naaman to dip himself in the Jordan seven times."

Louise smiled and nodded with the memory of the story.

"Now, the Jordan was no attraction. We're not talking about one of the cleaner rivers of

Damascus, but rather the muddy Jordan." Pastor Thompson straightened; his voice became more expressive with every word. "Naaman got angry and refused at first." He smiled. "But of course we know ultimately he did humble himself and in obedience to God did indeed immerse himself seven times in the Jordan and was in the end healed." The pastor settled back into his seat. "Who can know the mind of God, Louise? He so often works in ways we can't imagine."

"I quite agree. I think this is the way you must go," she said.

"You do?"

"Absolutely. I can see it in your eyes that it's right for you."

"Thanks, Louise." He rested his arm against the back of the booth. "I think we need to be reminded that we can't put God in a box. He will work in the way He chooses. Even in our ministry as pastors. We think things should run a certain way, this ministry is more important than that one, that kind of thing. But God is in charge. We are merely to trust and obey."

"So true," Louise said.

"You have something on your mind, I can tell," he said.

Louise smiled. "I was just thinking of those times that I had prayed for something to happen a certain way, and had God answered in that way, it wouldn't have been good for me. We have to trust that He knows what's best even though we don't always understand."

The pastor nodded and sighed. "It feels good finally knowing the message He wants me to give."

"I'm glad you feel at peace about it."

He smiled and looked as though he had more to say. She watched him. "Is there something else?"

A kind of shy, boyish look settled upon him. "I feel a little silly asking you something."

"What is it, Pastor?"

"Well, I was wondering if you'd consider hearing my message after I've prepared it?"

Before she could say anything, he hurried on. "I don't normally do such a thing, it's just that it will help me to hear myself present it, and well, Louise, I value your opinion. I want to do my best."

She smiled fondly at him, placing her mug back on the table. "I know precisely what you mean. I'll be most happy to listen."

He relaxed. "Thank you, Louise. You're a great friend."

Louise lifted a silent prayer, thanking the Lord for helping the pastor recognize the message he was to bring to the seminar, and she prayed that God would calm the pastor's anxious nerves.

After arriving home from work, Alice entered the living room where Catherine sat on the sofa reading a book.

"Hello, Alice," she said.

"Are you all alone in the house?" Alice asked.

Catherine nodded. "Louise is meeting with Pastor Thompson and Jane had to run to the store."

Alice noticed Catherine's red, puffy eyes. Concern for the older woman squeezed her heart. "Are you doing all right, Catherine?"

"I'm fine."

Alice wasn't convinced. She settled onto the sofa beside her, wondering if she could say or do anything to help the woman through her grief. "Catherine," she began with caution, "you seemed to be doing better until we had our discussion about the seizure dog. Did we say something that bothered you?"

Catherine waved her hand, tears swimming in her eyes. "It's nothing you said, Alice." Tears spilled onto her face, making wet tracks down her cheeks. "My sister was taking a nap. Her breathing machine malfunctioned. I was at the store when it happened. By the time I arrived home, it was too late." More tears. "Maybe if we'd owned such a dog . . ."

Alice put her hand on Catherine's. "Don't think that way, Catherine. We can't always make sense out of things that happen. It's during those times of utter despair, when our minds are exhausted from trying to figure everything out, that we need to rest in the Lord. A dog might not have made a difference—"

"He could have gotten her help since I was gone. Oh, why did I go to the store," she said more as a plea than a question.

Alice squeezed her hand. "Catherine, your sister's death wasn't your fault."

"They tried to tell me it was more than the machine malfunction. Her health was declining quickly. Still, I wonder." Catherine's shoulders shook slightly as she released pent-up tears.

Alice took a packet of tissues from her pocket and handed it to Catherine. "Might I pray with you?" Alice asked.

Catherine nodded, keeping her head down, a tissue pressed near her eyes. Alice prayed silently for the words to encourage their guest, knowing God alone could comfort her in her grief. Alice then spoke aloud, asking God to comfort Catherine, to give her grace, guidance and strength. Then, Catherine uttered her own prayer, thanking the Lord for bringing the Howard sisters into her life and asking Him to get her through her grief one day at a time. When they finished, Catherine turned and gave Alice a hug.

"Thank you, Alice. I guess I've just carried guilt over my sister's death, thinking I should have been there. Then when you talked about the dog, it made me think of something else I probably should have done." She wiped her face with the tissue.

"Bless your heart," Alice said, reaching over and giving her another hug. "We try to make sense of things that happen, even to the point of blaming ourselves. Life's events don't always lend themselves to neat explanations. That's where trust comes in."

Catherine nodded. "It feels so good to let go of that burden." She smiled and took a deep breath. "Thank you, Alice."

"You're welcome. Now," Alice said, slapping her hands on her knees, "how about some tea and Jane's homemade orange scones?"

"That sounds wonderful."

Chapter Twenty

"Alice, hi." Paula said into the receiver.

"Oh Paula, it's so good to hear from you. Are you home now?"

"Yes, and I'm dying for you to meet Paws."

Alice smiled upon hearing Paula already talking as if the dog was her dearest friend. "Well, I'd love to meet her. Would after dinner work for you?"

"That'd be great. Why don't you save some room for coffee and pie? We could go to the Coffee Shop together. Take Paws with us. It'll give her a chance to meet some of the fine folks of Acorn Hill."

Alice tried to ignore the hint of concern that wiggled through her stomach. "Sounds good. I'll pick you up around six?"

"Great, I'll see you then."

Returning the receiver to the cradle, Alice just stared at the phone, lost in thought.

"You okay?" Jane asked, on her way through the foyer.

Alice looked up. "Oh, I'm fine. Would you mind if I just made myself a sandwich for dinner tonight?"

"Oh sure," Jane said. "What's up? You have something planned?"

"Paula just called. She's back home. I thought I'd go visit her and meet her new roommate. Then we'll go to the Coffee Shop for dessert and introduce Paws to Acorn Hill." Alice smiled, deciding not to share her worries with Jane. Besides, there was probably nothing to worry about. Byrdie's brother-in-law's comments would blow over. Most things like that usually did.

"Sure, that's fine. There are all sorts of sandwich makings, and there's some leftover cream of carrot soup."

"Thanks, Jane. That will be perfect," Alice said.

Jane turned and headed for the stairway, leaving Alice alone with her jittery stomach.

Alice ate her dinner in the kitchen and then prepared to leave for Paula's house. As she got her coat from the closet, Louise said, "Please be careful and don't stay out too late, Alice. They're predicting more snow for tonight."

Alice smiled to herself. Louise still occasionally

took on the mother role. As a child, Alice had resented Louise's interference, but she now knew that Louise offered such comments out of loving concern. She turned to her sister. "Thank you, Louise. I won't be gone long."

Alice headed out the door to brave the winter winds. A few flakes had already begun to fall and the cold seemed to have more of an edge to it now than earlier in the day. A strong gust of wind blew against her, causing Alice to pull her collar up around her face. She ran to her car.

Inside the car was toasty warm by the time Alice pulled up to Paula's home. She hated to go out into the cold again, but she got out and walked quickly up to Paula's door and knocked.

"Hi, Alice, come on in," Paula said, stepping aside.

Alice walked in and immediately saw the golden retriever. "Well, hello."

"Alice, this is my new roomie, Paws. Paws, this is my good friend, Alice," Paula said as if introducing two dignitaries at a social event.

"I'm glad to make your acquaintance," Alice said, bending down to the dog as she spoke.

Paws extended her front paw.

"Oh dear," Alice said with a chuckle. She reached out, took hold of the furry paw, and shook it, then let go.

Her friend laughed. "Didn't I tell you, she's quite a dog?"

"Yes, you did. And I can see what you mean." Alice looked at the harness on Paw's back. The inscription read "Working Dog."

Paula followed Alice's gaze. "She has to wear that every time we go out so folks know she's a service dog, not just a pet. The sign also helps to discourage people from bothering Paws while she's working."

"Yes, I'm sure there is a great temptation to pet such a pretty dog."

Paula smiled proudly. "Oh, watch this." She turned to her dog. "Paws, fetch my slippers," she said.

Alice watched as the dog looked around the room until her gaze landed upon Paula's slippers. She ran over to them, nudged one with her nose until she could get a good grasp on it between her teeth, trotted happily over to Paula and plunked it down in front of her. Paws then went back and retrieved the other slipper in the same fashion, bringing it to rest at Paula's feet.

Paula looked up triumphantly. "Isn't she great?" She giggled, reached down and ruffled Paws' head. "Good girl, Paws."

Alice was almost sure Paws looked up with a doggie smile. "She really is something," Alice said.

Paula slipped on her coat and gloves. "Okay, I think I'm ready." She turned to Paws. "You ready, girl?" Paws stood up and barked once.

"I'll take that to mean yes?"

Paula nodded and laughed.

"Okay, let's go," Alice turned toward the door and stepped outside with Paula and Paws following closely behind her.

They arrived at the Coffee Shop in no time at all. Once inside, they settled into a booth. Paws sat as still as a lawn ornament next to Paula's side of the booth. Only when Paula removed her coat and relaxed into her seat did Paws curl on the floor by her feet.

Alice and Paula ordered tea and apple pie from Hope and soon fell into conversation. While they were talking, Byrdie Hutchison walked in with her sister and brother-in-law. Alice wanted to turn away, but Byrdie had already seen her. After a brief conversation, the trio walked over to Alice and Paula.

"Hello Alice," Byrdie said. Her eyes turned to Paula.

"Hello, I'm Paula," she said, extending her hand to Byrdie.

"How do," Byrdie said with a curt nod.

Paula looked at Byrdie's brother-in-law. "Hello." He grunted.

Paula looked at Alice but before she could say anything, the brother-in-law piped up. "That your dog?" he asked, obvious distaste in his voice.

"Yes," Paula said with pride until she looked at his face. Her smile quickly disappeared.

"Well, no dog should be in a business establishment, especially one that serves food," he announced.

Paula took a deep breath. "Well sir, she's not just any dog. She's a service dog."

"You blind?" he asked, making Alice gasp for breath.

She struggled to keep a tight rein on her tongue.

"No sir, I'm not blind." Her words were even, deliberate. A deep crimson flamed Paula's cheeks.

"Excuse me, Mister—"

"Mr. Grose. Luther Grose," he said, pinning Alice with a stare that said she'd better not take him on.

At that moment, the door swooshed open and in walked Lloyd and Ethel. Spotting Alice, Ethel waved and, tugging at Lloyd's arm, pulled him with her. "Well, hello folks," Ethel said in a neighborly fashion. With one glance at Mr. Grose, her smile faded.

"Ethel, you remember my sister and brother-in-law," Byrdie began.

"Yes, I do." Ethel eyed Luther Grose with suspicion.

Alice figured she wouldn't have to take on Luther Grose, as Ethel could do that single-handedly.

Grose turned to Alice. "You were about to say something," he said, as if daring her to argue with him.

Alice was not easily intimidated, not when it came to protecting her friends. "Mr. Grose," Alice began, "Paula has a service dog, as indicated on the harness." Alice pointed. "She has every right to bring this dog inside any public establishment."

He turned to Lloyd. "You're the mayor, is she right? Does this woman have the right to bring her pet into an eatin' place? I don't want dog hair in my coffee." The lines on his face deepened as he growled the words.

"Now, hold on, Luther," Lloyd said, raising his hand. Alice wondered how Lloyd knew Byrdie's brother-in-law since he was just visiting. No doubt this man made his presence known when he came to town.

"Excuse me," Paula cut in. Everyone turned to her. "My dog is not merely a pet—"

"What does she need him for?" Mr. Grose looked to Lloyd.

"Sir, I don't know that she must explain that to you," Alice said.

"No, it's all right, Alice." Paula looked up at the man. "I have seizures. My dog has been trained to help me through them, even get me help if I need it."

Mr. Grose didn't look convinced. He waved his hand. "I still don't see why you need to bring him into places where folks are trying to eat." With that he turned on his heels. "Let's get out of here, Byrdie."

Byrdie threw an apologetic look Paula's way, as did Mrs. Grose, but they quickly followed the man out the door.

Alice blew out a long breath. "Are you okay?" she asked Paula.

"I'm fine," she said, though her chin quivered slightly.

"Well, I'm sorry, Paula. You will find most folks in Acorn Hill are very nice, and they'll be pleased to have Paws in their midst," Alice said.

"I should say so," Ethel chimed in. Alice felt thankful to have her aunt on their side. One glance at Lloyd, however, made Alice a little uneasy. He had an uncomfortable air about him, one that suggested that he was undecided on the matter.

Paula nodded, her gaze fixed on the table. She took another breath and looked up at Alice. "Thank you. I'm sure we'll be fine."

Alice smiled and prayed that it would be so. She added a prayer for herself while she was at it, for her thoughts toward Mr. Grose veered more than a trifle from the Christian path.

Chapter Twenty-One

When Alice returned to the inn, she closed the door with more force than was necessary.

"Whoa, what's wrong with you?" Jane asked.

"Oh, sometimes I don't understand why the Lord puts up with us at all," Alice said, hanging her coat, then pacing the foyer. Alice was angry and, for the life of her, she couldn't seem to calm down.

Louise joined them. "Alice, come in and sit down," she encouraged in a warm voice. "Jane, perhaps you could get Alice some tea?"

"Sure thing." Jane headed for the kitchen.

Louise took Alice by the hand. "Now come in here and get yourself warm by the fire. You're obviously distressed and that's simply not good for your health."

Alice took a deep breath, feeling her pulse slowing a tad. Once she settled onto the sofa, Jane entered carrying the tea she'd prepared only moments before Alice had arrived home. She set a cup before her sister. After everyone was seated, they remained quiet, waiting for Alice to speak. Alice merely stared into the flames of the hearth, lost in thought. Louise and Jane wisely didn't press her for answers, but rather waited.

Finally, Alice told them about running into Byrdie's brother-in-law. Alice relayed what Luther Grose had said to Paula.

Jane shook her head. "That just makes me want to throttle the man. There's no reason for a person to be that unkind."

"I should say not." Louise's eyebrows pulled together in a frown.

Alice felt better after talking with her sisters. "Well, we must pray for him and for the situation.

I don't want Paula to get hurt. I know the good folks of Acorn Hill will stand behind her."

"That's true enough, Alice. You're so right, we do need to pray. Perhaps Mr. Grose is misinformed or doesn't understand Paula's need for her dog. It's interesting how unsympathetic we can be until we have a need ourselves," Louise said.

"Well, I agree with both of you, but we'd better hope that this man doesn't get anyone else stirred up. I'd hate for this thing to get out of hand," Jane said.

"The good news is he's a visitor, so he shouldn't have a whole lot of pull around here," Alice said.

"Yes, that's true. Unfortunately, the same can't be said of Byrdie. She can be quite outspoken at times." Louise said.

"Knock, knock," Ethel called out as she stepped through the front door.

"We're in here, Auntie," Jane said.

"Oh, there you are," Ethel said with a smile, while pulling off her coat. "May I join you?"

Ever the hostess, Jane said, "Absolutely. We're just having some tea, would you like some?"

Ethel nodded yes, and Jane headed for the kitchen.

"What brings you out on a cold night like this, Aunt Ethel?" Louise picked up the coaster she was working on and resumed her knitting.

"Well, I wanted to talk to Alice about what happened tonight."

Alice felt a knot form in her stomach. Though she loved her aunt dearly, Alice knew that Ethel could blow matters out of proportion.

"Yes, Alice has shared that incident with us, and we plan to pray about the matter," Louise said.

"Well, that's precisely what we should do. It's going to take prayer, that's what. Lloyd is in a dither about the whole thing. He's afraid people are going to start calling him about the dog and that things'll get out of hand."

"The woman has a right to her dog, Aunt Ethel," Alice said with as calm a voice as she could muster. "It's the law."

"I suppose Lloyd knows all about the law, Alice." Ethel shifted in her seat, acting slightly put out.

Jane entered the room carrying Ethel's tea. "Well, it's just not right for anyone to complain about it. How'd Mr. Grose feel if he were the one with the medical problem and needed a dog?"

"Yes, yes, I see your point, and I agree completely," Ethel said, stirring her tea. "Still, that doesn't eliminate the problem. We have to keep everyone happy, and well, frankly, having dog hair in a restaurant isn't a pleasant thought." Ethel took a sip from her cup.

"I think now would be a good time to pray," Louise said. She looked at Ethel. "Aunt Ethel, would you please join us."

Ethel was flabbergasted. It was obvious that she

had more to discuss and being cut short caught her off guard. "Well, of course, we should pray. It occurs to me—"

"Lord, we thank You for Your gift of love," Louise said. "We thank You that You know us better than we know ourselves. Your word tells us that You are familiar with all our ways."

Louise stopped for a moment. They sat in the quiet of the room, each lost in her own prayer, worshipping, trusting the Lord with their need. Then Louise continued, sharing their situation with the Lord, praying for Luther, that whatever his needs might be that God would help him. Louise prayed for him as if he were their dearest friend. Alice felt humbled. She realized her attitude had been wrong and she needed to care about this man even if she didn't care for his attitude.

By the time they'd finished their prayer, Alice felt a weight lift from her shoulders. "Thank you so much, Louise."

Ethel, too, seemed to have found peace in the prayer. In fact, she didn't pursue the matter any further.

Well, at least then.

After Alice excused herself and went upstairs to bed, Ethel took her cue and decided to leave. Jane helped her aunt down the porch steps. Ethel waved her arm. "I'm not an invalid, Jane. I'll be fine. I've got good boots," she said. She squared her shoulders and took deliberate steps, proving herself quite capable of crossing the yard to her home.

"Call us when you're all settled so we know you didn't fall."

"The way you carry on." She waved her hand, but Jane could tell it made Ethel feel good to be fussed over.

Jane watched Ethel walk toward the carriage house until she was out of sight. Then she went back in the house to join Louise. "Boy, it's turning nasty out there," she said as Louise stepped into the foyer.

"I hope most people are in the warmth of their homes and not running about outside," Louise said as she moved toward the stairs. "I must get something from my room, Jane. I'll be back down in a few minutes."

The phone rang, startling them both.

Jane nodded in response to Louise and went to answer the phone. "Hello?"

"This is Aunt Ethel. The way you carry on, I figured I'd better call right away or you'd have the entire town looking in on me. I'm inside and my doors are locked. I'm snug as a bug in a rug."

"Thanks for letting me know, Auntie. I'll feel better now."

Just as Jane replaced the receiver, the front door opened and a man and woman dusted with fresh fallen snow stepped into the foyer. Bundled in layers of warm quilts, a baby lay quietly in the woman's arms.

"May I help you?" Jane asked.

"Yes. We are Brandon and Suzanne Evans and underneath all those blankets is our daughter Zoë," he said with what looked like a forced smile.

"I wonder if you had any rooms available?" he asked. "I had a job interview in Lancaster today, and we were on our way back home to Delaware. Unfortunately, we have been forced by the weather to change our travel plans."

"You are most welcome to stay with us," Jane said with a smile. "I'm glad you didn't try to make it home. It's fierce out there."

The man nodded.

"If you'll come with me, I'll get you registered."

They followed Jane to the desk. She took down the pertinent information.

The man pulled his parka hood off his head. Thick dark hair tumbled onto his forehead and fell just short of his brown bushy eyebrows. His lips were set into a tight line. His jaw looked granite hard.

Jane figured the tension from driving in the snowy conditions had gotten to him. She gave instructions about breakfast and reached for the key to the Sunrise Room. "I'll show you to your room."

"We plan to leave right after breakfast," the man said as he climbed the steps behind Jane. "I have to get to my office as soon as possible. I can't afford to be gone too long." He said the words as if to warn her not to try to get them to stay longer. Jane thought the man a bit curious. She exchanged a glance with his wife, who gave her a hesitant smile.

"What kind of job are you looking for?" Jane asked in an effort to be friendly, hoping she didn't sound like a snoop.

"I'm a lawyer, and I interviewed with one of the top firms in Lancaster."

"I hope it works out for you," Jane said as they reached the door of the room.

"Do you have Internet hookup here?" he asked.

Jane turned to him and saw Suzanne place her hand on his arm. "Brandon, can't you leave work for one night?"

He glanced at Jane and quickly said to Suzanne. "Honey, you know I have to keep up with things. I've got several big cases pending."

Her sad eyes spoke volumes. She merely nodded and looked down at the baby, her fingers fidgeting with the blanket.

"We don't have Internet connections in our guest rooms, I'm afraid," Jane said, wondering if she should offer him the use of their computer, but then she thought better of it. After all, she'd only just met these people, and she didn't think it wise to offer strangers access to their private information.

He frowned and glanced at his watch. "Well, no

one would be there now. I'll just have to call in the morning."

Suzanne took a deep breath and exhaled.

Jane opened the door of the Sunrise Room and heard Suzanne give an admiring gasp. Jane followed the couple inside the room and watched with delight as Suzanne's gaze swept over the area. A pale blue ragged faux paint covered the walls. A patchwork quilt of blue, yellow and white covered the featherbed that perched high upon the thick mattress. Plump, decorative pillows lay against the ruffled pillow shams.

"Oh my, Brandon, this is lovely," Suzanne said, clearly pleased by her surroundings.

Brandon didn't seem to notice. He was already fiddling with his computer.

"I'm so glad you like it," Jane said. "My sister Alice is responsible for the décor. She has a very cheerful spirit and I think the room reflects that."

"I love it. I'm sorry the weather disrupted our trip, but I have a feeling it's going to be a wonderful interruption." Suzanne's eyes sparkled with excitement. The baby squirmed, her blue eyes squinting open for the first time since they'd arrived.

Jane leaned into the baby. "Oh, what a doll."

Suzanne pulled the blankets from the infant and lifted her at an angle so Jane could get a better glimpse. "She's only two months old. I'm having such fun with her."

"She's just beautiful. If you need to heat any bottles or anything, just let us know. We'll be happy to accommodate you."

"Thank you so much." The woman bit her lip. "I hope Zoë doesn't disturb anyone. She hasn't quite learned the sleeping through the night thing yet."

Jane smiled. "We have only one other guest and she's in one of the front rooms, so there'll be no problem. You'll be fine."

Mrs. Evans relaxed. "Thank you again."

"Well, I'll leave you to get settled." She glanced at Mr. Evans who was already engrossed in a work document.

Mrs. Evans lifted a what-can-I-do shrug.

"Good night." Jane closed the door behind her. Jane knew that life could get hectic and could distract one from what was important. She hoped Brandon Evans realized what was really important in his life while his daughter was still young.

Chapter Twenty-Two

The next morning Alice entered the kitchen, where Jane was checking on her baking. The open oven perfumed the room with a mouthwatering scent.

"Oh my, that smells scrumptious," Alice said as she came up behind Jane to peek at whatever was baking.

Jane looked at her and laughed. "Let me guess who woke up hungry this morning."

Alice chuckled. "I guess I am a little hungry at that. What are you making?"

"Fruited braid," Jane said. "It's basically sweet dough with raisins, candied orange peel, candied citron, confectioner's sugar, that kind of thing."

"You're doing nothing for my girlish figure, you know."

Jane shrugged. "What are sisters for?"

Alice walked over to the refrigerator and took out a pitcher of orange juice. "I understand that we got a couple of unexpected guests last night?" Retrieving a glass from the cabinet, Alice poured herself some juice and took a drink.

"Yes. Brandon and Suzanne Evans. They were forced to stop here because of the weather." Jane turned on the mixer to blend the icing ingredients for the braid. Once she finished, she snapped off the metal beaters and washed them off. "Oh yes, you'll be interested to know that they have a beautiful two-month-old daughter named Zoë." She brushed the white sugary glaze across the top of the braid.

"Oh, how lovely. It's been some time since we've had a baby here. Are they staying just for the one night?"

Jane nodded as she put the bread on a serving tray and sliced it.

"So what are they like?" Alice asked.

"The bread slices or the Evanses?" Jane answered with a teasing twinkle in her eyes.

Alice rolled her eyes. "I can imagine what the bread is like, why do you think I'm the first in line? I was referring to the Evanses."

"They seem like a nice couple, far as I could tell," Jane thought a moment, "though Mr. Evans did seem a bit . . . oh, I don't know . . . preoccupied."

"Oh?"

"It sounds as though he's a very busy lawyer," Jane said, walking over to the table and sitting down. Alice sat down across from her.

"What are you not telling me?" Alice asked with a smile.

"What do you mean?"

"I'm not sure. You just look like something is bothering you about them."

"I wonder if perhaps Mr. Evans works too hard. His wife appeared delighted that they were stuck here. I could be way off base, but he had all the signs of a workaholic," Jane said.

"Well, then perhaps the snow is an answer to her prayers," Alice said.

Jane shook her head. "You always find the silver lining, don't you, Alice?" She laughed. "I can't imagine snow being the answer to anyone's prayers right now, but then the pastor did remind us that God works in mysterious ways."

"Yes, he did say that," Louise said as she entered the kitchen. "Good morning, ladies."

"Good morning," Alice and Jane said in unison.

While Alice brought Louise up to speed on their discussion, Louise reached for a slice of the warm bread.

"Hey, I've been waiting for that," Alice said in a mock complaint.

"Girls, girls," Jane teased. "There's enough for everyone." Jane put slices on a plate for Alice and Louise, then took the serving tray into the dining room for their guests. Jane walked back into the kitchen to join her sisters. "It looks like no one is up yet. I hope that breakfast doesn't go to waste."

"Oh, I promise you that won't happen," Alice said, taking a bite of her treat. She closed her eyes to savor the experience. When she opened her eyes, she found Jane and Louise staring at her. They laughed. "Okay, I admit it. I love this bread," Alice said.

"I'm glad you do." Jane said, patting Alice affectionately on the back. Then she moved around the kitchen with her usual efficiency, preparing the rest of the breakfast for their guests.

"Well, maybe we can help this young couple relax while they are here at the inn," Alice said.

"That's what I'm hoping," Jane said. "If it's only a peaceful breakfast. He said they were going to leave right afterward."

"Is there something I missed?" Louise asked.

Jane shrugged. "Might be my imagination, but I think Mr. Evans might be a bit of a workaholic."

"Oh," Louise said with concern.

"I hope that I'm wrong, but in any case, we can make their time here as relaxing as possible—that is, if they don't leave in the next half hour."

Louise lifted her gaze toward the window and the swirling snow outside. "By the looks of things out there, I can't imagine they'll be leaving anytime soon."

"Well, we'll do what we can with the time we have," Jane said.

The sound of a baby's cry reached their ears. "Looks like we just might have that opportunity right now," Alice said with a smile. She got up and rinsed off her dishes and loaded them in the washer, then headed into the dining room.

"Good morning. I'm Alice."

"I'm Brandon Evans. This is my wife, Suzanne, and our daughter, Zoë." The couple smiled at Alice.

"This breakfast looks wonderful," Mrs. Evans said.

"Well, you can credit our sister, Jane, with that. I believe you met Jane last night when you checked in?"

They nodded.

"You will find that Jane is an excellent cook."

Mr. Evans smiled but said nothing. Catherine Schmidt stepped into the room. "Good morning, everyone," she said.

The Evanses turned to her.

"Catherine, this is Brandon and Suzanne Evans,

and their daughter, Zoë," Alice said, and then she turned to the Evanses. "This is Catherine Schmidt."

"Oh my," Catherine said, catching a glimpse of baby Zoë. "What a darling little thing."

Mrs. Evans beamed while her husband served himself from a crystal bowl of strawberries and blueberries.

"You know, I can still remember when my daughter was that little." Catherine appeared mesmerized by the infant. After a moment, she turned to them and smiled. "Of course, that was a very long time ago."

"Would you like to hold her?" Mrs. Evans asked Catherine.

The question seemed to take Catherine by surprise. "Would I?"

"Well, honey, maybe she would like to eat her breakfast first," Mr. Evans said with impatience.

His wife turned to the older woman. "Oh, of course. I shouldn't have—"

Catherine shook her head. "I would be delighted to hold the wee one."

Mrs. Evans relaxed and smiled, lifting her baby girl into the wrinkled but loving arms of Catherine Schmidt. The older woman immediately began to rock sideways, patting the backside of the little bundle in her arms.

Alice watched Catherine with great interest. Joy seemed to replace the shadows of grief on her face like sunlight replacing storm clouds. An idea began to take root in Alice's mind as she watched the older woman cuddle the baby. *God truly worked in ways beyond man's human reasoning.* The thought came to Alice's mind unbidden, suggesting to her that her idea might not be hers at all.

While Catherine visited with Suzanne Evans and baby Zoë in the living room, Brandon Evans feverishly worked on the laptop in his room, evidently struggling to finish a legal brief that was due by day's end. Louise poked her head into the kitchen where Alice had stopped to nibble on another piece of fruited braid.

"Come on in. I'm just sneaking an after-breakfast snack before Jane gets home," Alice said.

Louise frowned. "I do wish Jane hadn't ventured to the store this morning."

"She'll be fine," Alice encouraged. "It's not that far away. If she gets into trouble, she can easily get back home."

Louise thought upon that a moment and had to agree with Alice's reasoning. She entered the kitchen and poured herself a half glass of milk, took a slice of sweet bread, placed it on a plate and walked over to the table.

"Have you decided when you are giving the ANGELs their coasters?" Louise asked, slipping into her chair at the kitchen table.

"I'm giving them next week, although I will tell

you that on Sunday when I took the coasters from my bag to dig something else out for one of the teachers, some of the girls noticed them on the table. I wouldn't let them take the coasters until after our lesson next week, but they loved them."

"Really?"

Alice didn't miss the look of satisfaction on Louise's face. "Oh yes. In fact, they were so excited they wanted me to ask you if you would consider giving them some lessons in knitting. They thought it would be nice if they could make something for the shut-ins."

Louise's expression brightened. "That's a wonderful idea. I'd be happy to teach them what I can. I'll have to look through my books and see if I can find some patterns for beginners."

"Maybe we could start next month sometime. I haven't made any lesson plans yet for April, so that would help me out too."

"I'll make a note to get right to that. You know how I like to interact with your group," Louise said.

"Aha! I caught you two snacking. You just ate breakfast," Jane chided as she entered the kitchen, carrying groceries.

"We didn't get enough of that fruited braid," Alice said as she put the last small piece in her mouth. She and Louise got up to help Jane with the groceries. They went out to the car.

"You two had better get back inside, or you'll

catch your deaths out here without coats," Jane said.

"We'll just move very quickly," Louise said.

The sisters hurried to get the groceries inside. Once everything was in the house, Jane closed the door behind them and took off her coat.

"Did you stop in to see Sylvia?" Alice asked.

"Yes. I called her before I left here and was able to pick up the few things that she needed from the grocery store. I saw she was doing fine, so I didn't stay long. She's tired of being cooped up."

"I think everyone is tired of being inside," Louise said, as the sisters stocked the canned goods on the shelves.

"She hasn't had much business, thanks to the weather. So that doesn't help matters. With nothing to do all day, she just sits around feeling bored." Jane bent over and lifted more cans from the grocery bags.

"I can imagine," Alice said. "But I'm thankful I don't have to work for the next few days. I wouldn't want to drive to Potterston in this weather. How were the roads, by the way?"

"Not horrible, but I wouldn't want to drive far today." Jane moved a can of tomatoes from the baking section and placed it with the vegetables. "Have you spoken with Paula lately?"

"Yes. In fact, if the roads are okay, we're going to go to the Good Apple Bakery later." Alice brushed her hands together after they finished loading the shelves. The sisters made their way back to the table.

"That sounds like a good idea. It will acclimate Paws to another place. I hope that you won't run into Byrdie and her entourage," Louise said.

Alice sighed. "I certainly hope we don't either."

"I wouldn't worry too much, Alice," Jane said, "Luther and his wife should be going home soon. I mean, how long can they visit?" Jane laughed, then she looked at Alice's face and stopped.

"I'd rather not think about how long he could stay." Alice said, shaking her head. "I just don't want Aunt Ethel and Lloyd to join the bandwagon or we could be in trouble."

"How so? I mean, I thought you said by law they couldn't stop Paula from taking her dog into public places," Jane said.

"That's true. But even though the law allows her to do so, it'd sure make her uncomfortable if she felt the people of Acorn Hill were against her."

Understanding lit Jane's face. "Oh, I see what you mean."

"We're forgetting one thing," Louise interjected. Alice and Jane looked at her.

"We have a lovely town with good people. Oh, they sometimes get sidetracked, but they always seem to come through with the spirit of caring. I believe they will rise above the circumstances and show their true character."

"You are absolutely right, Louise," Alice said.

"We do have a lovely town, with good citizens. I'm allowing doubts to fill my mind because of the opinions of one person. I shouldn't have so easily given up on my dear friends. Thank you for reminding me."

"You would've come around, eventually," Louise said.

Jane looked at them both. "I hope one day when I grow up that I can be just like my sisters."

Louise and Alice smiled.

"We will teach you whatever you want to know if you will teach us how to cook like you," Louise said.

Alice figured they couldn't possibly live long enough for that to happen. Besides, some things just weren't meant to be.

Chapter Twenty-Three

Right on the chime, when the clock struck ten, Wendell's ears perked up, though his eyes stayed closed.

It was time.

Across from Jane, Louise sat and worked on her latest knitting project. Jane glanced at the filled pages of her journal feeling a sense of satisfaction with her commitment to writing in it. She placed the journal and pen aside. Catherine Schmidt and the Evanses were in their rooms, and Alice had gone to pick up Paula for their visit to the Good

Apple Bakery, so once again Jane would get the chance to work with Wendell on his trick. She didn't want the others to know about it until Wendell could perform to perfection. She'd have to be discreet.

Wendell's droopy eyelids reluctantly lifted. No doubt he wanted to sleep longer, but his stomach ruled. They say that the way to a man's heart is through his stomach. Jane figured it was true of every male, regardless of the species. Her eyes narrowed and she mentally rolled up her sleeves. She would teach this cat a trick or else.

Wendell's gaze locked with hers. She waited. The clock ticked off the seconds. His whiskers twitched. Jane stood . . . well . . . sat firm. He stretched. Yawned. Still Jane waited. Finally, he got to his feet. Jane blew out the breath that she had been holding. She'd won the battle of the wills.

This time.

Head held high, Wendell sauntered over to Jane. He rubbed against her legs, back and forth, a bit half-heartedly at first. Jane wanted to make sure Wendell was good and hungry before she moved. The nudges grew increasingly harder, making it obvious that he wanted his treat and he wanted it now.

When Jane decided that it was time to head for the kitchen, she said, "I'll be right back, Louise. It's time for Wendell's snack."

"*Hmmm,* all right," Louise mumbled, her attention focused on her pattern.

Jane slipped from the room with Wendell padding along behind. For the fraction of a second, she thought perhaps he'd forgotten the latest routine. His paws thumped alongside her like a playful kitten. Once they were out of Louise's earshot, Jane commenced to work.

Placing the plastic bag on the floor, she pointed. "Treat, Wendell. Pick up your treat."

His paws skidded to a halt. He looked at the bag, then up at her. He meowed. She could imagine what his "meow" meant. *Not again.*

"Treat, Wendell. Pick up your treat."

Jane's imagination took over. *Hey you with the hands. Give it to me,* she could almost hear Wendell say.

Jane wouldn't be moved. "Get your treat, Wendell."

His meow intensified. *Give me that treat. Now.*

"Treat, Wendell. Get your treat." She pointed to the plastic wrap, wanting him to lift the small bag from the floor. She wiggled the top of the package.

He stared at her, almost digging his paws into the floor. "Treat, Wendell. Get your treat."

Teaching a cat tricks wasn't for the fainthearted. After several more attempts, Jane finally gave in and opened the package. She poured the contents into his food bowl and stood watching while

Wendell nearly inhaled the goodies. "You may have won today, but just you wait until tomorrow, you . . . you stubborn cat." Jane turned on her heels and left the kitchen.

She rejoined Louise in the living room. "Are the plans all set for the concert, Louise?"

Louise looked up, placing the knitting in her lap. "Yes, indeed, and I can hardly wait, Jane. But then perhaps I've mentioned that a time or two?"

Jane paused a moment, then grinned. "Oh, maybe once or twice." She picked up a magazine and flipped a couple of pages. "I think it's wonderful that you have this opportunity."

"He's such a fine musician. I can only imagine how wonderful it'll be to hear him play the piano in person."

Jane turned a couple more pages. "By the way, how are things coming on Pastor Ken's message for the seminar?"

"I believe everything is coming along fine. He finally decided what message he'd present and is working on it. Once he finishes, I'm going to let him practice on me." She chuckled.

"Oh, Louise, that's nice. I'm sure he'll feel better giving it a practice run."

Louise nodded. "I think it'll help him to say it aloud." She picked up her knitting and added a couple of stitches. "At first I was surprised that he is so nervous about the presentation, but I've decided that I'd feel the same way if I had to present a recital in front of my peers. It's not an easy thing to do, I'd imagine."

"I agree. I wouldn't want to prepare a meal for a roomful of chefs," Jane said with conviction.

"Is it okay if we join you?" Suzanne Evans said as she and Catherine Schmidt entered the room. Catherine held the sleeping Zoë in her arms.

"Certainly," Louise said.

They settled onto the sofa.

Jane was surprised to see Mrs. Evans without her luggage since they had said they were leaving first thing this morning. "You're staying awhile?" Jane asked.

"Actually, that's what I came to talk to you about," she said.

Louise and Jane looked at her.

"I told Brandon some roads could still be slick, and having Zoë with us, we shouldn't take any chances of getting stuck in the snow. Besides, I've needed a break from things lately and I so love this place." She looked at them and smiled. "Well, if you wouldn't mind, I . . . I mean, we'd like to stay until Saturday morning."

"We would be delighted to have you stay on," Jane said. She was glad to see that Brandon was willing to take off from work for some family time. She didn't miss the smile on Catherine's face.

Mrs. Evans looked instantly relieved. "Oh, good. Since Brandon finished his legal brief, and you allowed him to send the document as an attachment on e-mail, he can relax a little." She waited and then added. "Of course, it's rare that I can get him to relax. He's kind of a workaholic." She lifted a weak smile before continuing. "Anyway, thank you for letting us stay. And thank you for letting him use your computer," she said.

"You're welcome on both counts," Jane said, feeling better about their decision to allow the young man to send his e-mail to the office. They had decided that it wouldn't hurt for him to sit at their computer long enough for that.

"I hope you don't think us nosy, Mrs. Evans, but if you don't mind, we'd love for you to tell us about yourself," Jane said. "We like to get to know our guests."

"Well, my first name is Suzanne. Please call me that. Mrs. Evans is way too formal."

"Oh, okay. Suzanne."

"There's not much to tell, really. I'm a stay-at-home mom, and I love it. I was a paralegal before Zoë was born."

Jane nodded.

"I'm involved with our church. I head up a group for young mothers. We meet once a week to share our joys and struggles, pray together and do a study for moms."

"That sounds great. I'm sure that's helpful to all of you," Jane said.

"It really is. I had no idea how draining having a

227

child could be. It's nice to know I'm not the only one who feels that way." She smiled. "It's especially hard when Brandon is always working. I need some adult interaction now and then."

Jane nodded, all the while hoping Brandon would not one day have regrets for spending so much time away from his family.

"Last night when we talked and he said we could stay here a few days, I couldn't believe it. I was hoping for some quality time together away from his work. I hadn't expected it this week." Suzanne laughed.

"We're so glad you can stay." Jane walked over and glanced out the window. The snow had stopped and a perfectly azure sky reigned over Acorn Hill, while the bright sunlight splashed warmth and dazzle upon the sparkling heaps of snow. "You know, today would be a perfect day to build a snowman," Jane said, thinking out loud.

"Let's do it," Suzanne said.

Jane turned around in surprise. "What?"

"I said, let's do it." Suzanne's eyes twinkled. "I haven't built a snowman in years." Her excitement seemed to grow. "Brandon could watch Zoë—"

"Or I could," Catherine offered.

Suzanne looked at her. "Really, you wouldn't mind?"

"I'd love to," Catherine assured her.

Jane eyed Suzanne curiously. "You're serious?"

"Very. Are you game?"

Suzanne's enthusiasm was catching. "Why not." Jane answered.

"You get your coat, and I'll join you as soon as I get mine."

Suzanne was off and on her way up the stairs immediately. By the time she came back downstairs with her coat on, Zoë slept peacefully in an infant seat beside Catherine.

"Does Brandon mind?" Jane asked.

"I didn't even tell him. He was too busy working on his laptop," Suzanne said.

Jane looked at the others. "Okay then, I guess we'll go build that snowman."

Catherine and Louise smiled.

Once outside Jane trudged through the snow in the front yard, leaving ragged footprints behind. "Let's build it near the maple tree," Jane said, pointing.

Suzanne laughed. "Okay." Jane figured Suzanne would have skipped over there had the snow allowed her.

Together they packed the snow and began to build the base of the snowman's body. They rolled it along the ground, allowing the ball to collect more snow with every push. "I can't believe we're doing this," Suzanne said, almost breathless with excitement. "The air is so invigorating, I feel like shouting from the rooftops."

Jane laughed. "It does feel quite good, doesn't it?

The sun takes the bite out of the chill, making it almost pleasant outside today."

When the base reached the desired size, Jane and Suzanne rolled it into the spot where they wanted the snowman to greet the passersby. Once in place, Jane brushed the tiny balls of snow from her mittens and stood, hands on hips, to survey their creativity. "So what do you think?"

Suzanne walked around their creation, scrutinizing their handiwork. She picked up a glob of snow and packed it into a dent in the base. "There. That should do it."

They both laughed. "Okay, now for the tummy." Jane and Suzanne collected another ball of snow and heaved it onto the base. Before they knew it, they had the head in place. Jane went into the house and brought out an old hat and scarf and other items to give the snowman a personality.

With the wind on her face and a leap in her heart, Jane couldn't remember the last time she had had so much fun.

"What are they doing?" Brandon asked, looking out through the window curtains at his wife and Jane.

"Looks to me like they're having a lot of fun," Catherine said.

He turned to her. "They're playing in the snow. Grownups playing in the snow." He said the words as if he couldn't believe what he was seeing.

"I don't think it's written anywhere that only children can play in the snow." Catherine smiled and cooed at Zoë, who was now awake and looking at Catherine.

Louise noticed the indecision on his face. She felt sure he wanted to join them, but struggled with the very idea. Maybe he needed permission.

"You should join them," Louise said.

He looked surprised. "I should?"

"Absolutely," Catherine joined in. "According to what Suzanne said, Zoë has another forty-five minutes until eating time. I can watch her until then. Allow yourself to have some fun."

"Well, I don't—"

"Oh, go ahead," Louise urged.

A look of mischief suddenly crossed his face. "Okay, I'll do it," he announced. He left the room and came back within minutes all bundled up. "Can I go through the back door? I want to sneak up behind them."

Louise smiled and nodded, feeling every inch a conspirator in crime.

He turned to her. "Here goes nothing," he said.

She laughed as he walked through the door and slipped into a winter wonderland.

Jane had just pushed the black button eyes into place when she noticed a movement at the side of the house. She glanced over and caught a glimpse of Brandon Evans sneaking around the house. It tickled her that he would stop working long enough to join his wife in the snow. She saw him bend over and pack a good-sized snowball. He caught her gaze and put a gloved finger to his lips. Jane glanced at Suzanne, who was concentrating on the snowman.

Jane watched with sheer delight as Brandon slinked through the snow like a wildcat after prey. He came within a short distance of his wife and zapped her with a snowball. Her eyes widened and she jerked around. The moment she saw him, she giggled and started packing her own snowball. Jane watched them a moment, then quickly slipped away, leaving the young couple to enjoy their play, away from ringing telephones, legal briefs and computers. When she peeked around the corner of the house, Brandon tackled his wife and they fell into a heap upon the snow. Laughter filled the air.

Jane smiled and stepped toward the back door when she saw something black dart across the yard. Another look told her it was the dog Alice had befriended not so long ago. She adjusted her mittens. What was he doing this time? They still didn't know where he lived. To Jane, it seemed that the dog had an uncanny ability of searching out people in trouble, but of course, no dog could be that smart.

Jane's thoughts turned to Wendell, and her mood went south. If that mysterious black dog could save people, surely Jane could get Wendell to fetch a simple little treat packet. Determination set in. She'd get that cat to do something if it was the last thing she did.

Chapter Twenty-Four

Later that morning Alice pushed open the door to the Good Apple Bakery, holding it open for Paula and Paws.

"Hello, Alice," Clarissa Cottrell, the bakery owner, called over the counter. "Take a seat, and I'll be right with you."

"Thanks, Clarissa," Alice said, pointing toward a place to sit. Once they settled into their seats, Paws plopped obediently beside Paula. "Now, you can get what you want, but I'm telling you, Clarissa's cinnamon rolls are out of this world. Right up there with my sister Jane's, and that's saying something."

"*Mmm,* that sounds good to me."

Before they could talk any further, Clarissa padded over to their table. Her gray hair was pulled under her hairnet, back from her thin, wrinkled face. The older woman's clothes always looked two sizes too big, emphasizing her thinness. Despite her bouts with arthritis, Clarissa had a warm and pleasant personality, and the townsfolk loved to share a morning visit with her over coffee and some of Clarissa's delicious baked goods.

Clarissa looked at Alice, then over at Paula.

"This is my friend, Paula," Alice told Clarissa. "And this is her dog, Paws."

Clarissa glanced down at the dog, who was wearing his harness that said he was on duty. "Nice dog," she said without any hesitation. She looked up and smiled at Paula. "Are you new to Acorn Hill?"

Alice allowed herself to relax a tiny bit while Paula explained where she lived.

"Well, I'm happy to meet you and your dog friend here." Without further comment, she said, "Now, what can I get you ladies this morning?"

Alice wanted to swipe her hand across her forehead and say "Whew." Instead she said, "I had a big breakfast, so I'll just have hot tea, please."

"Well," said Paula, "I left room for a treat this morning, so I'll have one of your famed cinnamon rolls and a cup of coffee."

Clarissa nodded. "Coming up right away." She cast another smile Paula's way, looked down at Paws and said, "You're a nice pooch," then hurried back toward the kitchen.

"She sure seems friendly," Paula said, obviously relieved to have found another friend in Acorn Hill.

"You will find most folks at Acorn Hill are like that, Paula. I'm sorry Mr. Grose made you feel less than welcome here. But remember, he's only a visitor to our town."

"I understand. Paws and I will be fine." She

looked down at her dog. "Won't we, Paws?" Reassuring dark eyes looked up at her.

Across the room, the door swooshed open and in walked Clara Horn. "Well, Alice, I keep running into you," she said with the cheeriest of smiles.

"Hello, Clara."

Clara looked at Paws and then to Paula. Her eyes lit with understanding. "You must be Paula," she said with enthusiasm. Clara pulled a chair up to the table and made herself comfortable.

Exchanging a glance with Paula, Alice shrugged and smiled. Though a bit eccentric, Clara meant well.

"So this is your special dog. What's his name?"

"Paws."

Clara giggled. "Oh, what a cute name."

Alice turned to Paula. "Paula, this is Clara Horn."

"Oh my, my," Clara said, "I'm forgetting myself here. I just got so excited when I saw you and the dog—I mean, Paws." She chattered on excitedly.

Paula gave her a warm smile. Alice relaxed, sensing Clara's acceptance of the dog. Clara didn't seem bothered in the least upon seeing Paws in a public place.

Clarissa came to the table with their orders. Clara asked for hot chocolate and a cinnamon roll.

"Well, I don't know if Alice has told you, but I have a potbellied pig. Her name is Daisy, and she's quite intelligent, if I do say so myself."

Alice hid her amusement behind her teacup.

"I've been wanting to get Daisy on the Acorn Hill Police Department, but the officers told me there was really no need at present." Clara looked disappointed but not for long. "They also told me she could be on call and if they had a need for her, they would surely call us." Clara leaned into the table and said with utmost seriousness, "It's kind of like my Daisy is in the military and could be placed on active duty at a moment's notice." She thumped back in her seat. "Well, what's a mother to do?"

That comment almost sent Alice into a full fit of laughter, but, fortunately, Clarissa arrived at that moment with Clara's order. The interruption allowed Alice to get control of herself.

They spent the next half hour listening to Clara speak of Daisy's antics and how Clara felt quite sure Daisy would be of great help to the Acorn Hill Police Department, should the need ever arise.

After finishing her snack, Clara announced that she had a hair appointment and took off in a flash. After her departure, Alice and Paula enjoyed a quiet chat, though Alice had to admit that she was glad Clara had joined them for a brief time.

Alice glanced at her watch. "Do you have time to go to the library? I wanted to pick up a mystery book they're holding for me."

Paula thought a moment. "I need to get some work done on the computer this afternoon, but I suppose it wouldn't hurt to stop in at the library first. I've been meaning to get over there anyway. Perhaps I'll sign up for a library card while you're checking out your book."

"Great." Alice left her tip on the table and paid their bill, and soon they were in her car. As they drove down Acorn Avenue toward the library, Alice spotted the mystery dog. "Look, over there," she said, pointing. "That's the black dog I keep telling you about. He appears out of nowhere and then disappears again. We have no idea who he belongs to. He has lost the tag that apparently was on his collar."

As Alice talked about the dog, she slowed the car. As if he expected an ambush, the black dog darted across the street and out of view. "Why does he always do that? How can anyone help him get home if he won't let people near him?"

"Well, from what you've told me, you'd have to be in danger in order for him to come your way," Paula said jokingly.

"You know, you're right."

"I was only kidding, Alice. You don't want to put yourself in harm's way just to take a dog home."

"Oh, I know it, but he's driving me crazy."

They arrived at the library. Though she was excited to have the mystery book for which she had been waiting finally in her hands, Alice could not help wishing that she could get her hands on the mystery dog just as easily.

Alice arrived home, put her coat away and stepped into the living room. There she found Catherine holding baby Zoë. Mother Suzanne sat nearby, reading a book. They looked up when Alice entered.

"Hi, Alice," they said in unison.

"Hello," Alice said cheerfully. "Where's Brandon?"

"He's upstairs composing a letter to a client. I don't mind, though," Suzanne said rather pensively. "He's been very attentive to Zoë and me today. I fear we're getting spoiled."

"You should have seen them playing in the snow," Catherine said with a chuckle.

"Playing in the snow?" Understanding hit Alice. "So you're the one who made the snowman?"

Suzanne glowed and nodded, telling Alice all about making a snowman with Jane and Brandon's coming out to join their play in the snow.

"Well, you deserve to be spoiled," Alice said with a smile.

"Brandon's different here. I mean, he's really taking time for us. He doesn't mean to ignore us. It's just that work can be quite demanding at times." She frowned a little. "Though I don't know why he's trying to get into this other law firm. It's bigger than his current firm, and I'm sure it will mean longer hours."

Alice felt her heart squeeze at the young couple's dilemma. There was a fine line between being a good provider and a workaholic. "I'll be praying for you and your family, Suzanne," Alice said, meaning it.

"Thank you."

Alice glanced at Catherine, who continued to cuddle the baby. When Catherine looked up, Alice couldn't miss the sparkle in the older woman's eyes. Was this the same woman who had come to them only a few days ago, burdened with grief? Alice thought again about the idea that had struck her earlier. She was even more convinced that it might work.

"Seems Zoë has another grandmother," Suzanne said, catching Alice's attention.

Realizing Suzanne must have seen her staring at Catherine and the baby, Alice decided this was as good a time as any to bring up the matter. "She does indeed."

Catherine beamed.

"Catherine, I've been meaning to talk to you about something," Alice began. "This may or may not be something you would be interested in, but I know you live in Potterston and the hospital is not far away from where you live."

Catherine nodded, clearly wondering where Alice was going with this.

"We always need baby cuddlers. Do you know what that is?"

Catherine shook her head.

"It's a volunteer who comes in once a week, usually in one and a half hour shifts. The work involves holding and sometimes even feeding the little ones whose mothers are unable to do so."

Catherine's eyes widened. She listened intently.

"The only requirement is that you love babies," Alice said with a smile. "Some volunteers might be asked to help with minimal housekeeping chores such as sweeping, laundry and cleaning, but nothing major. Just things that keep the area sparkling clean for the babies. State licensing requires that the volunteers take a tour of the hospital and fill out an application form. You would then be called for an interview. There you would be asked to complete some paperwork, like a criminal history background check—"

At this, Catherine chuckled. "I suppose I do look a tad like a gangster."

Alice smiled. "Hey, don't laugh. In Philadelphia they've had some problems with seemingly innocent little old ladies."

Catherine looked at Suzanne. "I assure you I am quite harmless. Unless, of course, the neighbor boy throws his football into my rose garden. Then I can get cranky." She winked at Suzanne, then turned back to Alice.

"The only other thing you have to do is take a tuberculosis test. No one is allowed to serve until they pass the TB test," Alice said.

"I'm glad they're careful about such things," Suzanne commented.

"After that, you go through a training process that takes about an hour. That's it."

Catherine smiled and nodded.

"It's just something to think about. I noticed how you love babies and thought it might be a good fit for you."

"I think it's a wonderful idea, Catherine. You are great with Zoë. Not everyone can handle babies so well. It's like the babies can sense the person's nervousness," Suzanne said.

"That's true," Alice agreed.

Catherine looked down at Zoë, tracing her finger across the sleeping infant's cheek. "Little ones are so precious." She looked up at Alice. "Still, I don't know."

"Well, it's a commitment, that's for sure. Once you sign up, the hospital will expect you to be there at the times agreed upon. So you need to think it over. No hurry, just let me know if you decide that you'd like to do it."

Catherine smiled. "Thank you, Alice, for thinking of me." She looked once more at the baby. "I wonder . . ."

After dinner, the sisters were in the living room when the phone rang.

"I'll get it," Jane said, getting up from the sofa.

Alice was captivated by the mystery book she was reading, and Louise was knitting, using the soft baby yarn she had purchased the day before. A woman at their church was expecting a baby in a couple of months, and Louise had decided that she had plenty of time to make a blanket and matching booties.

"Louise, it's for you," Jane said. "It's Martha Spangler."

"Oh, thank you, Jane," Louise said, quickly making her way to the phone.

"Hello, Martha."

"Louise, my dear friend, how are you?"

"I am fine. And you?"

"I'm fine, dear. Listen, I won't keep you. Charles and I are just leaving, but we hadn't talked in a while, and I wanted to make sure we were all set for your visit tomorrow."

"Oh yes. As we had discussed earlier, I plan to arrive at your home tomorrow in time to go to lunch together, do some shopping and then head to the concert that evening. Is that still convenient for you?"

"Most convenient, Louise. I can hardly wait to see you again. It has been such a long time."

"Indeed, it has. We'll have a wonderful time catching up. I can hardly thank you enough for inviting me to your home and to the concert, Martha. I'm so looking forward to it."

Martha chuckled. "Well, I couldn't let Eduardo Fink come to our fair city without letting you know. Why, you would have my head."

Louise laughed. "I suppose I haven't hidden my appreciation of his fine music."

"You're not alone. He certainly is a master pianist. And besides that, it has been much too long since we've had the chance to visit."

Louise heard a man's voice calling in the distance.

"Oh dear, Louise, I'm afraid I must go or we'll be late. Be safe driving, dear. I look forward to seeing you."

"Thank you, Martha. See you tomorrow." Filled with thoughts of her weekend, Louise absently hung up the phone. She couldn't remember the last time she'd so looked forward to attending an event.

Louise gave a sigh of pure pleasure, turned and walked back toward her sisters. She could hear Eduardo's music in her imagination.

Chapter Twenty-Five

It was Friday morning, and Louise had gone upstairs to finish packing for her trip. Jane was straightening up the reception area when she heard the clock strike ten. Despite her earlier frustration in trying to teach Wendell his trick, she now felt excited at giving it another try. Thoughts of a pig showing more intelligence than Wendell pushed Jane forward, almost as if the Howard family honor depended on her success.

"Wendell, do you want your treat?" Jane half expected Wendell to roll his eyes and then shield his face under his paws. Instead his ears perked up and his whiskers twitched. He didn't seem to mind this little ritual as long as he got his treat in the end. Jane sighed. It seemed like she was the one doing all the work here. "Come on, you," she said, crooking her finger at him.

Wendell licked his paw a time or two, then he stretched and yawned, prolonging Jane's agony. "Look, King Wendell, I don't have all day."

Seemingly making a decision not to push his luck, he rose to his feet. Like one of noble birth, Wendell lifted his chin and strolled toward her, his tail held high.

Jane let out an exasperated sigh. This cat beat all. "Let's go get your treat, Wendell. Get your treat," she repeated. She walked to the kitchen, Wendell's paws thumping playfully along beside her. When Jane reached the pantry, she repeated the phrase once more. "Get your treat, Wendell." She pointed to the package sitting within his reach on the lower shelf.

Wendell looked at the treat, then back to Jane. He stared at her for the longest time. Then his gaze turned and fixed on the treat. His pink tongue stretched and lapped his upper lip a time or two.

"Get your treat, Wendell," Jane said again, ever hopeful. She pointed at the package. Wendell cocked his head to one side and looked at Jane as if she had taken leave of her senses. Jane blew out another breath of frustration. "Just get it."

When all hope seemed lost, Wendell stretched his paw in the air ever so slightly. Jane gasped, not daring to blink for fear it would break the spell. Wendell's paw lifted a bit more. Excitement gripped Jane and for the span of a heartbeat she thought the feline just might pull this off. Suddenly, Wendell had a change of heart and dropped his paw gently to the floor. He looked—or was it sneered—at Jane and meowed.

Jane let out the breath she was holding. She shouldn't give him the goodies at all. "Patience," she told herself. "Rome wasn't built in a day." She reached for the package and gave the tabby his treat even though she felt sure building Rome would've taken less patience than teaching Wendell.

"Well, hello, Alice," Paula said, standing behind Alice in the grocery aisle lined with canned fruits and vegetables.

Alice turned. "Paula! Goodness, first the post office, now here." She smiled. "Looks like you and Paws are getting a lot of errands done this morning."

"Yes, my neighbor had to come to town, so she brought me. She's doing some shopping and we're meeting up in about forty-five minutes. It's allowed me to get a number of things done too. You know, it's been wonderful having Paws with me. I didn't realize how afraid I was to go out into the world until she came along and freed me from worry. Now I don't fret about a seizure, because I know she won't leave me." As if to reaffirm her comment, Paws heartily shook her fur and settled back beside Paula.

They chuckled.

"She is a great dog," Alice said, looking at Paws. She turned back to Paula. "How are your seizures, Paula? You haven't mentioned having one in a while."

"I'm doing much better. I still have them, though the increased medication has helped slow them down. Now when I wake up from a seizure, Paws is lying right beside me, her paw over my stomach so I don't move." She bent down and scratched Paws' head, obviously grateful for the dog's assistance. Paws lifted her chin, tilting her head to get a better scratch. Paula laughed, then stood upright. "You know, I think my seizures are better, too, because I'm not as afraid. With Paws around, I feel so much more independent than I used to."

"That is wonderful, Paula. I'm so happy for you." Alice could hardly imagine a life where one lived in fear of having a seizure when out in public. She knew Paula had been through a lot and Alice hoped somehow she could make Paula's life a little easier in the future.

A frown slowly formed on Paula's face.

"What is it?" Alice asked.

"It's just that I do worry that the townsfolk don't

want Paws around. If they don't want Paws, they can't want me around either. Without Paws, I'm pretty much homebound. I want to live with her someplace where people accept us. My life has changed because Paws has come to live with me."

Alice felt her heart twist. It hurt her deeply that anyone could be so cruel as to suggest that the dog stay out of public places. Just as guide dogs were eyes to the blind, Paws offered Paula assurance that she would never be alone in her affliction. "The only one I've heard complain is Byrdie's brother-in-law, and, as I told you, he's a visitor. He'll be gone in no time."

"That may be true, but until he leaves, he can stir up the people around him," Paula said.

Alice thought of the mayor and his concern about how people would react. Could Luther Grose poison the kind folks of Acorn Hill with his negative talk?

"I'm going to give it a little more time, but if I keep running into Mr. Grose, or if I see others are unhappy with our presence, I'll probably look for a new place to live."

"Paula, I would hate to see you do that," Alice said. "I don't believe for a minute anyone would want you to move. Things will settle down. You'll see." Alice forced a reassuring smile.

It looked like Acorn Hill needed another answer to prayer, and Alice couldn't begin to imagine how God might tackle this one.

· · ·

"Are you enjoying your stay here?" Alice asked Brandon and Suzanne Evans that afternoon as they relaxed in the living room. The smell of cherry wood burning in the fireplace perfumed the room. Alice loved a wood fire and the fragrance it produced. She couldn't imagine a cold winter's evening without a fire on the hearth.

"It's been an eye-opener," Brandon said, regaining Alice's attention.

"How so, Brandon?" Alice asked.

He reached over on the sofa and took his wife's hand in his. "When we came on this trip, it was in hopes that I'd get the job with the law firm I told you about. It would mean a lot more money, but it'd also mean more travel and more late hours." He smiled at Suzanne. "Spending these past couple of days at Grace Chapel Inn has opened my eyes to what's important." He paused a moment. "My wife." His eyes lingered on hers. "My baby girl," he brushed a finger alongside Zoë's cheek. The infant blinked and wiggled in response to her father's touch. He turned back to Alice.

"We get by. We're not rich, but we have enough. I don't know why I thought we needed more. I'd rather provide a sufficient income and spend time with my family than have more money than I know what to do with and risk losing them."

Alice swallowed past the knot in her throat when

she saw Suzanne squeeze his hand. *Who could have known they were facing such a decision?*

"I haven't told you this yet, Suzanne. The law firm sent me an e-mail this morning, asking me to call. When I did, they offered me the job."

Suzanne gasped.

"I have until next week to decide, but I've made up my mind to decline. Is that all right with you?"

Tears fell from Suzanne's eyes. She bowed her head and nodded. "I was hoping you would, but I didn't want to influence your decision. I want you to be happy where you work."

"As long as I have you and Zoë, I will always be happy. In fact, I've made up my mind that I'm going to work fewer hours when we get back home. Even my boss has been telling me to slow down. I think I'll take him up on his advice."

Alice thought she should leave them alone. The couple had much to discuss. She started to get up.

"Wait, Alice," Brandon said.

Surprised, she sat back down.

"I want you to know that you, your sisters, this inn . . ." he raised his arm in one sweeping gesture across the room, "have been an answer to our prayers. Actually, I guess the icy roads started it all." He smiled. "It gave me the time I needed to think, away from the noise and clamor of work. Thank you."

Alice smiled and shook her head. "I am con-stantly humbled at how the Lord can use our inn for His purposes. I'm thankful you've found your answer." Standing, Alice excused herself from the living room and headed toward the kitchen.

Who would have thought God could change the course of a family's future through a snowstorm, an inn and three prayerful sisters?

By the time Louise carried her bag down the stairs, she felt quite out of breath.

"Louise, you're getting ready to leave us?" Alice asked, when she brought the mail in the front door.

"Yes, I am," Louise said with a smile, trying to hide some of her excitement so that she would not appear childish.

Jane stepped out of the living room and into the foyer. "It's hard to imagine that Louise would prefer the company of some stuffy old concert pianist to ours, don't you think so, Alice?" Jane teased.

"Yes, it's hard to imagine," Alice joined in. "And I thought I knew my sisters." She turned to smile at Louise.

Louise waved her hand. "Oh, you two." Louise's fingers absently smoothed her hair into place. "Do I look all right?"

"You look wonderful," Jane assured her before giving her a hug. "Now, go and enjoy yourself. You have earned this time with your friend."

Louise glanced at her watch. "Well, if I am to meet Martha for lunch, I had better get started."

She smiled, picked up her suitcase and headed for the door, with Jane and Alice close behind. She turned around to face them. "Remember to pray for Pastor Ken. He speaks tonight at the seminar."

Alice nodded. "I covered him in prayer this morning."

"So did I," Jane said.

"I too. I am sure we needn't worry. When he presented his message to me the other night, it was wonderful. Still, it could not hurt to have his nerves calm down a bit." Louise smiled.

"With all of us bombarding Heaven, the Lord will surely answer," Alice said.

"Thanks. I will see you tomorrow afternoon." After hugs and well wishes, Louise turned and took her first steps toward what she hoped would be a wonderful day.

Jane and Alice stood at the door and waved good-bye. "I wonder how Pastor Ken is feeling," Jane said, closing the door.

"I would imagine he might be a little nervous right about now," Alice said. "I know I would be." She felt quite thankful she was not a public speaker.

The rich smell of chocolate reached Alice as she and Jane made their way into the kitchen. "*Mmm, what are you baking?*" Alice asked.

Jane turned and smiled. "Chocolate cheesecake for tonight's dessert."

"Oh Jane, I can feel the pounds coming on just thinking about it."

Jane laughed. "Then try not to think about it."

Alice watched as Jane turned on the oven light to check on the cake. "Looks good," Jane said, walking over to her chair.

They had barely seated themselves when the phone rang.

"I'll be right back," Jane said, going off to answer it. Alice relaxed in her chair. The warmth from the oven and the smell of chocolate were very soothing.

When Jane returned, she looked worried.

"What is it?"

"That was Pastor Ken. He wanted to talk to Louise, but I told him she had already gone. He asked us to pray about a matter."

"Oh?" Alice felt a thread of fear work through her nerves.

Jane nodded. "Seems he's been nauseated all morning and is beginning to think it might be more than a nervous stomach."

"Oh dear," Alice whispered.

Chapter Twenty-Six

Yoo-hoo," Ethel called as she stepped into the kitchen through the back door an hour later.

"Hi, Auntie."

Ethel pulled off her coat and laid it on a chair.

She rubbed her hands together. "The sun feels good out there. It's still chilly, though."

"I'll take chilly," Jane said, "but I hate frigid." Jane put the dishtowel back in its place and joined Ethel at the table. "So tell me about your class."

"One more week and it will be over."

Jane was surprised. "Has it been that long already?"

"Sure has. Hard to believe. That's why I came over. I wanted to thank you for the opportunity. I've had a great time teaching those people. The class was just what I needed during these slow weeks of winter."

Jane looked at her and smiled. Her aunt could be a bit, well, challenging at times, but Jane loved her dearly. "I'm so glad you enjoyed it, Auntie. I knew you'd do a wonderful job. You really helped me out. I'm glad that it turned out to be fun for you. I thought it'd be."

Ethel nodded. "In fact, my students and I have decided to get together every now and then for lunch."

"Oh, that's great." Jane couldn't have been happier that her aunt had developed some new friendships.

"So I suppose Louise already left for the concert?" Ethel asked.

"Yes, she did . . . well, she left for her friend's house anyway. The concert isn't until tonight."

"She certainly is excited about hearing that pianist."

Jane chuckled. "Yes, I haven't seen her that excited in a long time."

"She needs to get out more. All you girls do. It's not good to be chained to this house. You need a social life."

Oh dear, Jane could feel the "you-need-to-get-some-friends" speech coming on. She braced herself. "I do get out every now and then with Sylvia Songer."

Ethel perked. "How is Sylvia doing, by the way? I haven't heard you talk about her in a while."

"She is getting along quite well. I take her groceries when she needs them and on errands since she finds it difficult to drive. She's able to manage at the shop pretty much on her own, though."

"I've always liked Sylvia. She's a nice woman."

"And a good friend," Jane said with a smile. "She's so talented."

"You both are talented. I've never seen the likes of all that talent in two people. It makes you wonder if the Lord doesn't have favorites."

"Aunt Ethel," Jane said with a laugh, "you know that's not true."

"Well, either that or I was off fussing with someone when the talents were handed out."

"If you would just ask your bread class, I'm sure they would agree you have plenty of talent," Jane said.

Ethel shrugged. "I suppose I get by. People do like my peach tarts."

"They certainly do. You are known all around Acorn Hill for your tarts," Jane agreed.

"And tart words, maybe," Ethel said with a chuckle.

Jane thought her aunt had a point, but Jane wisely kept silent. She reached her hand over and placed it on top of Ethel's hand. "I'm thankful for you, Auntie."

Ethel looked up in surprise. She squirmed in her chair, as if she didn't know what to do. "Well, I guess we've got a mutual admiration society thing going on," Ethel said with a laugh.

Though it was a rare occurrence, Jane had to agree with her aunt.

"Martha, you look wonderful," Louise said, stepping through the front door into her friend's home. Though Martha was sixty-eight, she could easily pass for younger. She had styled her softly colored blond hair into a French twist. A fashionable black pantsuit flattered her thin frame and made her look every inch the woman of elegance that she was.

"Louise, it is so good to see you." Martha pulled her friend into a warm hug. "Come in, come in." She closed the door behind them.

Stepping into the entryway, Louise took in the marble tile underfoot and the beautiful crystal chandelier overhead. Martha ushered Louise into a living room decorated in beige walls, white detailed crown molding at the ceiling's edge, over-stuffed chairs and sofas in muted earth tones, and a baby grand piano against the backdrop of white French doors. Louise said, "What a lovely home, Martha."

"We are blessed, and I never take it for granted. Still, it all means nothing without family and friends." She sat on a sofa and patted the seat beside her. "Now, sit down and fill me in. How have you been, what are you involved in besides the inn and your teaching?"

They spent the next half hour in comfortable companionship, catching up on each other's lives. "Oh goodness!" Martha said, glancing at her watch. "It's time to go to lunch." She stood. "Leave your suitcase where it is. My husband will put it in your room for you later when he gets home."

"Thank you."

Louise and Martha spent the next few hours enjoying lunch at a cozy French bistro, traipsing through the Rodin Museum and taking a carriage ride through town.

Louise sat comfortably in the white, horse-drawn carriage and lifted her face toward the brilliant sunlight. "I cannot believe we have been blessed with such a lovely day, a perfect day, really."

Martha looked pleased. "I'm so glad you could come."

The clip-clop of the horses' hooves echoed upon the city streets. Louise loved the sound. "You know, I lived here many years, but it's been a long time since I've actually acted like a tourist," Louise said with a laugh.

Martha smiled. "That's why I thought it would be fun to do it today. We might as well take advantage of what we have in our fair city."

"Did I tell you our pastor is here to deliver a talk at a pastors' seminar tonight?"

"Yes you did mention that. When I talked to you, though, he hadn't yet decided on the theme of his talk."

"Yes, he was quite concerned, but of course, the Lord came through for him in time. I'll be eager to hear from him how it went."

Martha nodded. "I'm sure he'll do fine."

The carriage pulled to a stop at the curb and Martha and Louise climbed down.

"I thought we might visit a few of the specialty shops if you're up to it, Louise."

"That would be lovely."

Louise and Martha visited some shops and just enjoyed each other's company until they returned to Martha's house to freshen up before the concert.

"Martha, would you mind if I used your telephone? I want to call our pastor and encourage him before he speaks tonight."

"Oh certainly, but do you think he'll be in his room?"

"Probably not, but I thought I could leave him a message on voice mail."

"Good idea. The phone is over there." Martha pointed to the stand beside the sofa. "The phone book is in the drawer."

"Thank you."

"While you make your phone call, I'll collect our mail."

Louise nodded. She pulled out the phone book and searched for the hotel where Pastor Thompson had mentioned he would be staying. After pressing the numbers, Louise waited while the phone rang on the other end. "Yes, I would like the room of Pastor Kenneth Thompson, please."

"One moment, please," the woman said.

The phone rang about six times. Thinking that the voice mail was never going to kick in, Louise was about to hang up when she heard someone answer.

"Hello?" The man's voice sounded strained and weak.

"Yes, I am trying to reach Pastor Kenneth Thompson." She hoped she had the wrong room.

"This is Ken Thompson," he said.

"Oh dear, are you all right?"

"Louise?"

"Yes."

"I wish I could say I had a bad case of the nerves, but I'm afraid it's a bit more than that."

"Oh dear," was all she could say.

"I haven't been able to keep anything down, and I'm weaker than I've been in a very long time."

Louise's mind scrambled for how she could help him. "What are you going to do about your talk tonight?"

She heard him blow out a weak sigh. "That's just it, I don't know. I can't ask someone else to speak this late in the day. I've only just decided I have the flu. I kept thinking what was bothering me was just nerves and that it would go away. I suppose I'll have to gather the strength somehow. I know the Lord wants this message to be heard, so I can't understand why I'm so sick." They waited a moment in silence. "Pray for me, please. I feel better just knowing my prayer partner is in town."

Louise could hear the smile in his voice. "Yes . . . yes, Pastor Ken, I'll pray."

"Don't worry. I have hotel personnel here if I need help. The Lord will work this out somehow. I'm afraid my stomach is rumbling again. I have to go. I'll tell you tomorrow how God worked out all the details. Bye, Louise."

"Good-bye." Louise hung up the phone and stared at it. Why would he get sick now of all times? With all those pastors attending she would think at least one of them could deliver his message, but she knew that Pastor Thompson didn't want to impose upon anyone at this late time. But what could he do? He sounded terribly ill.

Martha walked in carrying a stack of mail. "Oh,

I wish we didn't get so much junk mail," she said, sorting through it. When finished, she looked up at her friend. "Louise, what is it?" Martha sat on the edge of her seat, waiting for an answer.

Louise looked at Martha and explained the pastor's predicament. "I just wish I knew how to help him."

"Well, I'm terribly sorry for your pastor, but I don't see how you can help, short of delivering the message yourself."

Louise shrugged. "I suppose not . . ." Louise stopped speaking, then looked straight at Martha. "What did you say?"

Martha tossed another envelope into a growing pile and looked at Louise. "When?"

"Just a moment ago, you said something about not seeing how I could help short of—"

Martha laughed. "Oh that." Her hand brushed the air. "I said I didn't see how you could help short of delivering the message yourself."

Louise felt like she'd been doused with cold water. Martha seemed oblivious to Louise's internal struggle.

Martha's phone rang and she went over to answer it.

While Martha took care of her caller, memories of Pastor Ken's sermon flooded Louise's mind. She remembered how he relayed his talk to her with great passion. It seemed a shame that he couldn't present the message on his heart to this group of people, but she knew the message. She had heard him present it. The very idea sent a shock through her system. It was preposterous. Why, she could hardly be the one to present something so important to a room full of ministers. *God can use whomever He wishes to do whatever He deems best.* Pastor Ken's words spoke clearly to her heart. Could it be that God would want her to present his message?

It seemed utterly absurd. What could she be thinking? She straightened herself on the sofa. And what of the concert? This foolish thinking would cause her to miss the concert. The idea of attending this concert had filled her thoughts every day and her dreams at night. Would God ask her to miss something so important to her?

Louise bit her lip. How could she be so selfish as to think about herself at a time like this? Pastor Thompson was in trouble. This is the message God had given him. Still, if God had given Pastor Thompson the message, God could also make the pastor well enough to deliver it.

God can use whomever He wishes to do whatever He deems best. Even Balaam's donkey. The words persisted, gnawing at her conscience like a beaver at wood. Her heart pounded hard against her chest. Could she do it? She wouldn't even have considered it had she not seen Pastor Ken's note cards. If he had them, she might be able to muddle through. Panic surged through her, but then quickly she calmed herself. *Wait a minute, Louise. If God can use a donkey, He can use you.*

The concert. Pastor Thompson.

Eduardo Fink. God's message.

Louise took a deep breath and slowly, reluctantly and finally willingly pushed aside her own wants. She would make the offer and trust God's will to prevail.

Martha hung up the phone. "That was our dear neighbor. She calls me just about every day to chat about nothing in particular." Martha smiled.

"Might I use your phone again, Martha?"

Martha looked at Louise, puzzled. "Certainly."

Louise picked up the phone book and searched for the number once again. When she found it, she called the hotel and waited for the receptionist to connect her to the pastor's room. After a little while, Pastor Thompson answered, sounding weaker than before.

"Pastor Ken, it's Louise again. Do you have your note cards with you?"

"Note cards?"

"Yes, the ones you used when you presented your message to me."

"Oh yes, I have those. Why?"

She gave a nervous cough. "Well, if you are still unable, I am willing to give your message." She half expected him to laugh at her. After all, who was she to present such a message to his fellow preachers?

Silence.

"Pastor Ken?"

"Louise, I just finished praying that God would send someone to me who would take my place. I confess I hadn't considered it might be you, but I believe God has chosen you to be the messenger."

"Oh dear," she uttered.

"I don't want you to get sick, so I will put my notes in an envelope, call the bellboy up here and give them to him. The notes will be at the front desk. You can read through them and call me if you have any questions."

She could feel herself shaking but then she knew God sometimes stretched her out of her comfort zone.

"Are you certain you want to do this, Louise?"

"I'm certain I have to do this," she said, trying desperately not to think about the concert she would miss.

"My prayers will cover you. Lance Spelling is the man in charge. I will call him and let him know what's going on. In fact, here's his number." He rattled it off. "You call him in the next hour to make the necessary arrangements." His words had practically weakened to a whisper. "I'll have the notes at the front desk within half an hour."

"All right. If you don't hear from me soon, I'll contact you after the seminar."

"Louise?"

"Yes?"

"God be with you."

"I'm counting on it."

Chapter Twenty-Seven

After spending time in prayer and going over the pastor's notes, Louise decided she was as ready as she would ever be for the seminar.

A knock sounded at her bedroom door.

"Yes?"

"Louise, are you ready to go?" Martha asked.

She walked over to the door and opened it.

Martha's expression showed her concern. "You're sure you want to do this?"

Louise nodded. She reached for her handbag and gave Martha a nervous smile. "I think I'm ready." The two made their way down the stairs.

Martha dropped Louise off at the conference center and then continued on to the concert. Louise wound her way through the center in search of Lance Spelling. She finally found someone to point him out to her, and she walked up and introduced herself. After exchanging greetings, he advised her of the night's schedule, where she would be sitting and answered a few of her questions. Once he introduced her to the pastors who made up the committee in charge of the event, Lance led her to the platform to find her seat.

Louise settled in and looked up across the large room to see people milling around, finding seats, stopping here and there to say hello to old friends. To her right a group of men huddled in prayer.

A glance at the clock told her it was five minutes to the start of the meeting. She fidgeted with the note cards in her hands. She didn't know a single person there. Not one. Music was her calling, not pastoring. Goodness, what was she doing here? She didn't know the first thing about speaking. She was a stand-in. Helping a friend. Why, these pastors would be bored to tears.

The effect of the pep talk she had given herself earlier evaporated like the last note of a concerto. Panic kicked in. Putting a hand to her throat, Louise struggled to swallow. Another glance around the room squeezed the very air from her lungs. She considered a quick getaway, looked across the room and actually planned the path of her escape.

The words of Isaiah 41:10 came to her. *"So do not fear, for I am with you; do not be dismayed, for I am your God. I will strengthen you and help you; I will uphold you with my righteous right hand."* No matter how panicked she felt, she knew she had to go through with this. She had given her word, after all. The verse came to her once again. As she took slow, deliberate breaths, her throat began to relax. She repeated the verse once more in her mind, allowing the truth of it to sink deep into her soul.

So lost was she in her thoughts, if she hadn't seen Lance Spelling motioning to her, she might have missed her cue.

This is it, Lord. Just like Balaam's donkey, I am ready to serve. Please go with me. Her prayer flew heavenward as her footsteps took her to the front of the audience.

A hush settled upon the room as Louise, God's chosen messenger of the hour, spoke to His gathered servants.

What took place over the next hour, Louise could not say. She knew only that the presence of God replaced all thoughts of the missed concert. Helping a friend, doing the will of God, far exceeded any pleasure she might have enjoyed at the concert.

Louise realized too that through her obedience, her faith had grown.

After breakfast the next morning, Jane and Alice loaded the dishwasher, folded laundry and dusted the rooms downstairs before pausing in the living room for a morning break.

"I can't wait to hear about Louise's evening at the concert," Jane said.

"Yes, I've been thinking about her too. You know, Louise never gets excited about things, so seeing her energy and enthusiasm just tickled me," Alice said.

Jane nodded. "Me too. She rarely allows herself the treat of going out. She's like you, always busy helping others."

"Excuse me," Alice said with a teasing grin, "but I believe you have the same problem."

Jane shrugged. "I guess it runs in the family."

Alice smiled. "You know, it's a family trait for which I am thankful."

"Yes, you're right, Alice," Jane said.

"Good morning, all." Catherine Schmidt entered the room with her luggage in hand.

"You're leaving now, Catherine?" Alice asked.

Catherine gave a crooked smile. "I'm afraid so. I had hoped to say good-bye to Louise as well, but my daughter has other things to tend to this afternoon, so she will be here momentarily." Catherine settled onto the end of the sofa. "I cannot tell you how much I have enjoyed my stay."

The sisters smiled in unison.

Catherine turned to Alice. "I have decided to look into the matter of volunteering as a baby cuddler. I think it may be just the thing I need. I can stop thinking about myself and do something constructive with my time. I can't think of anything I'd rather do than cuddle babies."

Alice clasped her hands together. "You would be a wonderful addition to our neonatal unit, Catherine." Alice proceeded to tell Catherine where to go in the hospital to fill out the necessary paperwork. While they were still talking, the Evanses entered the room.

"Well, they say all good things must come to an end," Brandon said, his hat in his hand and a smile on his face.

"You're leaving too?" Jane asked, putting her magazine aside and standing.

Alice stood to greet them as well. "We're losing everyone at once, I'm afraid."

Catherine got up and everyone surrounded the Evans family.

Alice told Suzanne of Catherine's decision to look into the baby cuddler position.

"Oh, Catherine, that's wonderful. You'll be great," Suzanne said. Right then Zoë let out a happy squeal, causing everyone to laugh.

Brandon Evans clasped Jane's, then Alice's hand. "I can't thank you enough for the past few days. This place has helped me to see things through different eyes." He looked at his wife and smiled. "Though it was quite by accident that we ended up staying here, I want you to know we will be back." Suzanne stood beside him nodding eagerly.

Tricia Burks arrived to pick up her mother.

Alice and Jane exchanged hugs with their guests and walked them to the front door.

"We are blessed, Alice," Jane said after they all had left and she had closed the door behind them.

"We truly are, Jane," Alice responded, then said a silent prayer of thanks.

Ethel came in the front door. "Yoo-hoo, anybody home?" she called.

Alice and Jane had just finished cleaning the guest rooms and came down the stairs carrying the linens for the laundry.

"Hi, Auntie. We'll be with you as soon as we put these in the washer. We've got the rooms ready for the next guests," Jane said.

"Well, I'll just make myself at home while you two do that. Then we can get down to some serious visiting," Ethel said.

Soon the three had settled in for a chat in the living room.

"What brings you out on such a cold afternoon, Auntie?" Jane wanted to know.

With a serious expression, Ethel looked at her niece. "I've been doing some thinking."

Alice's gaze darted to Jane. It always scared Alice when Ethel started a conversation this way.

"Oh?" Jane said with a smile.

"Well, Jane, you remember that day I practiced my bread making in your kitchen before the class began?"

Jane nodded.

"You remember how I put in double the amount of yeast and how the dough spilled over the sides of the bowl and practically took over your kitchen?"

Jane nodded again and chuckled.

"Well, I've been thinking about the Scriptures and that bread dough. You know the one that talks about how a little yeast works through the whole batch of dough?"

The sisters nodded.

"I've been thinking that's what that old Luther Grose has been trying to do, stir his negative attitude into the Acorn Hill community. I've made up my mind that it's not right, and I won't stand for it."

Now she had their attention.

"I talked to Lloyd this morning and told him that under no circumstances was he to let Byrdie's brother-in-law stir up trouble for that sweet young woman. Acorn Hill is a good town . . ." Ethel was standing now, pacing actually. ". . . a loving community." She stopped pacing. "And I aim to keep it that way."

Ethel had practically taken Alice's breath away. Alice didn't know whether to stand and clap or encourage her aunt to run for office.

"Auntie, I think it's wonderful that you stood up for Paula this way," Jane said. "We all know that Lloyd gives careful thought to what you have to say."

Ethel sat back in her chair, smoothing her skirt. "Well, I'll not have it. This backbiting and mumbling over a dog that is trying to help one of our very own. Why, that dog has as much right to live

270

in our town as Daisy the pig." Her voice rose in pitch as she climbed her invisible platform once again. "Paula deserves our help, not our complaints. I, for one, aim to see that she gets it."

Alice clapped.

"Well said, Auntie. Well said," Jane cheered.

"It's the truth. I'm meeting Lloyd for dinner tonight, and we're going to talk some more about this whether he wants to or not. I want him to hear both sides of the issue."

Just then someone opened the front door and stepped into the foyer. Soon, Louise stood at the living room entrance. "Hello," she said, smiling.

"Louise, come in, come in. We've been dying to hear what happened last night," Jane said.

Louise laughed and pulled off her coat. "Well, give me a moment to catch my breath."

The sisters and Ethel waited patiently . . . well, the sisters waited patiently.

"Doggone it, Louise, are you going to stand there all day playing with your coat or are you going to tell us what happened at that concert?" Ethel asked.

A look crossed Louise's face that Alice couldn't quite place. Was she happy or sad?

After Louise hung up her coat and returned to the living room, she sat down and began her story. "Well, first of all, I didn't go to the concert."

Alice gasped. "Oh Louise, no!"

"No concert? Are you sick?" Ethel chimed in.

Jane turned serious. "I'm so sorry, Louise. What happened?"

Louise took a deep breath. "No, I'm not sick, Aunt Ethel. In fact, I'm better than I've ever been." She spent the next fifteen minutes explaining just what had happened the day before, how the pastor had fallen ill, how she had felt the Lord had impressed upon her heart to help him, how she presented Pastor Ken's message to a host of ministers. When she had finished, they all sat completely still, saying nothing.

"Well, I'm downright flabbergasted," Ethel said. "I never thought you to be a preacher, Louise."

Louise laughed. "Well, I can assure you I don't feel God leading me in that direction, but I do know He needed me to fill in last night and that's exactly what I did."

"Well, if anyone could do it, you could," Jane said. She rose from her seat, walked over and gave Louise a hug.

"I must say, Louise, you never cease to amaze me," Alice said, also rising to give her sister a hug. "I'm sure the pastor is deeply grateful for your sacrifice."

"Sacrifice?" Louise asked.

"Missing your concert," Alice reminded her.

"Oh. You know, I really wanted to attend that concert, and I know I'd have loved it. But I know I did the right thing, and that feels good."

"Have you heard how Pastor Ken is doing today?" Jane wanted to know.

"He called before I left Martha's and said he had made it home and was feeling better. It's a good thing, because I had no intention of preaching at church tomorrow." She chuckled. "I'll take my music any day over speaking in front of a room full of people. Why, I nearly broke out in hives." She laughed.

"I don't blame you," Jane said.

They spent more time discussing the seminar, Paula and her dog, Sylvia's improved arm and their guests who had left earlier that morning. Before they knew it, the afternoon had turned into early evening. Ethel headed home and Louise went to her room for a quick nap before dinner.

"You know, I wish we could do something special for Louise to make up for the concert she missed," Alice said as she helped Jane set the dinner table.

Before Jane could comment, the phone rang, and she went to answer it. Alice finished placing the dishes around the table and looked up when Jane returned.

"Well, it looks like your wish will come true," Jane whispered.

Alice was puzzled.

"That was Martha Spangler. She feels terrible that Louise missed the concert. The conservatory gave a reception afterward, and Martha told

Eduardo how Louise loved his music and had looked forward to his concert and then explained what had happened. It seems Mr. Fink and his wife will be passing this way as they travel back home tomorrow afternoon, so Martha has talked him into stopping by our inn so that he might meet this avid fan of his."

Alice's breath caught in her throat. "You don't mean it!"

"I do," Jane said excitedly. "I don't know how long they will stay, but he suggested to Martha that since we have a piano, he might play for Louise."

"Oh my, she will flip," Alice said.

"Let's keep it a secret," Jane said, "just in case the plans change. If they don't, it can be a wonderful surprise."

"Hmm," Alice said

"What's the matter?"

"I think I'd better get some smelling salts so Louise isn't unconscious during his concert."

Chapter Twenty-Eight

Sunday dawned sunny. Though winter's chill still had a hold, sunshine fanned across Grace Chapel's front lawn, leaving puddles of melting snow scattered here and there. A hint of spring's freshness was in the air.

"Are you ready to go in?" Alice asked Paula once they reached the church's double doors.

Paula's fingers tightened around Paws' harness. "What if they ask me to leave?"

"They won't. Grace Chapel parishioners aren't like that, Paula." A softness touched Alice's voice, and she took note that Paula's shoulders somewhat relaxed. "Please don't think everyone is like Luther Grose. Luther is just . . . well, Luther." Alice smiled.

Paula chuckled in spite of herself, and then she pulled in a ragged breath. "I think I'm ready." Alice turned to open the door when she heard Ethel's voice behind her.

"Yoo-hoo, Alice, wait up."

Alice and Paula turned around to see Ethel scurrying up the walk with Lloyd Tynan struggling to keep in step beside her. When she reached them, she was quite out of breath. "Land's sake, I must be out of shape," Ethel said between gasps of air.

Lloyd tipped his Greek fisherman's cap and smiled. "Morning, ladies."

"Morning," they replied in unison.

"Are Louise and Jane already here?" Ethel asked after briefly scanning the area around them.

Alice nodded. "They walked over while I went to pick up Paula and Paws."

Ethel looked at Paula. "Good morning."

"Hello."

"Hi there, Paws," Ethel said.

Alice remembered Ethel's new determination to help Paula and looked over at Lloyd, who said nothing.

"I'm glad you're here," Ethel said to the dog. She looked up at Paula. "She belongs here with you."

Just then, they heard footsteps shuffling up the walk. Alice looked to see who was coming. When she spotted Byrdie, her brother-in-law and his wife, Alice felt uneasy. *Please, God, help us all to behave in a Christian manner and reach out to Paula in love.*

Byrdie said, "Good morning." Luther exchanged a glance with his wife, looked at the dog and at Paula, but said nothing. They stepped forward into the church.

Ethel was the first to speak. "Now you pay him no mind," she said, pointing toward the door through which they had disappeared. "We will march into that church and sit down for worship." Her face suggested "or else." She threw back her shoulders, tensed her muscles and pointed her nose heavenward. "You ready, Lloyd?"

Looking dapper in his navy double-breasted coat, Lloyd reminded Alice of a chubby Maurice Chevalier. Why, if he had a fancy cane, she could almost imagine him singing and dancing his way right into the church.

"I'm ready, Ethel." He crooked his arm for her to tuck her hand into it, which she did.

Alice and Paula shared a smile as they followed close behind.

Once again, the sunlight played behind the stained glass windows, causing bright colors to upon the wooden pews. Ethel and Lloyd scooted into their seats, leaving room for Alice and Paula to join them. Paws sat obediently beside Paula on the outside of the pew. People could not help giving curious looks, and Alice knew Paula must feel uncomfortable.

"Are you doing okay?" Alice said, leaning over to Paula.

"I'm fine. I knew the first Sunday would be difficult. I'm glad you invited me, Alice. Since I can't drive to my other church, I've really missed attending somewhere."

"Well, we are more than happy to pick you up and have you join us, Paula."

Paula looked around at the curious congregation. "I just hope everyone feels that way," she said in a nervous whisper.

"They do. They just need to get past the novelty of a dog in church. They will settle into the idea in no time."

"I sure hope so."

Before they could talk any further, musical chords rose from the organ as Louise's fingers moved with expertise across the keys, ushering the congregation into worship.

After the service, when the music subsided and the congregation began to file out of the church, someone stopped Alice to ask her a question. Paula moved down the aisle toward the door, evidently not noticing that Alice wasn't behind her. Alice listened to the woman talk about an idea for an ANGELs meeting, but she kept her gaze on Paula, wanting to make sure Luther Grose stayed away from her.

Alice watched Paula hold on to Paws' harness, as she made her way with Ethel and Lloyd right behind her.

As people walked out of the chapel, Paula got closer to the door, and Alice turned back to the woman, who had continued talking.

"Someone get Alice!" Ethel said loudly.

Alice turned with a start to see the frightened crowd separate, allowing Lloyd and Ethel to carefully place a limp Paula on the floor.

Alice rushed toward Paula, but before she could get there, a stirring occurred in the crowd.

"Do you see that?" someone said with awe.

"I've never seen the like," another marveled.

Whispers filled the chapel as the puzzled crowd watched the seizure response dog at work. Paws pushed to his charge and stretched out beside Paula, then placed her paw and head gently upon the woman's stomach.

"Well, will you look at that," one woman said.

"She's protecting her," another said, "so she won't hurt herself. I've heard about these dogs. They're remarkable."

Alice finally made her way through the crowd and looked down at Paula. Paula's eyelids fluttered, then opened. She looked around at the people, then at Paws' head upon her stomach. "I had a seizure, didn't I?"

"Yes, you did," Alice said, brushing a strand of hair from Paula's forehead.

Paula lifted her hand and stroked her dog. "Thank you, Paws."

"Are you going to be all right, dear?" Ethel asked, her face scrunched with worry.

"I'll be fine now. Thank you, Ethel."

Ethel looked at Lloyd. "Well, don't just stand there, Lloyd, help her up," she said in a staged whisper that made those around them snicker.

Paula looked at Alice. "I have something to tell you later."

Alice nodded and with Lloyd's help, got Paula to her feet. Members of the congregation patted her shoulder, gave her hugs and said how glad they were that she was okay. It was not until most of the folks had stepped outside, leaving only a handful behind, that Alice noticed Luther still standing there. He had evidently watched the whole episode with Paula. He walked their way, causing Alice's stomach to tighten.

"I want to talk to you a minute," he said in his usual gruff manner.

Paula nodded and Alice stood firmly at her side. Wild horses couldn't drag her away. If Luther didn't behave himself, Alice would do what she had to do to protect Paula.

Luther glanced at Alice, then looked back at

Paula. "I need to apologize, ma'am." He turned his hat nervously between his fingers.

Apologize? Surely Alice had misunderstood.

"I, uh, was wrong about the dog." He fiddled with his hat some more. "When I was a kid, I got bit by a mean dog, and I've been, well, *um* . . ." he stammered a moment, almost as if he didn't want to finish what he was saying "well, I'll just flat out tell you. I've been afraid of dogs ever since. I don't like to be around them." He stared at his hat. "I just didn't think people were safe when there was a big dog around." He looked up at her. "I didn't mean no harm."

Alice saw compassion replace Paula's fears.

"What made you change your mind?" Paula asked.

He looked at his wife, who had joined them and nodded her encouragement. After a hard swallow, he took a deep breath. "Yesterday I was getting ready to back my car out of the driveway when this dog came out of nowhere, stood by my door and started barking his fool head off. I was scared to get out. I was going to take off in a hurry, but after he barked at me, he went to the back of the car, so I couldn't move. I didn't know what to do. I sat there a moment, trying to get my wits about me, figure out what to do. Then I heard a child's squeal." He looked at his wife again, who had tears filling her eyes. Blowing out a breath, he continued.

"Well, I couldn't very well stay in the safety of

my car if this dog was hurting a child, so I got out and when I went to the back side, I saw the neighbor's two-year-old playing directly behind my car. The dog was standing nearby, looking on, his tail wagging."

He scratched his head and thought a moment. He looked choked up, as if he was trying to fight back the tears. "It was then I realized that dog had saved that little girl's life. If not for that dog, I would have pulled out of that driveway and run right . . ." His words trailed off.

His wife placed her hand on his arm and gave it a reassuring rub. "Well, ma'am, there are good dogs out there, and I'm sorry I made such a stink about your dog. I can see she takes care of you." Paws lifted warm brown eyes to the man as if to say she accepted his apology.

"Well, it seems to me if Paws can forgive you, I certainly can," Paula said with a smile.

Soon the little group was talking about how incredible these special dogs were, how they helped their owners and made the world a better place for those who needed them.

"What is it you wanted to tell me?" Alice whispered to Paula when the group began to break up and start out the chapel door.

They stopped walking for a moment. "I know it's far too early to tell, but remember I told you that some dogs are alert dogs, yet when you get your dog, you have no way of knowing?"

Alice nodded.

"It takes time for the dog to get to know you, get used to your seizures, that kind of thing. I've had a few seizures since I've been with Paws, which isn't nearly enough for her to recognize an onset of one yet. Still, before I had my seizure a moment ago, Paws started licking my hand furiously. That's not something she does. I thought she was nervous with all the people around, but the next thing I knew, I was on the floor with her leaning on my stomach. I know it sounds crazy, but I wonder . . ."

"Oh my, Paula. That would be wonderful, wouldn't it?"

"It sure would." She scratched Paws' head. "Time will tell, I guess."

As Paula and Alice edged out the front door of the church, Alice tapped Luther on the shoulder. He turned to her.

"I was wondering, what did that dog look like, the one who stopped you in the driveway?"

"Well, he was a big dog. Probably a Lab, a black Lab," he answered on their way out the door. He looked toward the lawn and pointed. "Say, he looked just like that dog right there."

Alice looked up with a start and saw the black dog with the red collar standing with Pastor Thompson and another man.

"Are you sure you're all right, Paula?" Alice asked.

"I'm fine, Alice."

"Okay, then I'll be right back. I need to talk to the pastor a moment."

Paula nodded.

Alice stood at a distance until the pastor and the other man had finished talking. One look at the dog told her that this was their mystery dog. The two men looked at her. "Good morning, Alice. We've had quite a lot of excitement this weekend, haven't we?"

Alice smiled at the pastor and the man beside him. "Oh, forgive me, Alice. This is my friend, Pastor Philip Daugherty. He pastors over in Potterston but is on vacation and thought he would visit us today."

The man extended his hand to Alice.

"It's very nice to meet you," she said, then she quickly turned her attention to the dog. "I presume that is your dog?" she asked, eager to learn about this mystery dog.

"Well, as a matter of fact, he is. I hope he hasn't caused you any problems," he said with a bit of worry in his voice.

"Oh no, not at all," she assured him.

The man's shoulders relaxed. "You see, the neighbor girl was watching him for me. When she took him outside one day, Parakaleo spotted a nearby cat and went chasing after it. The girl could not catch him. Since that day, I've been looking everywhere for him, put out posters, called every dog shelter I could think of. I'm from Potterston, and I have no idea how Parakaleo got all the way to Acorn Hill."

The dog barked, stood on his hind legs, then circled a couple of times. Pastor Daugherty laughed. "I don't know why you think you deserve a treat when you ran away from home."

Alice couldn't believe the talents of this dog. "Quite the contrary, he is very deserving of a treat," she said. The men looked at her and she began to recount the various measures Parakaleo had taken to ensure the safety of the citizens of Acorn Hill, down to righting a preconceived notion about dogs in general.

They discussed the matter. Pastor Daugherty was aware of his pet's penchant for good deeds, but his feats in Acorn Hill had surpassed anything he had done before.

"Well, I suppose he does indeed deserve a treat," Pastor Daugherty finally agreed.

"By the way, how did you come up with the name Parakaleo?" Alice asked.

"Do you know what it means?" he asked.

Alice shook her head.

"It's the Greek word for 'encourager.'"

Alice smiled. "Well, I must say, he has worked very hard to live up to his name. It's appropriate that Parakaleo associates with the clergy. He appears to have a ministry of his own."

They all laughed. Finally, Alice said good-bye.

She dropped Paula and Paws off at home, and then joined her sisters at the inn. She knew Jane would be preparing for the famous pianist and his wife, who were expected soon.

She could hardly wait to tell her sisters about the mystery dog. God continued to amaze her with His answers to prayer. Who would have ever thought God would use a dog, of all things, to soften Luther Grose's heart? But then, if God could use Balaam's donkey, He could use Parakaleo.

Chapter Twenty-Nine

Jane hurried her sisters through lunch as best she could without raising Louise's suspicion. She didn't know exactly what time to expect the Finks, and she wanted to be prepared. Louise and Alice helped Jane clear the dishes from the table and load the dishwasher.

"You know, I'm a bit tired. I believe I'll lie down for a while in my room," Louise said.

Alice and Jane looked at each other.

"Is something wrong?" Louise asked upon seeing their expressions.

"Oh no, no," Jane said. "You go right ahead." Knowing Louise would want to look her best when the Finks arrived, Jane's mind searched for what to say. "We may have company later today, would you like me to get you up before then?"

Louise turned. "Oh? Who?"

Alice stammered. "Well, he's an acquaintance of a friend from Philadelphia." She shared a glance with Jane.

Louise's eyebrows raised in their usual curious manner. "Oh? Mark Graves and a friend?" Louise teased. "Well, no matter. I'll just read for a while instead of taking a nap. Let me know when he—or they—arrive, and I'll come down and join you." She paused a moment. "Unless, of course, you prefer to be alone," she said, emphasizing the last word.

To give a pretence of annoyance, Alice stared at Louise a moment.

Louise raised a hand. "All right, I'm only teasing."

"I'll let you know when our company arrives," Alice said.

When Louise turned and walked from the room, Alice mimed a whistle and gave a look that said they had barely pulled it off.

Quickly, Jane and Alice finished cleaning in the kitchen, tidied up the parlor, fluffed pillows in the living room and prepared for the arrival of their surprise guests. After their chores were done, Jane and Alice settled in the living room to wait.

"Well, at least the Finks have a nice day for driving," Jane whispered.

Alice nodded. After turning a page or two in her mystery book, Alice let out a giggle.

"What?" Jane asked, looking up from the book that she was reading.

"I just thought of how surprised Louise will be when they show up. I can hardly wait to see her expression."

Jane covered a laugh behind her hand. "Me too." She felt herself warm with the thought. If anyone deserved such a special treat, it was Louise. "I'm so happy for her, Alice. This will be a memorable afternoon."

"It's been a memorable weekend already." Alice thought a moment. "You don't suppose Aunt Ethel will come over while they're here, do you?" Worry lines formed on her forehead.

Jane smiled. "Auntie went with Lloyd to Potterston for the afternoon. I think we're safe."

"It's not that I don't want her around, exactly, it's just that . . ."

Jane held up her hand. "I understand completely. Auntie has good intentions, but she does have a unique way of expressing herself."

They soon drifted into comfortable silence, each lost in what she was reading. In no time at all, the doorbell rang.

Jane locked eyes with Alice and took a deep breath. "This is it. You get Louise. I'll let our guests in the house."

Alice smiled and nodded. "I'll be right back."

Jane opened the door. A tall man with reddish blond hair and thoughtful brown eyes stood before her. A trim mustache gave him an artsy appearance, while a strong jaw suggested the determination so needed to excel in a musician's world.

"Hello, I am Eduardo Fink, and this is my wife, Tina."

The woman beside him had wide brown eyes and an abundance of chestnut hair that swept up from her neck into an elegant French twist. A stylish pearl comb held it into place. The woman's warm smile and sparkling eyes put Jane at ease.

"Hello, I'm so pleased to meet you. I'm Jane, Louise's sister. Do come in," she said.

Eduardo turned to Jane. "Does Louise know that we are coming?"

Jane smiled and shook her head. She took their wraps and hung them in the closet. Then, she led the Finks into the living room. There they spoke of Louise's sacrifice and her love of Eduardo's music. Jane thought it admirable that the man seemed genuinely pleased to stop to meet Louise. When they heard footsteps in the hallway, Jane shared a glance with the Finks.

"I think I'll make us some—" Louise's words stopped when she walked into the room. "Oh my!" She pulled her hand to her chest. She looked at Tina, then back to Eduardo, both of whom were heading her way. "Oh my," she repeated.

Jane glanced at Alice, whose stance suggested

that she just might bolt for the smelling salts. Together they reveled in the joy emanating from Louise's face.

"Louise Howard Smith, it is our pleasure to meet you," Eduardo said, shaking her hand warmly.

"So happy to meet you, Mrs. Smith," Tina Fink said, pulling Louise into a gentle hug.

Louise stared at them, totally speechless.

"Louise, are you all right?" Alice asked.

"You'll have to excuse me," Louise said, then pulled in a nervous breath. "This is such a surprise, such a wonderful surprise."

"We have heard the story of your sacrifice, Louise, and I am honored that you should treasure the music of my heart."

"But who told you—" Louise stopped short and then said, "Martha."

The Finks smiled and nodded. "She told us everything," Tina said.

"And she had the wonderful idea that we might stop by and see you. Perhaps I could play a song or two from the concert for you?" Eduardo asked.

At this, Jane thought Louise would need the smelling salts for sure.

"I . . . I don't know what to say," Louise replied.

"Perhaps we should just show Mr. Fink to the piano in the parlor," Jane suggested with a smile, already leading the way.

In the parlor, Eduardo seated himself at the piano and commenced playing selections from his concert. Finally, he asked Louise to join him and they quickly became absorbed in their music.

Louise played with her favorite pianist, while Jane's camera quietly snapped the memories. At last the Finks had to depart and the sisters waved from the front door. Then they headed back into their home, each lost in the memory of the day.

Later Jane found Louise in the parlor, sitting at the piano, her fingers tracing the keys, her eyes glazed with memories and tears of joy.

"Are you okay?" Jane asked.

"I will never forget this day as long as I live," Louise said. "My heart is as light as a child's on Christmas Day."

Alice joined them. "This has been quite a weekend for you, Louise."

"If I had died today, Alice, I would have died a happy woman."

Alice hesitated, then chuckled when she looked at Louise's face. "Well, I'm glad you're happy, but if it's all the same to you, I'd rather that you stick around awhile."

Louise grew pensive. "I wish Eliot could have been here today."

"He would have enjoyed watching you as much or more than actually hearing Eduardo's music. Your reaction was priceless," Jane said.

Louise laughed. "I imagine I was a sight."

Later that evening, when Jane finally slipped between her sheets, visions of Louise's special day filled her mind. Jane thanked the Lord for making the afternoon possible and asked Him to bless the Finks for their kindness.

Her thoughts briefly flitted through tomorrow's list of goals, her work with Wendell at the top of her list. Her efforts to train their stubborn tabby had become wearisome at the very least, but still, Jane planned to persist. After all, she convinced herself before drifting off to sleep, victory could be just around the corner.

Chapter Thirty

Jane waited impatiently on the living room sofa for the hall clock to strike ten. She finished an entry in her journal and closed it for another day. She peeked first at Louise, whose eyebrows pulled into a frown as she worked the stitches on her knitting needles. Then Jane looked toward Alice. Her wide eyes and white knuckles suggested Alice had reached a critical point in her mystery.

Jane looked at Wendell, trying not to fume over the stubborn cat. Perhaps today would be the day Wendell would shine. Then again . . .

The clock struck one, two, three—Wendell's right ear twitched—four, five, six—his left eyelid rose in slow motion—seven-eight-nine-ten. He stretched his legs, licked his paw, then looked over at Jane with an expression that said, *Can we just skip the preliminaries and go straight to the treat?*

Jane thought it a good sign that Wendell had come to expect their new little ritual. He had learned a little more patience while waiting for Jane to go through her routine. "Wendell, let's go get your treat."

Louise glanced up and smiled.

"Wendell, let's go get your treat."

Alice turned the page in her book and looked up. "Treat time, huh?"

"You guys want to see something? I haven't told you this, but I've been working with Wendell. I think today's the day he'll surprise us all."

"How do you mean?" Alice asked.

"Well, I've been trying to teach him to pull his treat from the bottom pantry shelf and onto the floor. Then I open it and give it to him."

"He does that?" Louise asked, incredulously.

"Well, *um,* not yet, but I think today just might be the day," Jane said with more enthusiasm than she really felt.

Louise winked at Alice.

"Well, it might be," Jane said a tad defensively.

Alice put her bookmark into place and closed her book. "As stubborn as that cat is, if he's learned a trick, I have to see it for myself."

Of course, that was exactly the response for which Jane was hoping. She felt an unusual confidence today.

"Well, if you're going to watch, I suppose I

should too," Louise said, laying aside her knitting and pushing herself from the chair.

As though he knew he was the object of their attentions, the lethargic Wendell sprang to life. He jumped and padded playfully around their feet.

"Goodness, he certainly seems to know what you are doing," Louise said, watching Wendell with amusement.

"Oh, he knows what I'm doing all right," Jane said.

Alice laughed.

When they reached the shelf holding his treat, Wendell stopped in his tracks and locked eyes with the now stooping Jane. "Get your treat, Wendell," she cooed.

"Meow."

"Get your treat," she encouraged sweetly with only a teensy hint of impatience.

The feline turned his nose upward and circled hard against her legs, almost causing her to topple. "Get your treat." Jane's voice had a definite edge to it now.

"Meow." More circling, head and tail held high.

"Your treat, Wendell," Jane growled through clenched teeth. She ignored her sisters' snickers.

He stopped, looked her over, then turned to face the treat. Right then and there he plopped his back-side down.

If there had been a St. Bernard in the house, Jane would have turned him loose.

"Wendell."

He stayed perfectly still, his eyes fixed on the treat.

Jane glanced at her sisters who now tried to control their snickers, though they were not having much success. Jane frowned. "Wendell."

Not so much as a muscle twitch.

She let out an exasperated sigh.

"Well, look at it this way, Jane, at least he knows what *treat* means," Alice said, finally giving in to a laugh. Louise joined her.

Jane fumed. She pulled the treat from the shelf, opened it, and practically threw it into Wendell's bowl. "I don't know why I've wasted my time," she finally said as she slumped onto a kitchen chair.

"You tried, that is the important thing," Louise said, sounding much like an older sister.

"I tried all right. A lot of good it did me."

"Now, Jane, I've never known you to give up," Alice said.

"No, you're right. But then I've never come across a challenge as great as King Wendell, either."

Right then, Wendell sauntered past them, ignoring their comments altogether. Jane looked at her sisters, who erupted into laughter.

Later that day, Jane scrubbed the stove in the kitchen while Louise practiced a piano piece, no doubt inspired by Eduardo Fink's visit. Alice headed for the stairway to place fresh towels in the bathrooms. The phone rang just as she reached the first step. Knowing her sisters were busy, she went to answer it.

"Hello?"

"Hi, Alice. How are you?" Paula asked.

"I'm so glad you called, Paula. I've been meaning to talk to you since yesterday's events at church, but we had a lot going on in the afternoon." Alice proceeded to tell her friend about the surprise visit from Eduardo and Tina Fink.

"Oh, I'll bet Louise was really surprised."

"Was she ever," Alice laughed. "I've never seen her stunned into silence before."

They discussed the church service and all that had happened, Luther Grose's comments and the congregation's reaction to her seizure and Paws.

"In fact, Alice, that is the main reason I called."

"Oh?"

"I wanted to let you know that somehow Pastor Thompson heard that I had assisted with the bell choir at my other church. He wanted to know if I would consider doing a concert for Grace Chapel."

"Paula, that would be wonderful. Our folks would really enjoy that."

"It would be my way of saying thanks for Grace Chapel's generosity. Without their help, I wouldn't have Paws today. I thought I might get a few of my former bell choir members to come with me, and I think we could put together a decent concert for the church."

"I will look forward to it," Alice said. "Are you feeling better about things now that Luther and the others have expressed their apologies?"

"Much better. I actually feel accepted now."

"I'm so glad."

The front door pushed open and in walked a middle-aged man and woman.

"I'm sorry, Paula, I have to go. We have someone at the door. I'll call you later, all right?"

"Sure. Talk to you soon."

Alice placed the phone back on the cradle and turned to the strangers. "Welcome to Grace Chapel Inn. May I help you?"

"Well, yes, as a matter of fact. We were on our way home from vacation and saw this place. The wife here wanted to check it out and see if you had any openings for a night or two."

Alice smiled. "We certainly do, and we would love to have you stay with us."

His wife looked pleased. The man smiled his approval.

Louise emerged from the parlor. At the same time, Jane rounded the corner and stopped short when she saw the strangers. She held a can of cleaning solution and a cloth rag in her hand. "Oh, I'm sorry. I didn't realize we had company."

The couple smiled. "I'm Dennis Walker and this is my wife, Sheila."

"Nice to meet you," Jane said. "Are you going to stay with us?" With her free hand, she tucked some loose strands of hair back into her ponytail.

"Well, it looks like it," Mr. Walker said.

Alice explained that the Walkers were on vacation and that they had noticed the inn and decided to come in.

The man piped up. "We were visiting her parents. Her dad has been sick. We stayed a week and helped them. He was doing so well, we decided to go home." He looked at his wife. "She's kind of worn out from caring for her folks, so when we spotted this place, we thought it might be nice to spend a night or two here so she could rest before we went back home to the usual work routine."

Alice saw the woman tuck her arm into her husband's and give him a warm smile.

"Well, we're glad you chose to stay here."

"It's funny," the woman said. "We had no plans to stop here at all." She looked up at her husband. "Thank you."

Alice quickly ran through the routine and paperwork with the couple, gave them the key to their room and took them upstairs so they could get settled. After they expressed their pleasure and closed the door, Alice went back downstairs and joined her sisters in the kitchen where they were making a batch of popcorn.

"You get them situated?" Louise asked.

She nodded. "Yes. His wife certainly is pleased."

"That's nice," Jane said. "Another of life's little interruptions, but in this case it's a welcome one."

"Interruptions, or could it be an answer to prayer?" Louise asked, pouring the cooked popcorn into a large bowl.

"What do you mean, Louise?" Alice asked, collecting bowls from the cupboard for their popcorn.

"Well, we know that God answers in unusual ways. I just wonder if this is another one of them. You know, they just happened by, saw the place, decided to stay." Louise shrugged.

Jane looked at her. "That's a good point. Isn't it humbling to think He uses our inn sometimes for His unusual answers?"

Alice shook her head. "We never know when He might use us. I suppose it keeps us on our toes."

Just then, Wendell moseyed into the kitchen. His eyes scanned his empty dish bowl, then looked up at Jane.

"Oh sure, you want me to feed you on demand, but you won't do anything for me. You've already had your treat today, thank you very much. Now if you don't mind, I'm going to enjoy my popcorn," she said.

The sisters chuckled and watched as Wendell took on his aristocratic walk and headed for the treat shelf.

"Look, Jane, he's headed for the treat packet."

Jane rolled her eyes. "Trust me, it means nothing. We've been at this for some time now and all he does is meow." She shook her head. "I just don't see how Clara can get Daisy to do anything. I mean, she's a mere pig after all." She dropped her chin into her palm propped on the table.

Wendell disappeared into the pantry. The sisters talked a little more, forgetting about Wendell altogether. Alice heard a crackling sound. "What is that?"

"What is what?" Louise asked, placing her teacup in its saucer.

Another crackle. "That noise."

The sisters looked at each other and listened. Understanding seemed to hit them all at the same time and before they could get up from their chairs, Wendell walked in carrying the treat packet clutched between his teeth.

Jane gasped.

"Wendell?" Louise said, as if an alien cat had taken over his body.

"I don't believe it," Alice said in awe.

"Okay, who are you and what have you done with Wendell?" Jane asked.

The clever feline simply stopped where he stood, dropped the packet on the floor and looked at Jane as though this was something he did every single day.

The sisters stared. Jane rushed over to ruffle the cat's fur. She cooed words of praise, scratched him behind the ears, ripped open the treat and poured the entire bag into his food bowl. "Daisy has nothing over you," she said with triumph.

"That's right, if the police department ever needs an animal to clutch a packet of cat food between its teeth, we have their feline," Alice said with a laugh.

Jane frowned. "Well, you never know. If God can use Balaam—"

"We know, we know," Alice said. "Just like when, in His providence, He answered our prayers using Paws to help Paula, and to help our town to reach out to others. God can use whatever means He chooses to get the job done."

Jane brightened. "I like that, Alice. Prayers, Paws and providence."

"Sounds like a good sermon title to me," Alice teased. She and Jane looked at Louise.

Louise smiled but said nothing. She merely got up from the table and left the room.

"Do you think we offended her?" Alice asked with some alarm.

Jane shook her head. "No way. If I know Louie, she probably went into the living room to scratch out some sermon notes—just in case she's ever called upon to preach again."

Butterscotch Pie

1 ten-inch pie shell
2 cups light brown sugar
8 tablespoons flour
¼ teaspoon salt
4 egg yolks
4 cups milk
3 tablespoons butter
1 teaspoon vanilla
Whipped cream for garnish

Use your favorite recipe for a baked ten-inch pie shell, bake and let cool.

Mix sugar, flour and salt in large mixer bowl. In a medium-sized mixer bowl, beat the yolks for approximately forty-five seconds on medium speed. Pour the milk slowly into the egg yolks and blend for twenty seconds; add the milk and yolk mixture slowly to the dry mixture until well blended—about sixty seconds on medium speed. When combined, transfer to large pot. Add softened butter in small chunks, then add vanilla, and stir constantly over medium heat until thickened (approximately twelve minutes, turning the heat down to medium low for the last three or four minutes). Place mixture in baked pie shell and let stand at room temperature for approximately one hour. Place in refrigerator overnight. Cut into serving slices and top with a dollop of ready-made whipped cream before serving.

An Invitation

Now you can visit Grace Chapel Inn online at

www.guidepostsbooks.com/gracechapelinn

Spend some time with other Grace Chapel Inn readers by joining our chat room. Life in Acorn Hill is never dull, and neither is our online community! You can discuss your favorite characters, talk about your favorite stories and maybe even make some new friends. You'll find a place that celebrates the blessings of family and friendship, and rejoices in faith-filled fun along the way.

You can visit www.guidepostsbooks.com to learn about other Guideposts Books. We'd love to see you!

&

Guideposts magazine and the *Daily Guideposts* devotional book are available in large-print editions by contacting:

Guideposts
Attn: Customer Service
P.O. Box 5815
Harlan, IA 51593
(800)431-2344
www.guideposts.com

Center Point Publishing
600 Brooks Road • PO Box 1
Thorndike ME 04986-0001 USA

(207) 568-3717

US & Canada:
1 800 929-9108
www.centerpointlargeprint.com

Bau

ES

1	31	61	91	121	151	181	211	241	271	301	331
2	32	62	92	122	152	182	212	242	272	302	332
3	33	63	93	123	153	183	213	243	273	303	333
4	34	64	94	124	154	184	214	244	274	304	334
5	35	65	95	125	155	185	215	245	275	305	335
6	36	66	96	126	156	186	216	246	276	306	336
7	37	67	97	127	157	187	217	247	277	307	337
8	38	68	98	128	158	188	218	248	278	308	338
9	39	69	99	129	159	189	219	249	279	309	339
10	40	70	100	130	160	190	220	250	280	310	340
11	41	71	101	131	161	191	221	251	281	311	341
12	42	72	102	132	162	192	222	252	282	312	342
13	43	73	103	133	163	193	223	253	283	313	343
14	44	74	104	134	164	194	224	254	284	314	344
15	45	75	105	135	165	195	225	255	285	315	345
16	46	76	106	136	166	196	226	256	286	316	346
17	47	77	107	137	167	197	227	257	287	317	347
18	48	78	108	138	168	198	228	258	288	318	348
19	49	79	109	139	169	199	229	259	289	319	349
20	50	80	110	140	170	200	230	260	290	320	350
21	51	81	111	141	171	201	231	261	291	321	351
22	52	82	112	142	172	202	232	262	292	322	352
23	53	83	113	143	173	203	233	263	293	323	353
24	54	84	114	144	174	204	234	264	294	324	354
25	55	85	115	145	175	205	235	265	295	325	355
26	56	86	116	146	176	206	236	266	296	326	356
27	57	87	117	147	177	207	237	267	297	327	357
28	58	88	118	148	178	208	238	268	298	328	358
29	59	89	119	149	179	209	239	269	299	329	359
30	60	90	120	150	180	210	240	270	300	330	360